BLOODSHED
OF THE
MOUNTAIN MAN

BLOODSHED
OF THE
MOUNTAIN MAN

WILLIAM W. JOHNSTONE
with J. A. Johnstone

PINNACLE BOOKS
Kensington Publishing Corp.
www.kensingtonbooks.com

PINNACLE BOOKS are published by

Kensington Publishing Corp.
119 West 40th Street
New York, NY 10018

PUBLISHER'S NOTE
Following the death of William W. Johnstone, the Johnstone family is working with a carefully selected writer to organize and complete Mr. Johnstone's outlines and many unfinished manuscripts to create additional novels in all of his series like The Last Gunfighter, Mountain Man, and Eagles, among others. This novel was inspired by Mr. Johnstone's superb storytelling.

All Kensington titles, imprints, and distributed lines are available at special quantity discounts for bulk purchases for sales promotions, premiums, fundraising, educational, or institutional use. Special book excerpts or customized printings can also be created to fit specific needs. For details, write or phone the office of the Kensington sales manager: Kensington Publishing Corp., 119 West 40th Street, New York, NY 10018, attn: Sales Department; phone 1-800-221-2647.

ISBN-13: 978-0-7860-3140-5
ISBN-10: 0-7860-3140-9

First printing: December 2015

10 9 8 7 6 5 4 3 2 1

Printed in the United States of America

First electronic edition: December 2015

ISBN-13: 978-0-7860-3141-2
ISBN-10: 0-7860-3141-7

CHAPTER ONE

"Earl Ray has his cap set for Katie, the foreman's daughter."

"No, I don't, Glenn, 'n you got no right talkin' like that," Earl Ray said. Earl Ray, Glenn, and Danny were riding night hawk, three-quarters of the way through a cattle drive, pushing five hundred head of beeves to the railhead at Coogan Switch. The cattle belonged to Ben Bartlett, owner of the Double B Ranch, and they had been on the drive for ten days.

"I agree with Earl Ray," Danny said. "Why would he be goin' after Kirkland's daughter, when he could have the owner's daughter?"

"Come on, Danny, Judy Bartlett ain't no more'n fourteen. You think I'm a cradle robber?"

"Well, hell, Earl Ray, you just barely out of the cradle yourself," Danny said, and the other two laughed.

There were eight men moving the herd, counting the cook and his helper. Earl Ray, who was sixteen, was the youngest of the crew, and this was his first cattle drive.

"Seems to me like we been on this drive forever," Glenn said. "What is it now? Two weeks?"

"Ha!" Danny said. "You boys don't know nothin' 'bout trail drivin'. Why, when I was workin' for the Hashknife, pushin' cows from Texas all the way up into Dodge City, Kansas, we'd be out for two months. But boy, howdy, would we ever tie one on when we got to Dodge."

"Tie one on?" Earl Ray said.

Danny and Glenn laughed.

"Boy, don't you know nothin'?" Danny asked. "I mean get drunk, find yourself a good lookin' bar girl to go upstairs with."

"I ain't never done none of that," Earl Ray said.

"That's all right, me 'n Glenn will get you good 'n broke in when we get to Coogan Switch."

Some of the cattle started bawling.

"I wonder what set them cows off," Glenn asked.

'You think those are cattle bawling? Hell, that's the cook's girlfriend," Danny said. "His real girlfriend."

"Damn, she sounds just like a steer," Glenn said.

"She looks like one too," Danny said, and all three laughed.

"I'd better go see what's got 'em all roused up," Earl Ray said.

"You ain't foolin' us none, Earl Ray. You pro'bly got you some girlfriend hid out," Danny said.

"No, I ain't," Earl Ray said as he rode off into the darkness.

"Maybe we should quit pickin' on 'im," Glenn said. "He's a good kid."

"True, but this is his first cattle drive, and we've all had to go through it. Next year we'll have someone new, and Earl Ray will be leading the charge."

"You got that right," Glenn said.

"Hey!" The shout was high and shrill.

"What the hell was that?" Danny asked.

"It sounded like Earl Ray."

The call was followed by the sound of gunfire, and Danny and Glenn could see muzzle flashes lighting up the night.

"Was that gunfire?"

They could hear thundering hoofbeats coming toward them. "Here comes Earl Ray," Danny said.

The horse appeared out of the darkness, but to the surprise of both Danny and Glenn, the horse was without a rider.

"What the hell? Did he get throwed?" Danny asked.

"Are you kiddin'? He's the best rider in the whole outfit."

The cattle had been still, but they started moving.

"Damn! What's going on here?" Glenn shouted.

Then, appearing out of the darkness behind Earl Ray's riderless horse, were six more riders galloping toward Glenn and Danny.

"What—" Glenn started to say, but that was as far as he got. All six riders opened fire, and both cowboys were shot from their saddles.

* * *

Earl Ray lay on the ground in the darkness, listening to gunfire and the shouts of the other cowboys.

"They're all dead, boys!" someone said. "Let's get these beeves out of here."

The young cowboy heard the sound of cattle being moved away; then a quiet settled in. He waited until he was sure the rustlers were gone before he called out.

"Danny? Glenn? Mr. Kirkland?"

There was no response.

He lay there for the rest of the night, fighting the pain of the bullet hole in his shoulder. When dawn finally broke, he could see that all the cattle were gone. The chuck wagon and hoodlum wagons were gone as well, but the bodies of the cook and his helper were lying on the ground, as were Danny, Glenn, the foreman, Mr. Kirkland, and the remaining two cowboys. Earl Ray was the only one left alive.

He saw Kirkland's horse standing over his owner's body, and he went over to retrieve it. It was hard, with his shoulder wound, to get the animal saddled, but he was able to do so.

It would be a long, troubled ride back to the ranch.

Coogan Switch, Colorado

Coogan Switch was named after John Coogan who, when the spur railroad was first built, lived in the switch house to change the tracks as needed.

A small town had built up around the switch, and now it was the railhead to which ranchers from as far away as a hundred miles brought their herds. Cattle brokers made their headquarters there, buying cattle and then arranging to ship them back to the processing plants in Kansas City and Chicago.

Merlin Lewis was one such broker, and he was there when a herd of five hundred cattle arrived, complete with drovers and chuck and hoodlum wagons.

"Hold 'em up here, boys!" the trail boss, a tall, blond man shouted to the others.

"Whose cows are these?" Lewis asked.

"They're from the Double B Ranch," the trail boss told him.

"Oh, yes, Mr. Bartlett," Lewis said. "What's he doin' sendin' so many drovers with such a small herd?"

"We're breakin' in a bunch of new boys."

"Yes, well, I guess this is as good a way as any to do it. I believe we had agreed upon a price of forty-five dollars a head."

"I thought it was fifty dollars a head."

"No, sir, forty-five dollars a head; you can take my offer or try and find another broker. But I'm telling you now, there are three of us here at the railhead, and we have all agreed upon the price. Not a one of us will be paying more than forty-five dollars a head."

"Mr. Bartlett isn't going to like it, but I don't guess I have much of a choice. All right, we'll take forty-five dollars a head."

"You have five hundred head, I believe?" Lewis asked.

"Five hundred and three, actually."

"Well, you can take three head back with you. Five hundred was what we agreed upon."

"Mr. Lewis, you drive a hard bargain."

"I represent McGill Meat Packing Company, and I have their interests to look out for," Lewis said.

"All right, you can have the extra three, it's not worth the effort to take them back."

Lewis smiled. "I thought you might see it my way."

Two hours later, thirty men were gathered just outside town. Behind them, the chuck wagon and the hoodlum wagon were burning. Twenty-eight of the men were wearing red armbands. One was wearing an orange armband, and the tall, blond man was wearing a blue armband.

The man with the blue armband was talking to the others.

"Men, this operation was conducted with military precision, and I'm very proud of you. There is not one regiment in the entire United States Army that could have pulled off this operation any better than you did.

"But, a better measure of your success than mere praise is money. Right, men?"

"Yes, sir!" the men shouted.

"I am pleased to report that your share for this job comes to six hundred and forty dollars apiece."

The men cheered, then gathered around to receive their pay.

Twenty miles northwest of Coogan Switch, buzzards were swarming around the bodies of seven of the cowboys who had started the drive for the Double B Ranch.

Ten miles beyond that, Earl Ray Dunnigan struggled to stay in the saddle as he made his way back to the Double B Ranch.

He thought about Mrs. Kirkland and her daughter, Katie. He dreaded being the one who would have to tell them that Mr. Kirkland had been killed.

LETTER TO THE EDITOR

Dear Editor:

After many successful forays in Wyoming, each of them conducted with military precision, I have decided to move my theater of operations to Colorado. Our most recent mission resulted in the theft of an entire herd of cattle, which we were able to sell without challenge.

Your city marshals, county sheriffs, and state rangers will try and stop us, but all their efforts will result in failure. I will take great personal pleasure in their frustration. I am Hannibal, Commandant of the Ghost Riders, the most efficient military unit in the United States.

Denver, Colorado, six months later

Having bought HRH Charles, a prize bull, and a registered heifer, Lady Bridgett, two years earlier, Smoke Jensen, Pearlie, and Cal—his two top men who were also his best friends—were looking at the first mature issue of the two registered animals.

The bull's name was Prince Dandy, and Smoke had entered him in a livestock show in Denver. So protective of Prince Dandy were they, that Smoke had arranged for a private car to transport the bull from Big Rock to Denver.

"You think Prince Dandy has a chance to win?" Pearlie asked.

"Of course he does," Cal replied. "There's not a finer bull in the entire state than Prince Dandy. No, and not in the whole country, either."

"You sure? You mean you don't think there might be a better bull in Wyoming or Texas or Rhode Island?"

"Rhode Island? What do they know about cows in Rhode Island? I mean, surrounded by water 'n all, they more 'n likely don't even have cows there, except maybe a few milk cows."

Pearlie laughed. "What makes you think Rhode Island is surrounded by water?"

"Because it's an island, and ever'one knows that islands are surrounded by water. That's what an island is."

"Smoke, how is it that we have someone this dumb workin' for us?" Pearlie asked with a laugh.

"Rhode Island is a state, it isn't actually an island," Smoke said.

"Well that doesn't make any sense," Cal said.

"Maybe not, but that's what it is."

At the moment, the three men were overseeing the unloading of Prince Dandy from his private car, the car having been shunted aside to be used again for the return trip to Big Rock. From the railroad depot, Prince Dandy would be transported in the back of a cattle wagon to the arena where all the animals were to be judged.

"Hey, Smoke, when it comes time to lead Prince Dandy around the show ring, I'm the one that should do it," Cal said.

"You are the one who *should* do it?" Pearlie asked.

"Well, yeah, I mean, it's pretty obvious, isn't it?"

"I don't know. What makes it so obvious?"

"Well think about it. This is all new to Prince Dandy, 'n you know he's got to be nervous. He knows me 'n he likes me a lot, so I think with me bein' the one that's leadin' 'im around the ring, well it'll make him feel a lot better. Besides, you don't want him all mopey come the judgin' now, do you?"

Smoke chuckled. "No, I sure don't want him all mopey."

"Hey, Cal, if Prince Dandy doesn't win first prize, maybe you will," Pearlie joked.

"Well, if it's for being good lookin', I'd sure come closer than you," Cal shot back.

When Prince Dandy was loaded into the wagon, Cal got into the back with him.

"Don't be nervous now," he said, speaking softly to the bull. "This is goin' to be your chance to shine."

"You think Prince Dandy thinks Cal is his mama?" Smoke teased.

"I don't know about Prince Dandy, but Cal sure thinks so," Pearlie replied with a laugh.

CHAPTER TWO

Once they reached the show arena, Smoke registered their entry; then they were assigned a holding pen. As they left the bull in the holding pen, Smoke saw Benjamin Bartlett. Bartlett too was showing a prize bull.

"How are you doing, Ben? A better question, how are your people doing, after that terrible event of having your men killed and your beeves stolen?"

"I can replace the cows," Bartlett said. "It's the lives of seven good men that grieves me."

"I know what you mean. You had one man who lived, I understand?"

"Yes. Earl Ray Dunnigan. He was shot in the shoulder, but is fully recovered now. He's a good kid, but he took this really hard."

"Did he see any of the men who did it?"

"Not so he could identify them by sight. He said it was just too dark. The son of a bitch that did this wrote a letter to the editor bragging about it. Can you believe that? The rustlers call themselves Ghost Riders."

"I've never heard of them," Smoke said.

"Well, whoever they are, they're an evil bunch of bastards," Bartlett said. "That's what Earl Ray said. And apparently, according to Sheriff Dennis, who has heard of them, that's the way they operate."

"Which bull is yours, Ben?" Smoke asked.

"High Dollar," Ben said. "Yours?"

"Prince Dandy."

The two men wished each other good luck, then started into the stands to await the judging. As they walked by the refreshment stand, they were assailed by a sweet-smelling aroma.

"Save me a seat, Smoke," Pearlie said. "I smell crullers. You want me to get one for you?"

"No thanks, I'm fine," Smoke said.

Smoke took his seat, and a few moments later Pearlie appeared eating one cruller and carrying another.

"I told you I didn't need one."

"I got two for me," Pearlie said. "By the way, they're about to bring out the bulls for judging."

The gate at the far end of the arena opened, and the bulls, each of them led by a handler, paraded around the arena. A crew of judges stood in the middle of the arena watching them walk by; then the handlers stopped and turned the animals to face the spectators. At that maneuver, the judges, each carrying a tablet and pencil, went by each bull and, after examining them closely, made notations on the tablet. Then the judges met in the middle of the arena to make a decision.

"Prince Dandy is goin' to win," Pearlie said.

"What makes you think so?"

"Well, you can see for yourself, Smoke, he's clearly the best lookin' bull out there."

"You sound like Cal."

As it turned out, Pearlie was right. Prince Dandy was awarded the honor of champion bull and High Dollar came in second.

"Miz Sally is goin' to be real proud of Prince Dandy," Cal said.

"Well, I'm proud of the money he's going to make when I sell him," Smoke said.

"Sell him?"

"Yes, sell him. The whole reason for buying HRH Charles and Lady Bridgett in the first place was to produce offspring I could sell."

"Well, yeah, I knew that," Cal said. "But I thought that maybe, now that Prince Dandy has been judged best of show . . . I mean, he really is a champion bull now, I thought you might change your mind."

"Cal, we came to this show hoping Prince Dandy would win so his value would increase. And I figure it just went up by about a thousand dollars."

"Yeah," Cal said. "Yeah, I guess you're right. Anyway . . . HRH and Lady can always have another calf," he said with a smile. "And maybe he'll win too."

Five miles south of Brown Spur, Colorado

Four men, all wearing red armbands, were waiting just off the road at the top of a long grade. The stagecoach between Big Rock and Brown Spur would have to stop when it reached this point in order to give the horses a chance to recover their breath after the long, hard climb.

"Ha!" one of the men said. "Look at that, Taylor. I just pissed that grasshopper off that weed."

"You piss everyone off, Moss," Taylor said, and the other two men laughed. "Fowler, do you see anything yet?"

"Yeah, it just come around the curve down there," Fowler replied. Fowler was standing up on a rock precipice, the vantage affording him a good view of the road from the curve at the bottom and all the way up the hill.

"I hope Reece is right," Newell said. "I hope this coach is carrying money. I would hate to think we waited out here half a day for nothin'."

"According to Reece, it's s'posed to be carryin' fifteen hundred dollars. If the money ain't there, Hannibal will deal with 'im," Taylor said.

By now the four men could hear the sound of the stage, the driver's whistles, the snap of his whip, and the squeak and rattle of the coach as the horses labored to pull it up the long grade.

"Get ready," Taylor said. "Don't nobody show yourself 'til the coach comes to a stop 'n all the passengers get out to take a piss, or whatever it is they're goin' to do. Then we'll shoot the shotgun guard. That'll get their attention."

It took another couple of minutes before the coach reached the top of the hill.

"Whoa!" the driver shouted, pulling back on the reins. The team stopped, one of the horses whickered, and another stomped his right foreleg. The driver set the brake on the coach.

"All right, folks," the driver called back. "We're goin' to be here about ten minutes to let the horses take a blow. You may as well take a break. If you've got a need for the necessary, ladies to the left side of the road and gents to the right."

Three men and two women got out of the coach. Apparently none of them had a need to do anything, because all five of them just stood by the right, rear wheel. A few of them stretched to work out the kinks from sitting so long in one place.

"Now!" Taylor shouted. He and the three men with him jumped out from behind a rock, with their guns drawn.

"What the hell!" the guard shouted, as he reached for the shotgun that was standing in the corner of the driver's boot.

Four shots rang out, and the guard fell back onto the seat.

One of the passengers drew his gun, and Taylor turned on him. The passenger was shot down before his pistol was able to clear leather.

The other passengers put their hands in the air.

"That's more like it," Taylor said. "Now, you, driver, throw down that strongbox."

"What makes you think there's any money in it?" the driver replied.

"Driver, the only reason you're still alive is because I don't want to go to the trouble of climbing up there to get the box myself. Now, I ain't a goin' to tell you again. Throw it down!"

The driver did as he was told. Taylor shot the lock off the box, opened it, then took out three bound packets of bills.

"Well, it seems our information was right, after all," he said, showing it to the others with a big smile.

"Can we go now?" the driver asked.

"Yeah," Taylor replied. The passenger he had shot was lying facedown on the road, groaning. "You folks get back into the coach and take him with you," he said, pointing to the wounded man.

The passengers reboarded, and the driver, after getting the go-ahead from Taylor, snapped his whip and called out to the team. Although they hadn't been given the ten minutes of rest time required by the stage-line, they moved forward in a brisk trot.

Half an hour later, Smoke stopped on a ridge just above the road leading into Brown Spur and took a drink of water as he glanced back toward the arriving stagecoach. Then, corking the canteen, he slapped his legs against the side of his horse and sloped on down the long ridge.

Upon being told that Ned Condon, a man who had a ranch just outside Brown Spur, might be interested in buying his prize bull, Smoke had ridden over today to see if he could close the deal. But after he arrived in town, Smoke stopped first at the saloon, deciding that what he needed after the long ride over from Sugarloaf was a cool beer. As he tied Seven off at the hitchrail out front, the stagecoach he had seen earlier came rolling into town. It was moving at a fairly rapid clip, and its driver was calling out loudly enough to be heard even over the sound of the horses' hooves and rolling wheels.

"We've been robbed! Stagecoach was held up! We need the doc!"

The coach stopped in front of the depot at the far end of the street, and several people, responding to the driver's shout, crowded around it. Smoke wanted the beer, but he figured it could wait for a bit. He was curious about the stagecoach robbery so he walked down to join the others.

"Hey, Lou, where's Toby?" someone asked. "What happened to your shotgun guard?"

"Toby was kilt, he was gut-shot. So was one of our passengers. We need a doctor."

"No need for the doctor now," a man called from inside the coach. "Mr. Thomas is dead."

"Who done it?" someone asked. Smoke saw that the questioner was wearing a star.

"It was Ghost Riders, Sheriff Brown."

"Ghost Riders? How many of 'em was it?"

"They was only four," the driver said. By now he had climbed down from the driver's box.

The star-packer shook his head. "If there was only four of 'em, it wasn't the Ghost Riders. There's more than two dozen of them."

"They was all wearin' red armbands," the driver said.

"They were? Damn, it might have been them, then. Or, it might have been a bunch of outlaws that wanted to make you think they were Ghost Riders."

"How much did they get?" one of the other men standing around the stage asked.

"I don't know. They got the strong box, but I don't have no idee how much was in it."

"Fifteen hundred dollars," another man said. While all the other men were wearing denim trousers and cotton shirts, the man who responded was wearing a three-piece suit. "It was a money transfer coming to my bank. What I don't understand, though, is how they knew about it."

"One of the outlaws said, 'our information was right.' They knew that the money was there," the driver said.

"Information?" the banker asked. "Where did they get the information? Did they mention any names?"

"No, sir. All they said was, the information is correct."

"As soon as you're finished here, Lou, I'd like for you and the passengers to come on down to the office and give me a report."

"All right, Sheriff Brown, we'll be right down there," the driver replied.

Smoke returned to the saloon, which was called Bagby's.

There were four bar girls working the floor as Smoke stepped up to the bar.

"Yes, sir?" the bartender asked.

"I'll have a beer," Smoke said.

The bartender drew a mug from the beer barrel. "They was some folks in here sayin' that the Ghost Riders held up the stagecoach," the bartender said as he set the mug down in front of Smoke.

"Yes, that's what the driver said."

"You know anything about these Ghost Riders?" the bartender asked.

"Not much," Smoke said, as he picked up the

beer. "A friend of mine had a trail herd of his cattle stolen a few months ago. Apparently, the rustlers who did that were Ghost Riders."

"Yes, I heard about that. They killed all the drovers, then took the herd on in and sold it off as cool as you please," the bartender said.

"They didn't kill them all. One survived."

"I hear tell that the Ghost Riders was up in Wyomin' before they come down here. I don't know what Wyomin' did to get rid of 'em, but whatever it was, I'd like to see Colorado do the same thing, so's maybe we could send them on down into New Mexico."

"If we did that, we would just be pushing them off on someone else," Smoke said.

"Yeah, that's what I'm talkin' about."

Smoke didn't try to explain his comment. Instead, he asked the bartender a question pertaining to his actual reason for coming to Brown Spur.

"I'm here to see a man named Ned Condon. I'm told his ranch is near here," Smoke said.

"Yes, sir, his spread is called Wiregrass Ranch. It's about five miles north of here. He and his wife live there. Nice young couple they are too."

"He contacted me about buying a prime registered bull."

"Yeah, he was in here just the other day talking about a bull he was wantin' to buy. Prince Dandy, I believe the critter's name is."

"Yes, that's his name," Smoke said. "I own Prince Dandy."

"Well sir, I'm sure he'll be glad to—"

Their conversation was interrupted by a scream from upstairs. Looking up toward the landing immediately above them, Smoke and the bartender saw a young woman running from her room with a man chasing her.

"Oh, I don't like the looks of that," the bartender said.

"Damn you! Quit runnin' from me, you bitch!" the man shouted, catching up with her just as they reached the top of the stairs.

"I gave you your money back! Leave me alone!"

"I don't want my money back! You know what I want!"

"Reece, you leave that girl alone!" the bartender shouted, pointing up at the man.

"You stay the hell out of this, Bagby! I paid for my time with her," Reece said. He grabbed the girl by her shoulder, but she twisted away from him.

"No, I don't want to be with you!"

"Damn you!" The man slapped her hard, the slap causing her to fall down the stairs. She cried out in shock and fear, but the scream was cut short. Silently, she fell the rest of the way, coming to a halt at the foot of the stairs. Her head was twisted to one side and her eyes were open but glazed. From the way her head was twisted, Smoke knew that her neck had been broken.

"Damn! Annie?" the bartender called in alarm.

CHAPTER THREE

"I guess you ain't goin' nowhere now, are you, you bitch?" The man called down to her. "Now, get your ass back up here before I come down there and drag you back up."

One of the young women who had been working the bar ran over to the still, twisted form lying on the floor, then knelt down beside her.

"How is she, Sue?" the bartender called.

"I'm afraid she's dead," Smoke said quietly.

Sue was holding her fingers to the girl's neck. "Annie is dead, Bagby," Sue replied, confirming Smoke's observation.

"Wait a minute!" the man who was standing at the top of the stairs said. "What do you mean, she's dead?"

"She's dead," Sue said again. "I can't find a pulse."

"You killed her, Reece," Bagby said.

"I . . . I didn't do this."

"The hell you didn't!" Bagby replied. "You knocked her down the stairs."

"How do we know she's dead, anyway? What does a whore know about findin' a pulse?"

"Sue, go get Sheriff Brown," Bagby said.

The young bar girl who had checked for the pulse stood up.

"No you don't! Now, you just hold on there," Reece said, pointing toward Sue. "You ain't goin' nowhere." He pulled his pistol. "If you start toward that door I'll shoot you. This was an accident. Yeah, maybe I hit her, but I didn't intend to knock her down the stairs. And I ain't goin' to get hung because some whore slipped on the stairs."

"Put the gun away, Reece," Bagby said.

"You go to hell, Bagby. And you, stay where you are," Reece shouted at Sue.

"Reece, if you don't put that gun away now, I'm going to kill you," Smoke said. He spoke the words calmly so that they became a statement of fact, rather than a challenge.

"Who asked you to butt into this? This ain't none of your affair," Reece said.

"Actually, it is my affair. You've taken this public, first by killing that girl, then by threatening this one. This is the last time I'm going to tell you. Put that gun away now or I *will* kill you."

"Who are you kidding, Mister? Maybe you're too dumb to notice, but it just so happens that I'm holding my gun in my hand. Your gun is still in your holster."

Smoke had already told him one last time, so he made absolutely no response to Reece's comment.

"I'm tired of talkin' to you. I think I'll just kill you now." Reece swung his gun toward Smoke. Smoke drew his pistol so quickly that to the witnesses in the room it seemed as if the gun had appeared in his hand, almost as if by magic.

Smoke and Reece fired at the same time. Reece's bullet hit one of the liquor bottles behind the bar, sending the aromatic liquid spraying into the air. Smoke's shot hit Reece high in the chest.

Reece grabbed his chest, then fell forward, sliding down the stairs. Unlike Annie, Reece didn't quite make it all the way to the bottom.

"Damn! I ain't never seen nothin' like that!" one of the saloon patrons said.

"Miss," Smoke said to Sue. "Maybe you should go get the sheriff now."

The bar girl stood there, looking on in total shock. In less than a minute, she had seen two people killed.

"Go ahead, Sue," Bagby said.

"All right."

Smoke turned to his beer as calmly as if nothing had happened.

"Mister, I've seen Wild Bill Hickok, John Wesley Hardin, and Clay Allison pull iron. But I've never seen anyone draw as fast or shoot as straight as the show you just put on here," the bartender said.

"I'm sorry it had to come to that," Smoke said. "And I apologize for it happening in your saloon."

"Are you kidding? Reece was a madman. You saw what he did to Annie. And there was no better-natured girl anywhere. I had no idea he was beatin' on her, or I would have never let him go upstairs with any of the girls in the first place."

Sue came back into the saloon with the same

man Smoke had seen a few minutes earlier down at the stagecoach depot.

"Bagby, I hear you've had a little trouble here," the sheriff said.

"Yeah, Sheriff Brown, we did. Reece killed one of the girls. Then this man . . . I'm sorry, I didn't get your name."

"Jensen," Smoke said.

"Mr. Jensen, here, killed Reece."

"I see." The sheriff turned to Smoke. "You want to tell me what happened?"

"I told you what happened, Sheriff," Bagby said.

"I know you did. But seems like I ought to also hear it from the man that done the actual shootin'," Sheriff Brown said.

"This man, Reece, knocked a young lady down the stairs, and the fall broke her neck. When Mr. Bagby asked this young lady to go get you, Reece threatened to kill her. Then, when I intervened, he turned his gun on me, so I shot him."

"And here's the thing, Sheriff. Jensen didn't even have his gun drawn when Reece tried to shoot him."

The others in the saloon backed up both Smoke and Bagby's account of the events.

"Do you need me to come to the office and sign any kind of statement?" Smoke asked.

"No, seeing as there's no one here who disputes what you, Bagby, and Elegant Sue have told me, I would say that it was a justifiable shoot."

"Elegant Sue?"

Sue smiled, displaying a dimple in her left cheek, and Smoke saw that there was an innocence about her, despite her profession.

"That's my name," she said.

"Well, Elegant Sue, you are a courageous young lady. You stood your ground when Reece threatened to shoot you." Smoke smiled at her.

"Thank you, sir," Elegant Sue replied.

"Anyone else want to tell me what they saw?" Sheriff Brown asked.

Half a dozen people started talking at once then, and Sheriff Brown had to slow them down so he could get one report at a time. Every one of the witness accounts was the same. The shooting was entirely justified.

"As far as I'm concerned, your shooting Reece probably saved the county the price of a new rope. If ever there was anyone goin' to wind up gettin' hisself hung, it was Lou Reece."

"Perhaps so," Smoke said. "But I would just as soon not have been the one to save the county money like that."

Sheriff Brown laughed. "I see your point," he said.

"Sheriff, if you don't need me for anything else, I'm going to ride out to visit some with Ned Condon about a bull."

"Ned and Molly are just real good people," Sheriff Brown said. "I wish we had more people like them. Ned would give you the shirt off his back if he thought you needed it. Tell them both that I said hi."

"I'll do that," Smoke promised.

* * *

After a ride of about twenty minutes, Smoke passed by a white sign that was posted just outside a white rail fence.

WIREGRASS RANCH
ESTABLISHED 1878
Ned and Molly Condon, proprietors

When Smoke rode up, he saw a young man who appeared to be in his late twenties or early thirties, pumping water into a bucket.

"That water sure looks good," he said.

The man smiled at him. "Well come down off your horse and have a drink."

"I appreciate the offer, and I believe I will. You are Ned Condon?"

"I am, sir," Condon replied as he scooped up some water with the dipper and handed it to Smoke.

"Thanks," Smoke said, accepting it, then taking a long drink. He tossed out the last few drops and handed the dipper back to Condon. "Mr. Condon, I'm Smoke Jensen and I—"

"Prince Dandy!" Condon said.

"Yes."

"Come in, come in," Condon said excitedly. "Have you had your supper?"

"No, I haven't; I thought I would get it at the hotel tonight."

"Nonsense. You'll take your supper with us, and you won't need a hotel either."

Ned Condon led Smoke into the house and called for his wife. "Molly, this is the man who is going to sell us Prince Dandy. He's going to have supper and spend the night with us."

"Oh, how wonderful!" Molly said. "I'm just starting supper. Do you like pork chops?"

"I love pork chops."

"While Molly is getting supper ready, come out with me and take a look at the place I've got fixed up for Prince Dandy. Why, he'll have his own private stall that's nicer than some of the hotels I've stayed at. But then, some of the hotels I've visited, like the ones in Hong Kong or Shanghai, are more like hovels than hotels."

"You've been to Shanghai?" Smoke asked. "How did you wind up in Shanghai?"

"My father owns the Pacific Trading Company. It's a fleet of clipper ships, and I was a junior officer on one of them for a while, until I realized I didn't want to make a career at sea. That's when I moved here and bought Wiregrass."

During and after the meal, Smoke learned a lot more about the couple who had invited him to stay with them. Molly's father was a college professor at the University of San Francisco.

"Interesting that you have been to sea. I have a friend who was a sailor for a while. And now that I think about it, I believe it might well have been with your father's company. He wasn't an officer though. His name is Elmer Gleason."

Ned laughed out loud. "Elmer Gleason? Well now, you talk about a small world. Gleason saved my life when we were attacked by pirates from Kuala Langat."

"That would be Elmer, all right," Smoke said.

"And trust me, you aren't the only one whose life Elmer saved."

"Well, as far as I'm concerned, Ned's is the most important life your friend ever saved," Molly said. "Had it not been for Mr. Gleason, Ned and I would have never been married."

"Have you been married long?" Smoke asked.

"We have been married for four years. Oh, and our wedding was beautiful," Molly said. "It was held in St. Patrick's Church and just everyone came. Why even Governor Perkins came."

"And why shouldn't he have come?" Ned asked. "My father certainly donated enough to his campaign."

"Still, he didn't have to come," Molly said. "And I thought it was very sweet of him to do so."

"Our folks, mine and Molly's, don't understand what has drawn us to ranching," Ned said, "but it's something I've wanted to do for my entire life. And with a seed bull like Prince Dandy, why, I've no doubt but that I'll have one of the finest herds in the whole state."

"He's a fine bull, all right," Smoke said. "But, Ned, you haven't even asked what I want for him."

"I don't care how much you are asking for him, I'll pay it," Ned said.

Smoke shook his head and laughed out loud. "Ned, Ned, never do that. You have to deal with people. If you don't, they'll rob you blind. Make an offer."

"All right, four thousand dollars."

"No," Smoke said, with a grin.

"Forty-five hundred?"

"No."

"All right, four thousand seven hundred and fifty dollars, but I have to tell you, I wasn't actually planning on spending that much."

Smoke laughed. "How about two thousand five hundred dollars?"

"What?" Ned asked, as a big smile spread across his face.

"Two thousand five hundred dollars."

"Yes! Yes!" Ned replied excitedly.

"Whew, what a tough negotiation this was," Smoke teased.

"Well, I've never really had to negotiate for anything," Ned said. "Generally if I wanted it, I just bought it."

"Don't tell people that," Smoke said with a laugh.

As it turned out, Ned was quite an accomplished pianist and Molly had a beautiful voice, so they gave Smoke a private concert that evening.

"I certainly appreciate the private concert," Smoke said. "But you didn't have to do that."

"Nonsense. It's no fun just performing for ourselves," Ned said. "We appreciated the audience."

After breakfast the next morning, Ned and Molly both came out to see him off.

"How long before you can get Prince Dandy here?" Ned asked.

"I've got some business to tie up, but I'd say less than two weeks."

Molly handed him a wrapped bundle.

"What is this?" Smoke asked.

"A couple of biscuits and some fried chicken," Molly said. "I thought you might get hungry on the way home."

Smoke chuckled and shook his head. "You didn't have to do this, but I will take it, and I do appreciate it."

"Hurry back with Prince Dandy. And do tell him how nice a place we have waiting for him," Ned said.

"I'll tell him, and I know he will be looking forward to it."

Smoke threw them both a wave as he rode off. He stopped by in Brown Spur after he left the Wiregrass Ranch, and stepped into the sheriff's office.

"Hello, Sheriff."

"Mr. Jensen," Sheriff Brown said. "What brings you by?"

"I just wanted to make sure that you didn't need to see me for anything about my run-in with Reece."

"No, it's like I told you. All the witness accounts say that you had no choice. Did you meet with the Condons?"

"I did, yes. And you are right, they are fine people. I'll be coming through here again in a couple of weeks with Prince Dandy."

"I know Condon is excited about that."

"He seemed to be. Well, if you have no need of me, I'll be on my way."

CHAPTER FOUR

The Vasquez Mountains, Colorado

The Ghost Rider Gang made their headquarters at Ten Strike, an abandoned mine that was in the Vasquez Mountains, near the town of Sorento. The buildings and structures that had once supported the mine were still in place. Here, there was a long, low bunkhouse that had been for the mine workers, as well as a small house that had been occupied by the manager of the mine. The men stayed in the bunkhouse, while the leader of the Ghost Riders, a man known only as Hannibal, stayed in what had been the mine manager's house.

Hannibal was a tall, blond-haired, well-proportioned man who at first glance might be considered handsome. But upon closer examination there was something about him that was rather off-putting, like a beautiful piece of crystal that had a minute imperfection in the casting that, while small, was nonetheless significant enough to destroy the overall illusion.

At the moment, the Ghost Rider Gang consisted of thirty men. The gang hadn't just happened into existence, Hannibal had planned every aspect of it and considered thirty men to be the optimum strength of his military unit, and a military unit is exactly the way he thought of the group. Thirty men might seem too large and unwieldy, but Hannibal understood the elements of command, so that didn't present a problem.

A gang that large would, of necessity, have to bring in enough money to make it profitable for all its members, and so far Hannibal had been able to do that. One advantage was their strength. There were too many of them for any single sheriff's department to deal with, and there was virtually no job that was too large for them to undertake.

Another advantage of having such a large group was that Hannibal was able to send out smaller groups for smaller jobs. Last week he had sent four men to hold up a stagecoach. He was supposed to give his informant fifty dollars for the information, but he didn't have to because Reece had gotten himself killed.

All the money, even the money that came from the smaller operations, was put into the unit treasury to be divided up among the men. And now Hannibal had happened across another lead for a job, and he didn't have to pay any informant for this information. The sale of a bull for the princely sum of twenty-five hundred dollars was news enough to have been picked up in newspapers all over the state, including the *Sorento Sun Times*.

"The rancher was a fool to allow the information

to be put in the newspaper," Hannibal said. "Now, all we have to do is pay him a visit at his ranch, relieve him of the money he is to pay for the bull, then when this Jensen person shows up, kill him and take the bull."

"Hannibal, how are we going to sell that bull?" Rexwell asked. "I mean if he is a champion bull, won't a lot of people know about him?"

"We'll change his name and fake his registration papers," Hannibal said. "And anyone who appreciates quality will realize that he is a purebred bull. I expect we can get rid of him in Wyoming or Utah easily enough."

"How many men do we want to use?" Rexwell asked.

"Pick five men out. It'll be no more than seven, counting you and me."

"All right. I'll get 'em together," Rexwell said.

Sugarloaf Ranch, Colorado

"The reason Smoke chose me to go with him is because he knows I'm better with cattle than you are," Cal said.

"What do you mean, better with cattle?" Pearlie asked. "You're not taking cattle, you're taking a cow. One cow. How can you have a cattle drive with one cow?"

"Yes, but it's a very special cow. It's Prince Dandy. And you know yourself, Pearlie, I near'bout raised that bull all by myself. I mean, think about it. Who did Smoke choose to lead him around the ring at the livestock show? And that's probably why Prince Dandy won, 'cause he knew I was with him."

"He didn't choose you, you practically begged him to let you lead Prince Dandy around."

"Yeah, well, Prince Dandy won, didn't he? It's like I said, Prince Dandy trusts me."

"You're not goin' to cry when you ride away and leave Prince Dandy with the Condons now, are you?"

"No, but I expect Prince Dandy is goin' to miss me somethin' awful."

Smoke and Sally came out of the house then. "Cal, are you ready to go?" Smoke called.

"Yes, sir, I'm ready. I've got both horses saddled, and Prince Dandy is in halter and leash."

Pearlie stood by as the two men mounted.

"Get along there, doggies," Pearlie called out. Then he laughed. "Oh, wait a minute. I guess what I really mean is, get along there little doggie."

"You're just jealous you ain't goin'!" Cal replied.

"Cal, you know better than that!" Sally said.

"Yes, ma'am," Cal called back. "Pearlie, you're just jealous that you *aren't* going."

"That's much better," Sally said with a little laugh.

It had been some time since Sally had been in a schoolroom, but she was a living example of the consummate teacher. She had left teaching, but teaching had never left her.

Near Wiregrass Ranch

Hannibal held up his arm as a signal to stop.

"Taylor, you and Moss approach as flankers.

Taylor, you go to the left and Moss to the right. Fowler, you go in as point. Keep your eyes open, and let us know instantly if you see anyone. The rest of you, stay with me," Hannibal said.

With the flank riders and the point man in position, Hannibal, Rexwell, Newell, and Hill approached the ranch. There was an attractive young woman hanging up clothes, and as they rode into the yard, she looked up with an expression of curiosity on her face.

"What can I do for you gentlemen?" she asked.

"Fowler, climb to the top of the windmill and keep an eye out."

"An eye out for what? Who are you men?"

"Madam, I suggest that you call your husband," Hannibal said.

"Ned! Ned, come out here, quickly!"

"What is it, Molly?" Ned asked, coming up from the barn. He saw Hannibal and the others. "Who are you men? What do you want?"

"We are here to collect the money for the registered bull that you bought," Hannibal said.

"What do you mean, you are here to collect the money? I'll pay when I get the bull."

"He has authorized us to collect the money for him."

"I would like to see that authorization."

"All right, I'll be glad to show it to you," Hannibal said. He looked at the other men. "Bands on."

At Hannibal's order, he and all the men with him put on armbands.

"Oh, my God, Molly," Ned said, pulling his wife close to him. "They are Ghost Riders."

"Oh, I'm glad that you recognized us," Hannibal said with an evil smile. "Now that you know who we are, I'm sure you well understand the importance of responding to my order. So I will ask you again to turn over the money you intended to pay for the bull."

"Mister, I don't know what you're talking about. Surely, you don't think I have the cash on hand, do you? I'll be paying for Prince Dandy with a bank draft."

Hannibal brought the back of his hand, hard, across Ned's face. "Wrong answer, Mr. Condon."

"I'm telling you the truth! I don't have the cash on hand!"

Hannibal hit Ned again. "You're not a very smart man, are you, Mr. Condon? All you have to do is give me the money; we'll be on our way, and neither you, nor your wife will be any worse for wear."

"Are you deaf? I don't have the money here!" Ned shouted.

This time Hannibal hit him with the butt of his pistol, and Ned went down.

"Take off his shirt," Hannibal ordered.

"Please! My husband is telling the truth!" Molly said.

"Hey, Hannibal, it comes to my mind that we took the shirt off the wrong person. How 'bout we take her shirt off too?" Taylor said.

"Good idea," Hannibal said. "Strip her down to the skin from the waist up. When Condon comes to and sees that, he might be a bit more cooperative."

Moss stepped up to Molly Condon, put his hands on the neckline of her dress, then ripped it open.

He then pulled her camisole down, exposing her naked breasts.

"Well now," he said, leeringly. "Ain't them thangs purty?"

Smoke and Cal were riding side by side, with Cal holding on to the leash that was attached to Prince Dandy's harness. They were taking the bull to Wiregrass Ranch and had been on the way for about three hours.

"Pearlie was teasin' me this mornin' when we left," Cal said. "He said he had never heard of a cattle drive with just one cow."

"That might be true, but Prince Dandy cost as much as fifty head of ordinary cattle, so you might say there are just two of us to handle fifty beeves."

"Yeah," Cal said. "Yeah, that's true, isn't it? I'll have to tell Pearlie that. Hey, Smoke, do you reckon Mrs. Condon will feed us? I mean, it'll be near'bout lunchtime when we get there, won't it?"

"I imagine she will," Smoke said. "She fed me quite well when I was here last."

"Good. I'm awful hungry."

"Cal, is it even possible for you to tell me when you haven't been hungry?"

Wiregrass Ranch

By now, Ned Condon was on his knees, with his shirt off. His arms were stretched out in front of him, and his wrists were tied to the water pump that rose from the ground. There were bleeding stripes across his back from the bullwhip that had been applied, and was still being applied, by Toon Taylor. Molly, who was also bare from the waist up, stood nearby. She was holding her arms across her breasts, providing her with a false sense of modesty.

Hannibal stepped around in front of Ned, so Ned could see him.

"You are being most obdurate, Mr. Condon. All you have to do to stop this unpleasantness is give us the money you were going to pay for the bull."

"I told you, I don't have the cash money," Condon said.

"And I told you that I don't believe you," Hannibal said, and he nodded at Taylor. "Lay it on again, and don't be so gentle in the application of the lash."

"No, please! Don't hit him again!" Molly begged.

"Mr. Condon, do you see how piteously your wife pleads for you? You could stop this, you know."

"Do you think I want to be beaten like this?" Ned replied. "I would give you the money if I had it."

Taylor brought the bullwhip around again, and it popped loudly as it fell across Condon's back, opening up another bloody streak.

Condon winced, but made no sound.

"Please!" Molly shouted. "He's telling the truth! Don't hit him again!"

"You know what, Hannibal, maybe we're whuppin' the wrong person here," Rexwell said. "I think if we started whuppin' his woman, why, he'd talk."

"No, please!" Condon said. "I've told you the

truth! I don't have the cash here! I'll write you a bank draft!"

"A bank draft, you say? And just what am I supposed to do with a bank draft?"

"Hey, Hannibal!" Fowler called down from the windmill. "Someone's a comin'!"

"How many?"

"Looks like two men. Two men, 'n they're leadin' a cow."

"That must be the bull Condon is buying. All right, keep an eye on them. When they get close enough, shoot them and we'll take the bull. Newell, Hill, get your rifles."

Suddenly, and totally unexpectedly, Molly Condon screamed.

"Son of a bitch! Shoot them!" Hannibal ordered. "Shoot both of them!"

"That sounded like a woman's scream!" Cal said.

"It *was* a woman's scream. Let Prince Dandy go! We'll recover him later. Come on, we have got to get there!" Smoke slapped his legs against the sides of his horse, and Seven bolted forward.

They heard two gunshots.

Smoke and Cal drew their pistols and galloped toward the sound of the guns.

Within moments bullets were whizzing by their heads. Smoke saw a shooter from the top of the windmill, and he shot at him. The windmill shooter pitched forward and did a somersault on his way down. A second shot brought down another of the shooters. Cal also brought one of the shooters down.

"Let's get the hell out of here!" they heard someone yell, and two of the four jumped onto their horses and galloped away. The other horses bolted away as well, leaving the two remaining shooters stranded.

"No!" one of them yelled, throwing down his gun and putting up his hands. "No, don't shoot! I give up, don't shoot!"

"Moss, you yellowbelly!" Taylor shouted, but as Smoke and Cal closed on them, he too threw up his hands.

CHAPTER FIVE

While Cal kept the two men covered, Smoke leaped from his saddle and hurried to Molly, who was lying on her back, a bleeding bullet hole in the middle of her chest, just below her bare breasts. Seeing Ned's shirt on the ground, he used it to cover her. She was breathing in wheezing gasps.

"Mrs. Condon, it's me, Smoke Jensen." Smoke took her hand.

"You are too late," she said, barely able to get the words out. "Tell Ned I love him."

Smoke glanced over toward Ned and saw him on his knees, his hands tied to the pump, his back raw with whip welts. There was a bullet hole in the back of his head.

"I will," Smoke said. "I'll tell him."

Molly took one last, labored breath; then she died.

Smoke put his pistol away, then walked up to the two men who were holding their hands in the air.

"It wasn't us who done this!" one of them said. "It was them two what done it! Fowler 'n Hill." He pointed to two of the three dead outlaws. "We told 'em there warn't no need to be shootin' these folks."

"That one was on top of the windmill," Smoke said, pointing to one of them. "How could he have done this?"

"Yeah, well, what I meant was, it was them two. The ones that run off, they was beatin' on 'em too, and—" That was as far as he got, before Smoke dropped him with a hard right hook.

"Hey, we've give up, you can't—" the other outlaw started to say, but his comment was stopped in mid-sentence because Smoke dropped him as well.

"Yes, I can," Smoke said. "Maybe I'm not sup-posed to, but that sure doesn't mean that I can't."

"What do we do now, Smoke?" Cal asked.

"Keep these two covered," Smoke said. "I'm going to get Ned and his wife into the house and in their bed. That's where they will be when the undertaker finds them."

"What do you think we should do with these three?" Cal asked, pointing to the dead outlaws.

"I'm tempted to throw them in the pen and let the hogs eat them," Smoke said. "But the sheriff may want to see them."

Smoke carried Molly in first, cradling her in his arms. As he carried her, he couldn't help but recall her laughter over the table when he had shared supper with them. He thought too of the songs she had sung in a clear, sweet voice.

A moment later he deposited Ned on the bed with Molly.

"I'm sorry I didn't get here an hour earlier," he said, as he looked down at the two.

The two outlaws were just coming to, when Smoke came back outside. "What are you goin' to do with us?" one of them asked.

"If I did what I want to do, I'd hang both of you from the barn rafters," Smoke said.

"No, don't! You got no right doin' somethin' like that!"

"What's your name?" Smoke asked.

"Taylor."

Smoke looked at the other man.

"Moss," he said.

"Cal, you keep Moss there covered, while I take care of Taylor. If Moss makes one move, shoot him."

"Nothing would please me more," Cal said.

"I ain't goin' to move! I ain't goin' to do nothin'!" Moss said.

"Smoke, there's Prince Dandy," Cal said, pointing to the bull they had been bringing to the ranch. "What shall we do with him?"

"We'll take him back," Smoke said. "The sale was never completed."

When Smoke had both prisoners bound, he put a loop around the neck of each of them.

"Oh, Lord, he's goin' to do it!" Moss said. "He's goin' to hang both of us."

"You lead Prince Dandy, I'll take care of these two," Smoke said, mounting Seven as he held on to the two ropes that were looped around the necks of Taylor and Moss.

"Hey, leadin' us like this is dangerous," Moss

said. "What if one of us was to trip? We could break a neck?"

"Yeah, you could, couldn't you?" Smoke said.

It was five miles from Wiregrass Ranch into the town of Brown Spur, and when Smoke and Cal rode into town they made a sight so unusual that by the time they were halfway through the town, there were fifty or more people following them. Smoke was leading Taylor and Moss, who were walking behind him, their arms securely bound down by their sides and with ropes around their necks. The two prisoners were wearing red armbands. Cal was leading a bull that even the uninitiated could tell was a magnificent animal. What no one could figure out was the connection between the bull and the two bound men, and Smoke heard that question being asked more than once.

By the time they arrived at the jail, word of the strange parade had already reached Sheriff Brown, and he was standing out front to greet them.

"I take it these two men are for me?" the sheriff asked.

"They are," Smoke said, dismounting.

"What did they do?"

"They killed Ned and Molly Condon."

"Oh, my God! Ned and Molly were killed?" someone gasped.

The news spread like wildfire through the crowd, repeated in tones of sadness, which quickly became sounds of anger.

"Let's hang the sons of bitches!" someone shouted.

"Yeah, they already got ropes around their necks," another said.

"We'd better get 'em inside before these people decide to take matters into their own hands," Sheriff Brown said. "Where are the Condons now?"

"They are out at the ranch," Smoke said. "I carried them inside and lay them on their bed. When you send the undertaker out there, he'll find three more bodies—friends of these two."

Ten Strike Mine

When Hannibal and Rexwell rode up alone, some of the others, seeing only two remaining of the seven who had ridden out, came over to them.

"Where are the others?" Peters asked. "Are they comin' along?"

"Fowler, Hill, 'n Newell was kilt, 'n they captured Taylor 'n Moss," Rexwell said.

"They'll more 'n likely hang 'em," someone said.

"You ever seen anyone get hung?" Rexwell asked.

"No."

"I have, 'n it ain't purty. Sometimes their eyes bulge out, 'n sometimes they swallow their tongue. They would of been a lot better off iffen they had got shot."

"They aren't going to hang," Hannibal said.

"I don't know, Hannibal," Rexwell said. "I mean we kilt that man and woman, 'n Taylor 'n Moss was captured right there with 'em. I don't know how they're not goin' to be hung."

"They will not hang," Hannibal repeated.

Sugarloaf Ranch

Cal was rubbing down Prince Dandy when Sally came out to the stall.

"Cal? Are you all right?" Sally asked.

"Yes, ma'am," Cal said, answering quietly.

"I'm worried about you. Ever since you and Smoke came back home you've not been yourself."

"No, ma'am, I guess maybe I haven't," Cal admitted. "It's just that, I can't get that picture out of my mind, Miz Sally. I mean, Miz Condon lyin' there, shot 'n half naked. And Mr. Condon was tied to the pump, 'n you could see how they had beat on 'im. I just don't know what kind of people can do somethin' like that."

Sally put her hand on Cal's shoulder. "Cal, you've seen your share of bad things in your life. You know that there are some people who are evil beyond all comprehension."

"I know. But I just can't get it out of my mind, is all."

Sally embraced him. "That's because you are a good person. I knew that the first time I ever met you."

"Ha!" Cal said, smiling for the first time. "I sure don't know how you could have known that then. I mean, considerin' how it was that you and I met."

"*You and I*, and not *me and you*. That's very good, Cal, I'm proud of you," Sally said. "And I was right. You are a good person."

"Yes, ma'am, I reckon I am. But that's because of you 'n Smoke."

"No, a good person is good from within. We recognized it, Cal, we didn't cause it."

"The trial is tomorrow," Smoke said at the dinner table that night. "Cal and I will have to go back over to Brown Spur to testify."

"Yes, I was sure you would," Sally said.

"I don't mind. Sally, I wish you could have met the Condons. They were really good people; I can see how everyone there thought so much of them. Justice needs to be done."

"Yes, and I think for Cal, especially," Sally said.

"For Cal?"

Sally told Smoke about her conversation with their young hand, earlier today. "Maybe, when he sees justice done, it will help him get over this. This has had quite an effect on him."

"He'll get over it."

"I'm sure he will. But Smoke, we've always known that Cal is different from Pearlie. Cal is, and always has been, a very sensitive young man."

Brown Spur

The cowboy, who had told Elegant Sue that his name was John, got up from bed and began dressing. It was over very quickly, they had come to her room upstairs at Bagby's no more than ten minutes ago.

"You're a sweet kid," John said in a low, gravely voice.

"Thank you," Elegant Sue responded quietly.

John had already put one boot on, but he paused before putting on the other and looked back at Elegant Sue, who, though naked, had the bed sheet pulled up to her shoulders.

"No, I mean really. I've been with a lot of whores, 'n some of 'em is just really hard, you know what I mean? Oh, it ain't always in what they say. But you can see it in their faces 'n their eyes. Especially in their eyes. Sometimes they look at you, but you get the feelin' they ain't really lookin' at you. You know what I mean?"

Elegant Sue didn't answer and wasn't even sure that he expected an answer.

"I don't feel that way about you. I know you can see me. But, and I don't know why, there's a sadness in your eyes. Even downstairs, when you're laughin' 'n drinkin' with us, your eyes ain't laughin'. They're sad."

John pulled on his boots, then stood up and tucked his shirttail into his jeans.

"Bye, Elegant Sue. It was nice," he said.

"Good-bye, John."

John closed the door behind him, and Elegant Sue lay in bed for a long moment after he left.

"Sweetheart, are you going to lie in bed all morning? You have to get up and get ready for school."

Elegant Sue could hear her mother's voice as clearly as if she were in the next room.

Tears came to her eyes. What would her mother think if she realized what her daughter had become?

Elegant Sue threw aside the sheet, got out of bed, and padded, barefoot and naked, over to the dresser where sat a porcelain vase and basin. After attending to her toilet she got dressed, then put water in her eyes to wash away the tears.

The men who came to Bagby's didn't want the bar girls to look sad. They wanted smiles and flirtations. And even after Annie's funeral, attended only by the other girls from the saloon, they had to come back and greet the patrons with smiles.

Elegant Sue started down the stairs and was greeted with a loud burst of laughter from one of the men, followed by Lilly's laughter.

"Elegant Sue, there you are!" Lilly said. "You need to come listen to some of these stories Jimmy is telling. They are really funny."

Elegant Sue put on a smile and walked over to join the others.

CHAPTER SIX

Brown Spur courthouse

"Oyez, oyez, oyez, this court will now come to order, the Honorable Judge Andrew Dixon presiding," the court bailiff shouted. "All rise."

"You may be seated," the judge said when he took his seat at the bench.

Judge Dixon picked up a pair of wire-rim glasses from the bench before him and slipped them on very carefully, hooking them on one ear at a time. For a long moment, he studied the document before him as if just now learning what the trial was to be, though so heinous had been the crime and so widespread the publicity, that he well knew.

Finally he put the paper down and glanced over toward the prosecutor's table.

"Mr. Fenton, you are handling prosecution?"

"I am, Your Honor."

He looked toward the defense table. "And you are from Denver, I believe?"

"Yes, Your Honor, Theodore Dawes."

"You aren't a public defender?"

"No, Your Honor."

"Pro bono?"

"Your Honor, as my clients are not destitute, I have been hired by them to act as their defense counsel. My credentials have been submitted to the court."

"Yes, I have seen them," Judge Dixon said. He turned his attention back to Arnold Fenton. "Mr. Prosecutor, make your case."

"Your Honor, the prosecution calls Mr. Kirby Jensen to the stand."

Smoke was sworn in.

"Mr. Jensen, are you known by any other name than Kirby?"

"Most people call me Smoke," Smoke replied.

There were a few reactions from the court when they heard the name. Not many had connected Kirby Jensen with Smoke Jensen, even those who had witnessed the swiftness of his draw when he had killed Lou Reece.

"Would you please tell the court what happened on the fifth of this month?"

Smoke told how he and Cal were delivering a bull to Ned Condon when they heard a woman scream, followed by gunshots. He told how Ned had been beaten before he was shot in the back of the head, and how Molly, who had been partially stripped, died shortly after he and Cal arrived.

"Thank you, I have no further questions. Your witness, Mr. Dawes."

"Mr. Jensen, did you actually see either Mr. Taylor

or Mr. Moss fire the fatal shots?" defense counsel asked.

"No. Both had been shot before we arrived."

"Then you can't say, with certainty, that my clients are the ones who killed them, can you?"

"I don't care whether they did it or not," Smoke said.

Dawes, thinking he had scored a point, turned toward the jury to measure their reaction, but when he heard Smoke's unexpected response he turned quickly back toward Smoke.

"What do you mean, you don't care?"

"Taylor and Moss and at least five more were there. As far as I'm concerned, all seven of them killed Ned and Molly Condon. I killed two and Cal killed one. We captured these two, and I fully expect the state to hang them."

"That means you are prejudging them, Mr. Jensen."

"You're damn right I am. And if I had had even the slightest thought that they wouldn't be hanged, I would have killed them myself. And if the state doesn't hang them, I will kill them."

There was another audible gasp in the audience at Smoke's words.

"Your Honor, I object!" the defense counsel said.

"Sustained. Court reporter will strike Mr. Jensen's last four words," the judge said. "Mr. Jensen," the judge said, admonishing Smoke. "What you have just done constitutes a threat to murder. I caution you, sir, to measure your words and respond with restraint."

"Yes, Your Honor."

"I have no further questions of this witness, Your Honor," Dawes said, putting as much contempt in his voice as he could.

Cal's testimony was identical to Smoke's, and Dawes waived his cross-examination.

Sheriff Brown was next on the stand, testifying about the fact that they were Ghost Riders.

"Even if you don't find them guilty of this killin', there is absolutely no doubt in my mind that they're guilty of at least a dozen more," the sheriff said.

After the prosecutor finished his presentation, it was time for the defense attorney to make his case for his clients.

Taylor and Moss both testified in their own behalf, both of them claiming that it was Eli Newell, one of the men killed by Smoke and Cal, who had actually shot Ned and Molly Condon.

"We didn't neither one of us have nothin' to do with it," Taylor said.

"The reason we didn't run away like the other three done, was 'cause we figured we should stay and tell the law who it was that actual done the killin'," Moss added during his time on the witness stand. "Neither one of us thought that killin' them two nice people was right, and we figured it was our duty to hang around and see to it that justice was done for them poor folks."

"I have no further questions, Your Honor."

"Mr. Prosecutor, cross?"

"No, Your Honor. I've heard enough of their lies."

In his final statement to the jury, the defense attorney reiterated the fact that neither Kirby Jensen, nor Cal Wood had been an actual witness to the murder of the two victims. "This is a fact that was admitted by both of them. Both witnesses testified that when they arrived, Fowler, Newell, and Hill were dead . . . by their hands, I hasten to add, and that my clients surrendered to them without putting up a fight.

"You cannot find my clients guilty of murder if you have no eyewitnesses to the crime."

The defense attorney sat back down, amidst the smug smiles of both Taylor and Moss.

"Mr. Prosecutor, your closing?" Judge Dixon said.

When the prosecutor approached the jury, he had in his hand a rather large, red book. He opened the book to a page marker and, without a word of introduction, began to read.

"An accessory is a person who assists in the commission of a crime, such as murder, but who is not actually a principal in said murder. In this case, there is no distinction between the crime as committed by the principal, and in support of the *actus reus*, which is the role of one who is the accessory."

He closed the book. "What that means, gentlemen of the jury, is that under the law of man and morality, these two men," he pointed to Taylor and Moss, "are guilty of the murder of Ned and Molly Condon just because they were there. It doesn't matter one whit whether or not they are the ones who pulled the trigger.

"And I ask you to find them guilty and to recommend that they both receive the death penalty."

The jury retired to consider the verdict, but given the barbarity of the act, nobody believed the jury would be out for any extended length of time, and that supposition turned out to be correct. The jury returned within less than half an hour and the gallery nodded and congratulated each other, because the evil sons of bitches who killed two of the finest people anyone is likely to find anywhere are going to pay for their crime.

There was a scrape of chairs and a rustle of pants, petticoats, and skirts as the spectators in the courtroom stood for the return of the jury.

"Gentlemen of the jury, have you reached a verdict?" Judge Dixon asked.

One of the jurors stood. "We have, Your Honor. My name is Douglas Wheeler, and I am the foreman of the jury."

"Would you publish the verdict please, Mr. Wheeler?"

"Your Honor, we find the defendants, Toon Taylor and Carl Moss, guilty of murder in the first degree. And it is the recommendation of the jury that they pay the extreme penalty for their act."

"Thank you, Mr. Wheeler and gentlemen of the jury,"

"Bailiff, would you position the prisoners before the bench for sentencing, please?" Judge Dixon asked.

"Yes, Your Honor."

The two men were brought before the bench. Though Moss stood with his head bowed contritely, Taylor stared defiantly at the judge.

"How long do we have to stand here and stare at your ugly face?" Taylor asked.

"Not long, sir. Not long at all," Judge Dixon said.

"In fact, sir, you have very little time remaining to stare at anyone, because I hereby order that a gallows or some similar contrivance for hanging be built as quickly as is practicable, and once done, that the sheriff of this community lead you to that place of your execution. There, a noose will be placed around each of your necks, the trapdoor lever will be pulled, you will fall to the end of that rope, and your necks will be broken. You will be nothing but dead meat then, and your miserable remains will become food for the worms.

"Now, Sheriff, take these worthless sons of bitches out of my courtroom. Court is adjourned," he said with a loud rap of the gavel.

The gallery broke into a spontaneous cheer.

Sheriff Brown approached Smoke and Cal at the back of the courtroom. "Smoke, I do hope that you and Cal will be present for the hanging."

"Oh, we intend to be," Smoke said. "How long do you think it will be before the gallows is constructed?"

"Joe Warner assures me that he will have it done within less than a week. So I don't expect it to be very long."

"We'll be here."

Ten Strike

The story of the upcoming hanging had appeared in newspapers all over the state, including the *Sorento Sun Times*.

"I thought you said that Taylor and Moss wouldn't hang," Rexwell said, showing the paper to Hannibal.

Hannibal read the paper, then smiled. "They won't, thanks to this article."

Rexwell got a confused look on his face. "What do you mean, thanks to that article?"

"A great warrior named Sun Tzu once said that the opportunity of defeating the enemy is provided by the enemy himself."

"I don't understand," Rexwell said.

"No, I didn't expect that you would. But the newspaper has provided us with all the information we need to make certain that Taylor and Moss do not hang."

CHAPTER SEVEN

Brown Spur

Carl Moss paced back and forth in the eight feet of cellblock that he was sharing with Taylor. Taylor was lying on his bunk. Outside the cell, the sound of the pulley straining with the sand-weight floated across the town square and in through the tiny barred window. As the weight slammed down against the trapdoor, Moss jumped and let out a little cry of alarm. Taylor laughed.

"What do you think, Moss? You think when we drop through that trapdoor that we'll sound like those sandbags? 'Course, sandbags don't scream or nothin', 'n I'm thinkin' you'll pro'bly squeal like a stuck pig."

"Why you talkin' like that, Taylor? I ain't the only one that's gettin' hung you know. You're gettin' hung too."

"Yeah, but the difference is, you'll land in hell screamin' 'n cryin', but me, I'm goin' to walk right up to the devil and kick him square in his ass."

Taylor finished his comment with a high pitched, insane sounding laugh.

"That's where we're both a goin', ain't it? We're both goin' to hell."

"I expect so."

"Ain't you some scared by that?"

"I'd rather visit the whores in hell, than listen to angels singin' in heaven," Taylor said.

"You are insane," Moss said.

Letter to the editor of the *Brown Spur Herald:*

> Dear Editor:
> I take this means of a letter to the editor to communicate, not only with you, but to the lawmen of Brown Spur and to the citizens of your town. You have recently tried and condemned to death by hanging, two of my men. I tell you now to disabuse yourselves of any idea that Toon Taylor and Carl Moss will hang. I adhere strictly to the principle of one for all, and all for one, and I will not let this hanging happen.
>
> > I am, sir, Hannibal,
> > Commandant of the Ghost Riders.

Because of the impending hanging of the two outlaws, Taylor and Moss, Bagby's Saloon had no more than a couple of customers, and Bagby had even contemplated closing the saloon.

"Why are you talking about closing it?" one of the two customers asked.

"Because of the hanging," Bagby replied.

"Hell, didn't you read Hannibal's letter in the paper today? He says there ain't goin' to be no hangin'."

"Yeah, well, he's wrong. All you have to do is look right outside 'n you can see for yourself."

All the way across the room from the bar, Elegant Sue, Lilly, Candy, Sweet Sal, and Maggie were sitting around a table. There had been a few customers in this morning, and everyone expected that business would be even more brisk after the hanging, so all five of the girls were wearing the revealing clothing that was the uniform of their profession.

"Do any of you plan to watch the hanging?" Maggie asked the other girls.

"Not me," Sweet Sal replied with a shudder. "That's not somethin' I care to see."

"Me neither," Lilly said.

"Surely, you don't plan to watch, do you, Maggie?" Elegant Sue asked.

"No, it's not something I want to see. I think when somebody murders someone, especially someone as nice as folks say Mr. and Mrs. Condon were, why, they should have to pay for their crime. I just don't want to watch it, is all."

"We'll know when it happens, though," Candy said.

"How will we know?" Lilly asked.

"I expect we'll hear it. They've been testing out

the thing all morning, and you can hear when the trapdoor opens, even from here."

"That's true," Elegant Sue said. "And we'll probably hear the crowd reaction as well."

"As long as all we do is hear it and don't have to watch it," Maggie said.

Candy got up and walked over to the door to stare across the batwings.

"What do you see, Candy?" Lilly asked. "Can you see the gallows?"

"Yes. There is a big crowd around it."

It was to be a public hanging, and a crowd was already beginning to gather in the middle of town. And because Ned and Molly Condon actually lived outside of town, other ranchers and farmers, feeling that the Condons were part of their own, had come to town as well.

As a result, Smoke and Cal, who had just arrived, saw that the town was not only crowded with people, but also with buggies, surreys, buckboards, coaches, and wagons. The two found a hitchrail with room for their horses, tied them off, then walked back down the street to the gallows. That's where they saw the sign.

TO BE HANGED ON THESE GALLOWS
TOON TAYLOR and CARL MOSS
Found guilty of the murder of
Ned Condon and his wife Molly
Justice Will Be Done

The sign was nailed to the front of the recently constructed gallows. The platform of the gallows stood thirteen feet high, the underpart hidden from view by canvas sheeting. It stood in the center of town, its grisly shadow stretching under the morning sun. From this moment it was less than fifteen minutes from the appointed time, and the crowd, already thick, grew even larger as many of the spectators began jostling for position.

Several hundred people were gathered around the gallows, men in suits, shirtsleeves, and overalls and women in long dresses and bonnets. Children, who weren't fully aware of what was about to happen, threaded in and out of the groups as they chased one another around the square. At the window of the cell a face would sometimes appear, look nervously through the bars at the crowd, then withdraw to the gloomy shadows within. A couple of young boys approached the cell and tried to peer in through the window, but a woman called out to them and they returned to the crowd.

A few enterprising vendors were selling lemonade, beer, and sweet rolls.

"Did any of you see that letter to the editor this mornin'?" Smoke heard someone ask.

"What letter to the editor?"

"It was from that fella that calls hisself Hannibal."

"Who?"

"Hannibal. You know, he's the one that's the head of the Ghost Riders. Or, the Commandant, he likes to call hisself. Anyway, he said he wasn't goin' to let this hangin' happen."

"Did he now?" the other man replied with a laugh. "Well, it's all bluster. As you can see," he pointed to the gallows. "It's about to happen. And there ain't no way in hell that he's goin' to be able to stop it now."

A black-frocked preacher climbed the thirteen steps up to the platform of the gallows, then stood there, awaiting the opportunity to give the condemned men one last chance at soul salvation.

"Hey, Padre!" someone from the crowd called. "We got a few a minutes left, why don't you give us a fire-eating sermon?"

"I am not here for that," the parson replied. "I am here only to succor the souls of the sinners."

"Well, hell, Padre, we're all sinners, ain't we?" one of the others shouted. "Leastwise, that's what you preachers is always a sayin'."

That comment got a nervous laugh.

"This is no place for levity," the preacher said, wagging his finger back and forth. "In a few moments two men are going to be sent to meet their Maker with blood on their hands and sin in their hearts. And if they do not repent of their sins, they will be cast into the fiery furnaces of hell, doomed to writhe in agony forever!"

Some of those in the crowd shivered involuntarily at his powerful imagery and looked toward the gallows. One or two of them touched their necks fearfully, and a few souls, perhaps weak on willpower, sneaked a drink from a bottle.

But the preacher, seeing that he had a captive and willing audience, decided to take advantage of the situation. He stepped to the front of the platform to preach his message.

"It's too late for them, but it's not too late for you! Repent! Repent now, I say, for the wages of sin are death and eternal perdition!"

"That's enough, Preacher," Sheriff Brown said. The sheriff looked up at the hangman. "It's about time, Mr. Cahill. Are you ready?"

"I'm ready," the hangman answered.

The sheriff turned toward the jail cell and waved his arm. A moment later the two prisoners, flanked on either side by deputies, were brought from the jail to the gallows.

"Burn in hell for what you did to Ned and Molly!" someone in the crowd shouted.

The sheriff met the two men at the foot of the steps.

"Come along you two," he said. "The show is about to start, and you two have top billing."

"You go to hell," Taylor said in a growling voice.

"Funny you would say that, Taylor, since I imagine you'll be there in just about three minutes."

The sheriff walked up onto the gallows platform with the two men; then he stepped out to the front, pulled a piece of paper from his pocket, and began to read.

"Toon Taylor and Carl Moss, having been tried by a jury of their peers and found guilty of murder, are on this day, at this time, and in this place, to be hanged by the neck until dead, by order of Judge Andrew Dixon."

The sheriff stepped back to the two men and

positioned them over the trapdoor. The hangman started to put the noose around Taylor's neck, when both trapdoors unexpectedly opened, and Taylor and Moss fell through. As the rope had not yet been put around either one of their necks, there was nothing to impede their falls.

"What happened?" the sheriff shouted.

"I don't know," the hangman answered.

"Well, get 'em back up here."

At that moment shots rang out, and all three of the men who were still standing on the platform—the sheriff, the hangman, and the preacher—went down under a hail of bullets.

The shooting continued and the spectators, who were waiting to witness the hanging, panicked and began to run. The center of town echoed with women's screams, men's yells, the crying of children, and the sound of gunfire, with so many guns shooting at the same time that it sounded almost like the rattle of musketry on a battlefield.

As many as two dozen mounted gunmen rode into the crowd, their horses trampling some and their indiscriminate shooting striking others. In the crowd, only Smoke and Cal had the presence of mind to engage the mounted gunmen, and they began shooting back. Smoke's first shot was at almost point-blank range, and because he was on the ground and his target was mounted, the bullet entered under the rider's chin and exited through the top of his head.

Cal also brought one of the riders down; then Smoke shot another one, and yet another.

Smoke saw one of the riders, a big, bald-headed man with a scar, shoot toward them.

"Uhnn!"

The grunt came from Cal.

"Cal!" Smoke shouted.

"I've been hit in the shoulder!" Cal said.

Then, even as Smoke was looking at him, Cal was hit two more times, once in the thigh and a third bullet hit him in the stomach, just above his belt buckle. Cal's eyes rolled back in his head and he fell.

"Cal!" Smoke shouted again. Turning, he looked for the bald-headed man, but he was gone. He did see the smiling face of the man who had been the second to shoot Cal. Smoke squeezed off a round and had the satisfaction of seeing a black hole appear in that man's forehead. He saw another one of the riders who was staring right at him. The rider fired at Smoke. The bullet missed Smoke, but he heard it strike someone behind him.

Smoke turned to see if he could be of any help, but the man was already dead.

By now the center of town was total pandemonium.

"Ghost Riders!" someone shouted. "Let's go!"

The mounted gunmen stopped shooting, then galloped away, leaving five of their own lying dead in the street behind them.

"Son of a bitch!" someone shouted. "Taylor and Moss! They're in the back of that wagon!"

Looking in the direction the man was pointing, Smoke saw the remaining riders converging on a fast-moving wagon. He realized then what had happened. The Ghost Riders had managed to get a harnessed wagon in position under the gallows, hidden by the canvas sheeting. Then just before the ropes were looped around the necks of the two prisoners, the man underneath the gallows opened the trapdoors and let the two condemned men fall into the wagon. The rest of it, the killing of the sheriff, hangman, and preacher, as well as shooting into the crowd, was just to cover the escape.

And Cal was one of those in the crowd who had been shot.

"Cal!" Smoke said, grabbing Cal's hand. "Cal!"

Cal opened his eyes. "Get me home, Smoke. I don't want to die here. Get me home, please?"

"I'm not going to let you die here, and I'm not going to let you die at home either," Smoke said.

Now some of the people were slowly beginning to work their way back into the center of town. Looking around, Smoke saw several bodies scattered around, including at least three women and one of the children. The wailing began. Smoke noticed that all five of the men he and Cal had shot, had a piece of red cloth tied around their arms, and he realized now, that it was probably for events like what happened here, today, that they wore the red bands. Such a thing would help them identify each other quickly in a melee such as just occurred.

Smoke saw someone that he assumed was a doctor looking at some of the people.

"Doctor, I have a wounded man here, I'd like for you to take a look at him if you would, please."

"Mister I have at least five more to look at, two of them women. You'll have to wait your turn," the harried doctor told him.

"Yes, I understand," Smoke said.

Smoke walked back over to Cal, scooped him up in his arms, then carried him into Bagby's Saloon.

CHAPTER EIGHT

"What are you bringing that man in here for?" one of the customers asked as Smoke stepped in through the batwing doors, carrying Cal in his arms as a mother would carry her baby. "This ain't no hospital."

"Let him in," Bagby said. "I know who this man is. He's the one who kilt the son of a bitch who kilt Annie."

"Bring him over here," one of the bar girls said.

"Thanks," Smoke replied. He recognized the girl who had spoken.

"I remember you," Smoke said. "You're Elegant Sue."

"Yes," Elegant Sue said. "Maggie, Lilly, Candy, help me get these two tables together," she said, and two of the tables were quickly put together. "Bagby, bring me a bottle of whiskey and some clean towels. All the clean towels you have."

Bagby brought the whiskey and the towels, and the girl poured the whiskey over Cal's three wounds; then she made compression bandages from towels.

"You look like you know what you're doing," Smoke said.

"I wasn't always a bar girl. My papa was a doctor, and I used to help him some."

"Thanks, Elegant Sue. I'm glad you're here," Smoke said.

"Elegant Sue is my bar girl name. My real name is Julia Pr . . . that is, Julia McKnight."

"Julia, I want to take Cal back home, so I'm going to go lease a buckboard and a team. I'll give you one hundred dollars to go with me and look after him on the way back."

"You don't have to give me that much money," Julia said.

"I know I don't have to. But this boy means that much to me," Smoke said. "The offer of a hundred dollars still stands."

"I'll go with you," Julia said. "But, if you're going to put him in the back of a buckboard, you should put him on a mattress. He doesn't need to be riding on the hard wood."

Smoke nodded. "Yes, that's a good idea. Not sure where I'm going to get a mattress on such short order, though."

"We can use the mattress from my bed. If I'm going with you, I won't be needing it."

"Thanks, again. I'm going to get a buckboard and a team," Smoke said, hurrying out of the saloon.

"Wow, you just wait until it gets around that he was here," Bagby said. "Why people will be comin' from all over, just to have a drink where the famous

Smoke Jensen kilt Lou Reece," Bagby said. "I didn't realize when he was here before, who he really was."

"Who is he?" Julia asked.

"Why, that's Smoke Jensen."

"Yeah, I got that much. But who is Smoke Jensen?"

"He's about the most famous gunfighter in the whole country, that's who," Bagby said. "Only he ain't evil. There has been books wrote about him. And from what I've read, he only uses his gun for the good. Sort of like a knight in shinin' armor, you might say," he added with a laugh.

"Julia," one of the other girls said, using her real name since Julia had already told Jensen what it was, "if you're going off travelin' with somebody like Smoke Jensen, don't you think maybe you ought to change clothes first?"

Julia glanced down at the exposed, creamy tops of her breasts.

"Oh, yes," she said. "Maybe I'd better do that. You stay here with him, will you, Maggie?"

"All right, but I don't know anything about nursing. So what do I need to do?"

"Nothing, really. Right now about the only thing you can do, is just make certain he doesn't roll off onto the floor."

Maggie chuckled. "Well, I can do that, at least."

Ten minutes later Smoke returned. "The buckboard is out front," he said.

Julia was much more modestly dressed now, and she had a packed bag of clothes with her. The mattress from her bed had also been brought down and was lying on the end of the bar. There were a few more people in the saloon now, who hadn't been here earlier, but seeing Cal laid out on the two tables, were quickly caught up with what was going on.

"Gordon, Ike, why don't you help Mr. Jensen carry this man?" Julia asked.

"I'll get him," Smoke said, scooping Cal up in his arms with little effort. "But I would appreciate it if you two would carry the mattress out to the buckboard."

"Sure thing, Mister," Ike answered.

Smoke and Cal's horses were tied to the back of the buckboard. The two men put the mattress down, and Smoke lay Cal upon it; then he helped Julia climb in beside her patient.

"Here, Sue," Lilly said, holding up a carpetbag. "I mean Julia," she corrected with a smile.

"Thanks, Lilly," Julia replied.

"Better hold on back there, Miss McKnight," Smoke said. "I'm going to drive as fast as I can without killing this team."

"Who is Miss McKnight?" Ike asked.

Gordon shrugged his shoulders. "Beats the hell out of me."

Smoke snapped the reins over the backs of the team, and the buckboard left Brown Spur at a rapid trot. As he drove out of town, he saw the carnage that had been brought on by the Ghost Riders' raid. The dead had been lined up alongside the street—the dead Ghost Riders separated from the slain citizens of the town. There were five of the Ghost Riders and eight townspeople, four men, three women, and one child. There were people standing over the bodies of the citizens of the town, many of them openly weeping.

As the buckboard travelled along at a rapid clip, Cal, unable to hold on, started bouncing around in the back. Julia lay down on the mattress beside him, put the sheet over them, and wrapping her arms around him, pulled Cal close to her.

Smoke had to pass by his ranch, Sugarloaf, before he reached Big Rock, but he didn't stop. Instead he drove on by, seven more miles to Big Rock, making the entire trip in a little over two hours. Smoke pulled up to the front of the doctor's office, yelling at him even before he came to a complete stop.

"Doc! Doctor Urban! Doc!"

Doctor Urban not only heard his name being called, but recognizing Smoke's voice, hurried out of his office to meet him. The buckboard slid to a stop, only to be wreathed for a moment in the rooster tail of dust that had been kicked up by the whirling wheels.

"It's Cal," Smoke said, setting the brake and jumping down. "He's been shot." Smoke looked toward Julia. "Is he—"

He didn't have to finish the question.

"He's still alive," Julia said.

"Get him inside quickly, Smoke," Doctor Urban said.

As he had before, Smoke scooped Cal up in his arms and carried him into the doctor's office.

"Back here," Doctor Urban said, leading the way into the back room he had set up in order to allow him to conduct surgical procedures.

"The bullet in his stomach has to come out first," Dr. Urban said after a quick examination. "This is going to be very tricky. We have to pray that no internal organs are involved, but I think they may not be, or he would, more than likely, be dead by now. And I not only have to get the bullet, I'll have to find the piece of cloth from his shirt that the bullet took in with it."

"Smoke?" someone called from the front of the office.

"Monte, I'm back here," Smoke replied, recognizing Sheriff Carson's voice.

"What happened?"

"Cal's been shot. Do me a favor, Monte, and ride out to my ranch to get Sally. She'll want to be here. Pearlie too."

"How bad is it?"

"It's very bad," Doctor Urban said. He shook his head. "Smoke, you have to be prepared to lose him."

"I know," Smoke said. "That's why I want Sally here."

"I should give him some chloroform, but it has to be done just right, or it is more dangerous than helpful. And I can't do that and operate at the same time."

"I know how to administer chloroform," Julia said. "My father was a doctor and I did it for him."

"Excellent," Dr. Urban said. "Well, we had better get started. Smoke, you stand by too. Sometimes folks act rather peculiar when they are under the effects of chloroform, they dream some strange things and they don't know the difference between dreams and reality. And I would start by taking his gun out of his holster."

"Right, I should have done that before, but I didn't think of it."

"I'll get started out to your place, Smoke, and I'll be back with Sally as soon as I can," Sheriff Carson said.

"Thanks, Monte."

Sally had just gathered some eggs and was walking back to the house when she saw Sheriff Carson approaching. Seeing him wouldn't, in itself, cause her to be curious, but he was coming at a gallop, and that was not only curious, it was also a little troubling.

"Sheriff, what is it?"

"Smoke wants you to come to the doc's office quick. Cal's been shot."

"Oh! How bad is he?"

"He's real bad, Sally. If you want to see him while he's still alive, Doc says you'd better get there fast. Smoke said to bring Pearlie, too."

"Pearlie!" Sally shouted.

Pearlie was in the barn and he came running. "Yes, ma'am, what's wrong?"

"We have to go to town! Cal's been shot!"

"I'll get the horses saddled," Pearlie said without having to be told. He turned back to the barn on a run.

"I'm goin' to start on back," Sheriff Carson said. "I plumb wore out my horse gallopin' out here so fast, I'm going to have to walk him back, so you two will more 'n likely pass me on the way."

"Thank you, Sheriff."

"Yes, ma'am. I sure hope Cal pulls through all right."

"A prayer would be good too," Sally said.

"Yes, ma'am, I been doin' that ever since I left town," the sheriff said as, touching his fingers to the brim of his hat, he turned his horse and started back.

In no time at all, it seemed, Pearlie was back riding one horse and leading Sally's.

"Oh, please, Lord, let him live until I get there," Sally said as she mounted the horse.

"Do you want to go at a gallop?" Pearlie asked.

"Yes!" Sally replied, breaking into a gallop, even as she shouted the word back.

Within less than three minutes, they thundered by Sheriff Carson, who was now proceeding at a brisk trot.

"God be with you!" Sheriff Carson shouted, the words trailing off in the distance as Sally and Pearlie galloped by.

As Sally bent forward into the wind, she knew that the time might well come when she would have to respond to a call to Smoke's side, just as she was, now, to Cal. She was thankful that it wasn't Smoke she was galloping to see, but almost as soon as she had that thought, she felt guilty, as if she was saying she was thankful it was Cal instead of Smoke.

Twenty minutes later, the two riders were thundering down Front Street, past Delmonico's and Longmont's Saloon; then they turned up Sikes Street.

Dr. Urban's office was right across the street from the courthouse and tucked in between the Big Rock Theater and the Brown Dirt Saloon.

"You go on in, Miz Sally, I'll tether the horses," Pearlie said, as both of them dismounted.

Sally tossed the reins to Pearlie, then ran into the office. "Smoke! Where is Cal?" She shouted. "Smoke!"

"We're back here," Smoke replied as Pearlie came in.

Sally and Pearlie hurried into the back.

"How is he?" she asked Dr. Urban. "Oh, please tell me he is still alive."

"He's still alive, but as to how he is, it's too early to tell yet. I've got the bullets out, but he's still under the effects of the chloroform. We'll just have to wait to see how he responds."

"Oh, please, God, let him come through this," Sally said aloud.

"Amen," Julia said.

Sally looked at Julia then, as if seeing her for the first time.

"Sally, this is Julia," Smoke said. "She helped me get Cal back here."

"I'm pleased to meet you, Julia," Sally said. "And thank you so much for your help."

CHAPTER NINE

Cal was dreaming.

"Your mama is a whore."

Cal was twelve years old, living in the town of Eagle Tail, Kansas, and he was sweeping the floor of the Beer Barrel Saloon, the saloon where his mother worked.

"You know that, don't you, boy?"

The man who was talking was one of the cowboys who frequented the saloon. "Your mama is a whore and you don't even know who your pappy is, do you? Hell, for all I know, I might be your pappy. I've sure bedded your mama often enough."

Cal's face burned as the two men who were at the table with the cowboy, laughed.

"How does it feel to be a whore's kid?"

Cal didn't answer.

"Your mama's upstairs right now with some drummer that ain't even from here. Tell me, boy, if he decides to spend the night with her, where do you sleep? Do you get to watch?"

"For crying out loud, Bill, let the boy be," the bartender said. "He's a good boy, and he comes here every day after school and works hard. He's never give me no trouble."

"I'm just funnin' him," Bill said.

"I doubt that he's havin' much fun from it."

"Whore's got no business havin' kids anyway," Bill said. "They ought to know that if they birth some brat, he's goin' to be nothin' but trouble. This little bastard will no doubt be in jail by the time he's sixteen years old."

Cal had made no response to the cowboy's brutal teasing, and now he picked up the trash he had swept up and put it in the can.

"I'm goin' to take the trash out, Mr. Fitzgerald," Cal said.

"All right. When you come back in, I'll have a lemonade waitin' for you."

"Thank you."

"Put some whiskey in it, Paddy," Bill said. "Hell, he's goin' to turn into a drunk someday anyway, he may as well get an early start."

Again the other two men laughed.

Cal went out back to dump the trash; then he ran up the side of the saloon to reach the street. There were six horses tied to the hitchrail in front of the saloon. Cal knew which horse belonged to Bill, and walking out to it, he looked around to make certain he wasn't being observed. Then, he cut the girth strap nearly all the way through. That done, he hurried back along the side of the saloon so that he would come back in through the same door he had used to leave.

The lemonade was sitting on the bar and he went over to pick it up. He was very hot . . . he didn't know why he was so hot. Somehow, the lemonade made his forehead feel cooler, though he didn't know how that could be.

With the floor swept, Cal stepped behind the bar and began washing shot glasses and beer mugs.

"You know the bunk is back there for you if you need it, Cal," Fitzgerald said in a comforting voice.

"Yes, sir, thank you," Cal said.

A few minutes later, Bill and the two cowboys with him got up to leave the saloon.

"Boy, tell your mama it's too bad she had an all-night customer," Bill called to him. "I would'a given 'er just a real good time."

"Don't pay any attention to him, Cal. He's nothin' but a loudmouth," Fitzgerald said.

"I don't pay no attention to people like that," Cal said. "I mean I don't pay any attention to people like that. Miz Sally would want me to say it that way."

Fitzgerald didn't react to the mention of Sally's name, and Sally, slipping into Cal's dream, didn't seem at all out of place to him.

Fitzgerald rubbed his hand through Cal's hair. "That's the way to do it."

"I'll get the glasses off their table," Cal said.

As he walked around from behind the bar, he looked outside through the front window. He saw the three cowboys mount up and start to ride off, but Bill went only a few feet before the girth strap snapped, the saddle slid off to one side, and Bill was dumped into the street. And, as it so happened, he fell into a big pile of horse apples.

The other two cowboys with him laughed out loud. "Damn, Bill, can't you stay on a horse?" one of them asked.

There were about six other men in the saloon, cowboys from one of the other ranches, and one of them happened to be looking outside when Bill fell.

"Ha! What the hell? Bill Dumas just fell off his horse!"

The others, looking outside, laughed.

Angrily, Bill got up from the pile of horse apples and stormed back into the saloon. He pointed to the group of laughing cowboys.

"All right, which one of you sons of bitches cut my saddle strap?" he shouted angrily.

"Damn, Bill," one of them said, waving his hand in front of his nose. "Why don't you go home and change shirts? You smell like horse shit."

The others laughed.

Bill stared at them for a moment, then with a shouted curse, went back outside. He mounted his horse and with the saddle thrown across in front of him, rode away bareback.

"Whooee," one of the cowboys said, slapping his leg in laughter. "I don't know who cut his strap, if anyone did. But if I knew who it was, I'd buy him a beer."

"I did it," one of the other cowboys said.

"No you didn't, Jed, hell, you been right here since before he even come here."

"Yeah, but I'll say I did it to get Arnie to buy me a beer."

The others laughed.

"Cal, did you do that?" Fitzgerald asked, quietly.

Dr. Urban's office

"Yes, sir, I did that," Cal said aloud. "I truly did." Cal laughed.

"What do you think it is that he did?" Sally asked.

"I don't know," Smoke said. "But whatever it is, he seemed to find it funny."

Cal opened his eyes, and when he did, he was looking into the face of a beautiful young woman. The woman was holding a cool, damp cloth to his forehead.

"Are you an angel?" he asked.

"How are you feeling, Cal?" Smoke asked.

"I thank you for the lemonade, Mr. Fitzgerald. It sure hit the spot."

"What?" Smoke looked at Dr. Urban. "Doc, is he all right?"

Dr. Urban laughed. "He'll be fine as soon as all the effects of the chloroform and the laudanum wear off. It's probably some dream he was having, that's hanging on.

"It's going to take him a while to recover, but I'm more hopeful now than I was when you first brought him here."

"Oh, thank God!" Sally said. She hurried to his bed and leaned over, then stopped and looked at Dr. Urban. "Will it be all right if I give him a hug?"

"I think that might be just what the doctor calls for," he replied with a smile.

"Miz Sally," Cal said.

Sally gave him a big hug. "Oh, Cal, you frightened me to death."

"I'm sorry I did," Cal said.

Pearlie came over to the bed as well. "You've scared all of us, pardner," he said, reaching down to put his hand on Cal's shoulder.

"Pearlie, you're not going to give me a hug too, are you?"

Pearlie laughed. "You and I are friends, Cal, but we ain't that friendly." He looked over at Sally. "Excuse me for saying ain't."

"Under the circumstances, Pearlie, you are forgiven."

"I'd like to ask a question," Cal said.

"All right, ask away," Smoke said.

"Where am I? And why is everyone making out over me so?"

"You don't remember anything?" Smoke asked.

"The last thing I remember is cuttin' the girth so that Bill fell on his ass in a pile of horse shit."

Cal's eyes grew big and he put his hand over his mouth. "Miz Sally, please forgive me. I'm sorry I said that in front of you 'n my angel."

"That's quite all right," Sally said. She chuckled. "And I'm sure your *angel* doesn't mind, either."

"You mean you can *see* my angel?"

"Yes, of course I can. She's standing right here."

"I didn't know anyone else could see her. But

nobody answered my question. Where am I, 'n why is ever'one makin' over me so?"

"You're in Dr. Urban's office," Smoke said. "And the reason we're all *making over you* as you say, is because we've been very worried about you. You were shot."

"I was shot? Who shot me?"

"You don't remember anything at all?"

"I remember . . . wait, didn't we go over to Brown Spur to see a hangin'? Yes, I remember that. The people that killed the Condons, we went over to watch them hang. I remember being out on the street waitin', but I don't remember anything after that. I don't even remember seein' 'em hang."

Smoke looked at Dr. Urban. "Is that something to worry about, because he can't remember?"

"No," Dr. Urban said, shaking his head. "It's called traumatic amnesia, and it's quite common. Sometimes the memory comes back, and sometimes it doesn't. But even if that particular memory never comes back, it won't matter. As long as it is isolated like that, it doesn't seem to have any lasting effect. And it is a good sign that he knows everybody."

"To answer your question, Cal, we didn't see them hang, because they didn't hang," Smoke said. "The Ghost Riders came in with guns blazing, they killed the sheriff, the hangman, the preacher, and some of the people in the crowd. You were one of the people who got shot but, luckily, you weren't killed."

"I hope you got a few of them," Cal said.

"We both did."

"Good."

"Doctor, how soon can we take him home?" Sally asked.

"Let him stay here for a couple more days; then we'll talk about you taking him home," Dr. Urban said.

"All right."

"Miss McKnight," Dr. Urban said. "I have an extra room here, in my office. I don't have a nurse, and you seem quite proficient. I wonder if you would consider staying on for a while longer? I'll be glad to pay you."

"All right," Julia answered.

"You don't have to pay her, Doc. I'll pay her," Smoke said.

"Is there anything you need, Julia?" Sally asked. "Anything I can get for you?"

"No ma'am, thank you just the same," Julia said. "I brought a grip with me. It's out in the buckboard."

"I'll get it," Pearlie said. "Anything for Cal's angel," he added with a broad smile.

"I'm glad you folks can see my angel too," Cal said. "She sure is pretty, isn't she?"

"Yes, Cal, your angel is very pretty," Sally said.

"You aren't going to go away or anything are you?" Cal asked Julia. "I mean, just 'cause I didn't die, that doesn't mean you have to leave me, does it?"

"I'm not going to leave you," she said.

"That's good. I sort of like having my own angel."

* * *

Smoke made arrangements with the Big Rock Livery Stable to take the buckboard and team back to Brown Spur; then he, Sally, and Pearlie rode back out to Sugarloaf, leading Cal's horse.

"Oh, Smoke, I don't know what I would do if we lost Cal," Sally said.

"He's a strong kid," Smoke said. "And now Doctor Urban is sure that none of his vital organs were hit. I think it's just going to be a matter of time until he heals up. Julia knows what she's doing, and Cal seems to get along with her all right, so I think I'll pay her to stick around until Cal is fully recovered."

"He more than just *gets along with her*. He thinks she's his angel."

"You might say that she is," Smoke said. "Sally, I really don't think I could have gotten Cal back alive, if it hadn't been for her."

LETTER TO THE EDITOR

Dear Editor:

Readers of the newspapers in which my missives now appear, and I am happy to report that this includes most of the newspapers in the state, will recall that I said that my two men, Toon Taylor and Carl Moss, would not hang. By now, everyone in the state must know that I was true to my word, carrying out a brilliant rescue operation.

Success was assured because I planned every aspect of the operation before I launched the attack.

In the words of the great military tactician

Sun Tzu, "The general who wins a battle makes many calculations in his temple before the battle is fought. The general who loses a battle makes but few calculations."

I am Hannibal,
Commandant of the Ghost Riders.

CHAPTER TEN

Hannibal knew that there were some in his organization who questioned why he wanted them to wear armbands. Initially, he had told them that they were wearing red armbands so that in the confusion of battle, they could quickly determine friend from foe. But there was more to it than that. Wearing the red armbands provided a cohesiveness, a unity, just as uniforms did for the army. He knew that, even though they might not realize it, the red armbands gave the men of his command a sense of belonging to a whole that was greater than themselves.

Hannibal wore a blue band, setting himself apart from the others, while still belonging to them. The blue band indicated that he was their leader. Bo Rexwell, who was second-in-command, wore an orange band.

Rexwell wouldn't have had to wear an armband at all; his appearance was so distinctive that he could be picked out from any crowd. He was bald-headed and his neck was so short that his head looked as if a cannonball was balanced on his shoulders. He also had a purple scar that ran from just above his left eyebrow up across his forehead to just where his hairline would have been if he had hair.

The outfit had been decreased by eight men, Hannibal having lost three at the Condon Ranch and five in Brown Spur when he rescued Taylor and Moss.

"It don't seem like it was all that good of a trade-off to me," Rexwell had said after the Brown Spur incident. "We saved two men but it wound up costing us five."

"That's because you don't understand the concept," Hannibal said. "I want every Ghost Rider to know that we are there for them. Only when you know that it is one for all, and all for one, can you be sure that there will be absolute and unquestioned loyalty. Remember, that is the motto of the Ghost Riders; one for all, and all for one."

Hannibal had stolen that motto from *The Three Musketeers.*

Hannibal believed that he needed to find another operation for the men, one that promised a high return for a minimum risk. Such an operation, he knew, would accomplish three things. One, it would make up for the unsuccessful Wiregrass mission. Two, it would take their minds off the men they had lost in the Brown Spur rescue mission, though in Hannibal's mind, as he had written in his letter to the editor, that had not been a failure. The mission objective had been to rescue his two men who were about to be hanged. And though it had cost him five men, the mission objective had been achieved, and Hannibal believed that achieving the mission, whatever the objective might be, was worth any cost.

And finally, he needed a mission that would provide another infusion of cash, and he knew exactly where, and how, he would do that.

At the moment, because of the loss of eight men, his company was understrength. When he set about building up the Ghost Riders, he had established a table of organizational manpower with a count of thirty men, including himself and Rexwell.

Now, there were only twenty-two, but for what he had in mind, that would be enough. And after this operation, he would recruit more men.

Ten Strike was near the town of Sorento, and Hannibal allowed his men to have a pass into Sorento, but never more than four at a time. And he cautioned them never to wear their red armbands and to always be on their best behavior while they were in town. Any violation of his rules, and they would be court-martialed. And he warned them that if they were found guilty by court-martial, the penalty would be quite severe.

So far there had been no need for a court-martial.

Tonight, as four men were in town and the rest of the men were entertaining themselves with card games and other amusements, Hannibal was planning the next mission. He had, spread out on the table in front of him, a map of Laurette, including the roads approaching the town.

As he examined the map, the plan of operation came to him and he smiled.

"Yes," he said aloud. "I know exactly how to do it."

Two days later, Hannibal and the Ghost Riders were gathered just outside the town of Laurette. It was nine o'clock in the morning, and the bank in town had just opened.

"We will split into two groups," Hannibal said. He had already laid out the plans of the operation to them, but he believed in the old dictum to *tell them what you are going to tell them; tell them; then tell them what you told them.* That way, there would be no chance of a misunderstanding.

"Rexwell, you will take half of the men and ride down the right side of the road; Taylor, you take the rest and go down the other side. I will be in the middle. Please understand that, for all intents and purposes, we are at war and war is an absolute. To that end, we will shoot everyone who is on the street."

"Women and children?" someone asked.

"Yes. The shock effect must be terrible and absolute. Believe me, nothing will have a greater shock effect than to see wounded or dead women and children. Ride all the way through to the far end of the road, continuing to shoot everyone you see, then come back to the bank. At that time I will take two men inside. Rexwell, you and the others will fan out into an arc just in front of the bank. I want at least two of you to be armed with rifles, and you will shoot anyone you see, no matter how far away from the bank they are.

"Smith, you and Peters are the best shots with the long guns, so that will be your assignment. But don't get them out until we reach the bank. You'll need short guns to huzzah the town."

Smith and Peters nodded.

"All right, men, draw your pistols."

Every man drew his gun and awaited Hannibal's order.

"Charge!" he shouted.

The armed unit galloped into town.

Because it was a warm, sunny morning, the boardwalks on both sides of the street were crowded with pedestrians as people were taking advantage of the weather to get their shopping done. The thunder of galloping horses caught everyone's attention, and people stopped talking in midconversation to look toward the curious sight.

"What is this?" someone asked. "Who are those fools, galloping into town like that? Someone could get hurt."

"I don't know, but we'd better stay out of the street."

"Engage!" the loud, and to the townspeople, meaningless word, could be heard even above the thunder of hooves.

Suddenly there was the staccato sound of gunshots. Bullets whizzed by the pedestrians, slamming into the buildings, and through the glass windows behind them.

"They're shooting at us! They're shooting at—" That was as far as the caller got before he went down.

After the first few bullets, the shooting became more accurate as men, women, and at least three children went down under the gunfire. The sheriff and his deputy, hearing the shots, came out of their office to return the fire, but they got off only a few shots, none of which hit their target, before they too went down.

By now the screams and shouts were nearly as loud as the gunfire, but the human voices quickly died out as so many of the citizens were shot down and the others fled. In accordance with Hannibal's plan, the group of riders galloped to the far end of the street, then returned, where they stopped in front of the bank. By now there was no one out on the street.

"Shoot into the bank!" Hannibal ordered.

Everyone began shooting into the bank. After several rounds, there was practically no glass left in the building, and not until then did Hannibal and two more men dismount.

"Peters, Smith, take out your rifles and shoot any target you can see," Hannibal ordered just before he stepped into the bank.

Inside they found two men and a woman. All three were dead. That left no one alive to open the safe door but that wasn't necessary. Hannibal had planned this operation with as much precision as he planned any operation, striking just at the start of the day's business. Because of that, the door was standing wide open.

"You two, empty the cashier's drawers. I'll clean out the safe," Hannibal said.

From outside they heard the sporadic bark of Winchester rifles as Smith and Peters fired at targets of opportunity.

"Let's go!" Hannibal said, once he had the safe emptied. Coming back out front, Hannibal and the other two mounted their horses.

"We'll leave the same way we came in," he said. "Shoot anyone you see."

The Ghost Riders galloped out of town, but this time there was no gunfire because there was no one left to provide a target. Behind them strewn on the boardwalks and in the street and in the bank, were bodies of men, women, and children.

Forty miles north of Laurette, and totally unaware of the massacre that had just taken place in that town, Smoke was taking Cal back home. Cal was lying on a mattress in the back of a buckboard, and Julia was sitting with him.

As they turned off the Big Rock Road, Julia looked up to see the great arch that stretched across the drive. The words SUGARLOAF RANCH were worked within the arch in wrought-iron letters.

The drive ran at least one hundred yards up to a huge, and Julia thought, beautiful house. She had already seen enough of Smoke Jensen to know that he was courageous and very good with a gun. She also knew that he was one of the nicest men she had ever been around, and in the last couple of years she had been around many men. What she hadn't known until this moment, was that he was a very wealthy man.

Smoke stopped the buckboard in front of the house, where he was met by Pearlie and one of the other ranch hands. They had a litter, and carefully, they moved Cal onto the litter, then carried him into the house. For the duration of his recovery, Cal would be in what the cowboys called the big house, rather than the bunkhouse.

"I'll put the buckboard away," Smoke said.

"Before you do that, shouldn't you take me back into town?" Julia asked.

"Why do you want to go to town?"

"Well, now that we have him home, I think I should go on back to Brown Spur," Julia said.

"Must you?" Sally asked. "It is obvious that you know how to nurse. I would be very pleased if you would stay on for a while, at least until Cal is much improved. We would be more than happy to compensate you for your time."

"Uh, ma'am, I would love to stay, but . . . uh . . . you might not want me to, when you find out who I am."

"You two work it out," Smoke said, as he headed toward the barn.

"What do you mean, find out who you are?" Sally asked. "Do you mean your name isn't Julia McKnight?"

"Oh, no, Julia McKnight *is* my real name," Julia said. "But the folks back in Brown Spur know me by my *working* name as Elegant Sue."

"I see," Sally said.

"Yes ma'am, I figured you would see, I mean once you heard what my working name was. So I'm sure you don't want me to stay around, now that you know."

"Julia, I had some very good friends once, named Flora and Emma, both of whom worked for someone who called herself Fancy Lil. Now, if I could have friends like that, why couldn't I have a friend named Elegant Sue?"

"But, were they . . . I mean, these friends of yours—"

"Are you asking me if they were ladies of the evening?" Sally asked.

"Yes ma'am, I guess I am."

"The operative term in *ladies of the evening*, Julia, is that they were ladies. They were also my friends, and I would like you to be my friend as well."

"Oh," Julia said. "Why, Mrs. Jensen, I would be honored to be your friend."

"Good. We'll start with you not calling me Mrs. Jensen. I'm Sally."

"Sally," Julia said with a wide smile.

CHAPTER ELEVEN

Pearlie and the cowboy who had helped him carry Cal into the bedroom where he would be staying, came back out onto the front porch.

"We've got him all situated, Miz Sally," Pearlie said.

"Thank you, Pearlie."

"You know what I was thinkin'?" Pearlie asked.

"What's that?"

"He'd more 'n likely love to have some bear claws. That is, if you felt up to makin' some."

"Oh, I don't think it would be good for him to have a whole batch of bear claws all by himself. I mean, with him having a stomach wound, I'm sure it wouldn't be good."

"No ma'am, I don't think so either," Pearlie said. "That's why I'd be glad to take some of 'em, just so that he doesn't eat too many."

Sally smiled. "Pearlie, that is awfully nice of you to volunteer like that."

"Well, Cal is my friend, so I just want to do right by him, is all."

"I'm sure you do. I'll get some made," Sally said.

"Of course, that's only if you want to do it, you understand."

"I understand," Sally said.

Sally looked at Julia and both of them laughed.

"Come on into the parlor, make yourself comfortable, and we'll talk. But first I want to check on Cal."

After showing Julia into the parlor, Sally went to the downstairs bedroom where she had told Pearlie to put Cal. She thought she would just check on him, thinking he would probably be asleep. But she saw that he was scratching at the wound on his shoulder.

"Cal, don't do that, you shouldn't scratch at your wound like that."

Cal looked at Sally for a moment, and she saw the confusion in his eyes. "I'm in your house, ain't . . . I mean, aren't I?"

"Indeed you are."

"Miz Sally, have I been shot?"

"Cal, don't you remember? Smoke told you all about it."

"No ma'am, I don't remember it."

"Yes, you have been shot. What do you remember?"

"I remember the angel."

Sally smiled. "Oh yes, the angel."

"Yes ma'am, I was lyin' in bed, 'n the angel was lyin' in bed with me." Cal held up his hand. "Only, don't get the wrong idea, 'cause we didn't do anythin' bad, what with her bein' an angel 'n all. I mean, she was just lyin' beside me in the bed, sort of makin' me feel better, you know? I think it was an angel, 'cause I don't have any other way of explainin' it."

"Wait here for a moment," Sally said.

Sally went into the parlor and saw Julia just sitting there, as if not yet quite sure of her place.

"He wants to see his angel," Sally said.

"Is he still calling me his angel?"

Sally smiled and crooked her finger. "Come with me."

Julia followed her down the hall and into a bedroom, where she saw Cal lying on the bed.

"I brought someone to see you," Sally said.

Cal looked over and, seeing Julia, he gasped. "It's my angel!"

"Yes, she is your angel," Sally said. "Oh, maybe she doesn't have wings and she doesn't sing in a celestial choir, but she is your angel, and according to Dr. Urban, you would have died had it not been for her. Cal, this is Julia McKnight."

Cal tried to get up from the bed, and both Sally and Julia rushed over to him.

"What in the world do you think you are doing?" Sally asked.

"I just want to be polite."

"The way you can be polite for us, is to stay right there in your bed, unless we tell you otherwise."

"Yes, ma'am. But what if I have to . . . uh—"

"Let one of us know, and we'll get one of the cowboys to come in and help you," Sally said.

"Yes, ma'am, thank you." Cal looked at Julia. "Uh, Miss Julia, did you get in bed with me?"

Julia smiled. "I lay next to you on the mattress on the way back from Brown Spur," she said.

"I knew it!" Cal said with a broad smile.

Ten Strike

"How much did we get?" Rexwell asked.

"Nine thousand six hundred and fifty dollars," Hannibal replied, holding his hand over the green bills that lay in stacks on the table. "That is three hundred and eighty-six dollars for each of you. I think you will all agree with me, that's pretty good money for half a day's work."

"It sure as hell is!" Smith said, with a broad smile.

Hannibal allocated the division of the money by assigning himself three shares and Rexwell two shares. And because he managed to maintain a good cash flow, none of the men complained about his three shares.

When the Ghost Riders first arrived in Sorento, the residents of the town were told that some Eastern investors had reopened the mine. Everyone knew there was nothing to be recovered from the mine, but when the *mine workers* did come to town, they were generally well behaved, and they spent money. They spent a lot of money, and if a few of the local businessmen wondered how such men always seemed to have a lot of money, nobody wanted to question what was turning into a most profitable relationship.

"Mr. Rexwell," Hannibal said after the money had been divided. "I think the time has come to replace the losses our ranks have suffered. Do you suppose you can find eight suitable replacements?"

"Yes, sir, I'm sure I can."

"Good. Then I charge you with undertaking the mission."

Sugarloaf Ranch

"Ma! Ma!" Cal said.

"Oh, Cal, you're having another one of your dreams, aren't you?" Julia said. "Only, I think this one is a nightmare." She reached down to take his hand, and when she did, he squeezed her hand so hard that it hurt, but Julia didn't take her hand away.

"Ma!" Cal said. "Ma!"

Cal opened his eyes and looked up at Julia. "You're still here, aren't you?"

"Yes, I'm still here. You were dreaming again."

"Was I?"

"You called out for your mother."

"Oh," Cal said. "I'm sorry."

"What a strange thing for you to say."

"I suppose it is."

Cal turned his face away and stared through the window. Julia sensed that he didn't want to talk now, but neither did he want to let go of her hand, so she let him hold it.

He seemed so deep in thought. What was he thinking?

Cal wasn't thinking, exactly. What he was doing was remembering, only it was much stronger than a memory. He could almost feel as if he were actually reliving it.

Cal was in the doctor's office. His mother had *left the line* three years earlier, no longer young enough or desirable enough to interest any of the cowboys who frequented the Beer Barrel Saloon. To support herself and her son she began taking in laundry. To help out, Cal got a job mucking out stalls at Miller's Stable. Between the two of them they managed, though barely, to make enough money to pay the rent and buy food.

Then this morning Cal was unable to awaken her, and he ran to get the doctor.

"Who'll be paying my bill?" the doctor asked. "From what I hear, your ma isn't working over at the Beer Barrel for Fitzgerald anymore. When one of his women gets sick, he generally pays the bill."

"Ma 'n I have enough to pay you," Cal said. "Please, come make her well again."

"Hook up my buggy while I get the things I'll be needing," the doctor said.

Cal hurried out to the barn and got the horse in harness as quickly as he could. Then the doctor came out and drove to the outer edge of town, to the one-room cabin where Cal and his mother lived.

The drive, it seemed to Cal, was agonizingly slow. "Tie my horse off, I'll go in and look at your ma."

Cal tied off the horse, then hurried inside. When he did he saw the doctor standing at the side of the bed, looking down at his mother. The doctor had his arms folded across his chest.

"You could've saved yourself a trip, boy," the doctor said. "You should have just gone straight to the undertaker."

"What?"

"Your mother is dead. She more than likely died during the night, which is why you couldn't wake her this morning."

The words weren't sugarcoated, and the doctor made no attempt to break the news gently. "Do you have folks who will take you in?"

Cal shook his head. "Ma had no relatives and I don't know who my pa was."

"Yes, that's the problem with women who make their living the way your mother did. They almost always have babies and they seldom, if ever, have any idea of who the father was."

"I don't understand," Cal said. "She wasn't sick yesterday."

"It was probably her heart," the doctor said. He shook his head. "We still don't have any idea why it happens, but often a person who seems perfectly healthy will have a heart attack. Do you have enough money to pay the undertaker?"

"We keep money in the sugar bowl. I don't know how much is there," Cal said.

"I think he charges twenty dollars to bury a person," the doctor said. "If you don't want her to wind up in potter's field, you'll need to come up with the money."

"Do I owe you anything?"

"Well, I should charge you five dollars just for coming out here. But seeing as your mother is dead and there wasn't anything I could do for her, I won't charge you anything."

"Thanks," Cal said.

After the doctor left, Cal examined the sugar bowl, and found twenty-seven dollars. He took it to the undertaker.

"When she was whorin' she was called Belle. But her real name is Gertrude. Gertrude Wood, 'n that's the name I want on her tombstone," Cal told the undertaker.

"What makes you think there will be a tombstone?" the undertaker asked.

"You mean there won't be?"

"Yes, if you pay fifteen dollars more," the undertaker said.

"I thought one came with the twenty dollars."

"Well, you thought wrong. Do you want one for another fifteen dollars?"

Cal shook his head, but he said nothing.

It rained the next day, the day his mother was buried. Nobody was present for the burial except for Cal and the gravedigger. His mother's coffin, a plain pine box, lay on the back of the wagon with rain drumming down and forming little pools on the wood. Cal stood there in the rain watching the gravedigger, who was a black man, open up the hole. His mother was being buried in the main cemetery, but it was separated from potter's field only by a very narrow pathway. And as there was no tombstone, there was little difference between her grave and the ones on the other side of the path. Had she been buried ten feet father to the south, he could have saved twenty dollars.

The gravedigger breathed hard as he worked, but said nothing until the hole was finished. Then he climbed out of it.

"If you'll get that end of the coffin, boy, we can let her down real gentle like," he said. "Otherwise I'll have to drop her into the hole one end at a time. Won't hurt her none, of course, but sometimes it does bust open the coffin."

Cal took the head and the gravedigger took the foot of the coffin, and they let his mother down gently into the hole . . . which was already filling with water.

"You got somethin' you want to say?" the gravedigger asked.

"Say?"

"Most of the time there's words spokc," the gravedigger said. "But most of the time there's lots of folks present for the buryin'. Bein' as there's just me 'n you, I reckon you don't have to say nothin', but if you want to, I'll stand here real respectful."

"Thanks," Cal said. He cleared his throat. "I know that you tried to be as good a ma to me as you could be, 'n I don't hold nothin' against you, you bein' a whore 'n all, 'n I hope you're in a better place now." He was quiet then.

"That was spoke just real nice," the gravedigger said.

"Thanks. You can cover her up now."

Cal looked over at the gravedigger. The raindrops running down his black face looked like tears.

Cal hoped that his tears looked like raindrops.

CHAPTER TWELVE

Big Rock, Colorado

Smoke was in Longmont's Saloon playing cards with three of his friends: the owner, Louis Longmont; Tim Murchison, the owner of the Boot and Leather Store; and Ed Gillespie, owner of Ed's Gunshop.

"Pair of jacks," Smoke said, turning up his hole card. His face-up cards had been a jack, queen, king, and ace.

"Damn, I knew you were bluffing. I knew you didn't have a straight," Murchison said.

"Then why didn't you call?"

"Well, you *could* have had that ten," Murchison said, and the others around the table laughed.

"Makes no difference, even a pair of jacks has me beat," Gillespie said.

"I didn't know my three little old sevens would

be so powerful," Louis said, chuckling as he drew in the pot.

"Damnit, Louis, I knew you were just sitting there holding back from us," Smoke said with a laugh, tossing his cards into the middle of the table.

"How is Cal getting along?" Murchison asked as Longmont raked in the pot.

"He's doing as well as can be expected," Smoke said. "Doctor Urban says the thing we have to be most careful about is infection. But Sally and Julia are keeping a pretty close eye on that."

"Julia?" Murchison asked.

"Julia McKnight. She's a nurse, a real nurse, who once worked for her father, who was a doctor. She was in Brown Spur when Cal got shot, she helped me get him back home, and she's been helping Sally look after him ever since."

"Well it's good Cal has a nurse looking out for him," Murchison said.

Sheriff Carson came into the saloon then and stopped at the bar to get a mug of beer before he walked over to the table.

"Hello, Monte," Smoke said.

Sheriff Carson was carrying a copy of the *Big Rock Journal* which he lay in front of Smoke.

"Have you seen the paper today?"

"No, I haven't had a chance to look at it."

"You might want to read this story." He pointed to a story on the front page. "Looks like you ran into a pretty evil bunch."

Smoke picked the paper up to read.

CARNAGE IN LAURETTE

*Twenty-Three Killed,
Seven Wounded*

Had Genghis Khan returned to life, it is doubtful his warriors would have shown more cruelty than the recent attack of a band of outlaws. On the 15th instant, a terrible gang of outlaws descended upon the tranquil town of Laurette while its citizens went about their peaceful morning pursuits.

With all guns blazing, they cut a swath through the town, pausing only long enough to empty the bank vault before riding away, once more firing indiscriminately into business buildings and private homes.

When all the smoke had cleared, twenty-three lay dead, including Sheriff Jarrod Holder; Deputy John Clinton; president of the bank, Eric Kerry; both tellers, Wes Reid and Harry Clark; and six other men, as well as the schoolteacher, Miss Valerie Rice. Five other women and three children, one a babe in arms, were also killed. Seven were wounded.

Although the identity of the attackers hasn't been validated, survivors have stated that the riders were wearing red armbands. That is known to be the identifying characteristic of a group of outlaws known as the Ghost Riders. Sometime past, the Ghost Riders were terrorizing the good people of Wyoming. Why they left Wyoming in order to ply their evil avocation here in Colorado is unknown. All that is known is that they are here now, and they are our problem.

"This article just suggests that it might have been the Ghost Riders," Smoke said, putting the paper back down. "But it was them; there is no doubt in my mind."

"Oh, it was them, all right, he admits it," Monte said.

"He admits it? What do you mean? Who admits it?" Murchison asked.

"Let me guess," Smoke said. "Another letter from Hannibal?"

"Yes. It was addressed to the *Commerce Commercial Press*, but it was picked up by our paper and I expect dozens of other papers throughout the state as well."

Letter to the editor of the *Commerce Commercial Press:*

Dear Editor:

Once again the Ghost Riders have conducted a military operation that surpasses anything ever done during the recent Civil War. Neither Grant, nor Sherman, nor Sheridan, nor Lee, nor Longstreet, nor Stonewall Jackson could have conducted a military strike that was as brilliantly conceived or masterfully carried out as our strike against the town of Laurette.

We attacked the town with the strategic maneuver of shock and intimidation, accomplished our task of relieving the local bank of all its funds, then withdrew with not one casualty.

I am Hannibal,
Commandant of the Ghost Riders.

"This man, Hannibal, is one arrogant son of a bitch," Smoke said after reading the letter. He put the paper back down.

"He is actually bragging about killing women and children," Monte said. "Not since the bloody raids of the Missouri Raiders like Quantrill and Anderson, has there been one group of people visit such cruelty upon another group."

"Not all of the Missouri guerrilla bands were like Quantrill and Bloody Bill Anderson," Smoke said. "And Kansas had its own share of bloodthirsty raiders. James Henry Lane and Doc Gunnison for example."

"Yeah, I know," Monte said. "I didn't mean to deal an uneven hand there." Monte was one of the few who were aware of Smoke's Missouri background. During the Civil War, when he was only sixteen years old, Smoke had ridden with the guerrilla, Asa Briggs.

"Why hasn't this bloody bastard been stopped?" Smoke asked.

"Who's goin' to stop him?" Monte replied. "Nobody knows where the gang hides out, and he makes his raids from county to county so he never stays in one jurisdiction for very long. And he has so many men that it is a virtual army. How could one sheriff deal with all that? For all his self-aggrandizement, we don't even know whether Hannibal is his first or his last name."

"It is neither," Louis Longmont said.

"How do you know? Louis, do you know this man?" Smoke asked.

"I don't know who he is, but I know him," Louis said.

"What do you mean, you know him?" Monte asked.

"Let's say that I know his personality. He fancies himself a great military leader. That's evident in all his letters to the editor. And his name, Hannibal? I've no doubt but that he has taken his name from Hannibal Barca, a Carthaginian military commander generally considered one of the greatest military commanders in history."

"Is that the fella that took the elephants over the mountains?" Smoke asked.

"Good for you, my friend," Louis said. "I'm impressed."

"Don't be. I would have never heard of him if it hadn't been for Sally. She told me about him one day."

Tim Murchison laughed. "Wow, I would like to have been there for that conversation." He went falsetto. "Honey, did you know that a man named Hannibal took some elephants over the mountains?"

The others, including Smoke, laughed.

"You know, Louis, you may be right. Our friend Hannibal might be a frustrated military commander," Smoke said.

"Or someone who wanted to be and failed," Louis said.

"Well whoever or whatever he is, he sure needs to be stopped," Sheriff Carson said.

"He could be stopped if the governor would give someone the same legal authority as the Colorado Rangers, but let him act independently of them."

"I don't think he'll do that," Monte replied. "Anyway, what could one man do?"

"Maybe I should go talk to the governor," Smoke suggested.

"Smoke, wait a minute. You aren't planning on going after the Ghost Riders by yourself, are you? You read the paper . . . hell's fire, you saw them at Brown Spur. This is an army we're talking about."

"I admit, whether he is a failed army commander or not, he has put together quite a formidable gang," Smoke said.

"But you're planning on going after him anyway, aren't you?"

"Yes."

"Smoke, I've never known of anyone, nor have I ever heard of anyone, who is as good with a gun as you are, and I've never met a man with more courage. But think about it, my friend. I don't think even you have ever tried to fight an entire army all by yourself."

"Maybe you're right. Maybe I shouldn't go after them all by myself."

"Thank God I've talked some sense into you," Sheriff Carson said with a sigh of relief.

"I'll take Pearlie with me."

"Oh, for crying out loud," Monte said. "Even

with Pearlie, and I admit, Pearlie is nearly as good with a gun as you are, there would still just be the two of you."

Smoke smiled. "Worried about us, are you, Monte?"

"Damn right I'm worried about you."

"I'm worried about Cal," Sally said when Smoke returned home.

"Why? I thought he was doing well," Smoke said, surprised and distressed at the news.

"I thought he was as well, but he's been running a temperature most of the day, and that's not good. Julia said it could mean that infection is trying to set in."

"Is Julia with him?"

"She won't leave him," Sally said. "Even when it was time for lunch, she ate in there with him."

"She can't do anything for him by just being there, can she?"

"She's been bathing his forehead with cool water. She says that will help keep the temperature down."

"I'm going to step in to say hello to him."

Sally shook her head. "He won't even know you are there, Smoke. But you can certainly say hello to Julia."

"Then I'll do that," Smoke said as, giving Sally a quick kiss, he walked down the hall to the bedroom where they had put Cal. The door to the room was ajar, and even though it was only midafternoon, the room was dark, the result of the shades being pulled down and the drapes closed.

He could see Julia sitting on a chair pulled up

beside the bed. On a nearby table, there was a basin of water with a wet washcloth draped over the edge of the basin.

Julia was holding Cal's hand in hers.

It had been a fortunate turn of events that Julia had been working at Bagby's at exactly the time he most needed her. What were the odds of finding a bar girl who not only had the compassion but the training and the skill needed to save Cal's life? He knew that every bar girl had a story, but this was unique. He would love to know her story, but he would never pry.

He stepped into the room

"How is your patient doing?" Smoke asked.

"Oh!" Julia replied, startled by Smoke's unexpected intrusion. She started to stand up, but Smoke put his hand on her shoulder and gently pushed her back down into the chair.

"No need for that."

Julia lifted her hand, and in so doing, also lifted Cal's hand.

"He's been in and out of consciousness all day," Julia said. "But when he is conscious, I want him to be able to feel that I'm holding his hand. I don't want him to think that he is all alone."

"Good," Smoke said. He nodded. "That's a good idea."

"Of course, I don't know if he even feels it or not," Julia said.

"He feels it," Smoke said.

"Cal was calling for his mother, earlier."

"He was?" Smoke replied, made curious by the

remark. In all the time Cal had been with them, he had never once spoken of his mother.

"Yes, I thought he meant Sally, but when I asked her if she was his mother, her answer confused me. She said, 'as far as I'm concerned, I am'."

"I'm sure she does feel that way," Smoke said. "Sally adopted him when he was a boy of no more than sixteen. When I say *adopted*, I don't mean that she had papers drawn up or anything like that. But we couldn't set any more of a store by him if we really had adopted him."

"I thought it might be something like that," Julia said.

"I can't come right now. Pearlie and I have to get the cows in from the west pasture. Smoke's likely to be some upset if we don't get it done."

Cal's words, coming unexpectedly as they did, interrupted the conversation between Smoke and Julia.

"That's all right, Cal, you can leave them there," Smoke said with a little laugh. "I won't need them back for a while."

"Did ya' hear that, Pearlie? We don't need to bring 'em in yet. What do you say, we go into town 'n get us a beer?"

"He's been talking like that ever since his temperature went up," Julia said. "Most of the time he's saying things that make no sense at all."

"I expect they make sense to him," Smoke said. "And that's all that matters right now. Fever can give a man some very strange thoughts. I know because I've been there myself."

"I guess you're right."

"Are you getting enough rest?"

"When I can. I want to be here if he wakes up and needs me for something."

"Julia, you aren't going to do any good for anyone if you get sick yourself. I appreciate all you're doing for Cal. But you have to think of yourself as well."

"I know," Julia said. "I promise you, I won't push myself until I get sick."

"You've been very good for Cal. You don't know how much Sally and I appreciate you being here. I know your father would be very proud of you."

To Smoke's surprise, Julia's eyes welled with tears.

"I have been nothing but a disappointment to my father, starting with the day I left home. And if he knew what . . . I had become." She wiped the tears away. "You said that you and Sally appreciate me, you have no idea how much I appreciate the opportunity I have been given to do something worthwhile. I'm a long way from recovering my self-respect."

"Don't put yourself down, Julia. I know people. I can read people better than just about anyone. And you have a good soul."

"I can't tell you how much that means to me."

"*Yes, sir, Mr. Miller,*" Cal said.

"Who is Mr. Miller?" Julia asked.

Smoke chuckled. "I don't have the slightest idea."

CHAPTER THIRTEEN

After he paid for his mother's burying, Cal had just enough money to pay the month's rent and buy some bacon and beans. He lived on bacon and beans for a whole month until he got paid for his job mucking out stalls at the livery stable.

He quit school so he could work full time, and that increased his pay from ten dollars a month to twenty dollars a month. Even though his pay was doubled, that still left him with barely enough to pay the rent and buy food. But he knew that a boy his age, and with his background—everyone in Eagle Tail knew his mother had been a prostitute—would be unable to get work anywhere else, so he stayed there. He worked for Elmer Miller for six more months and would've stayed there even longer, had it not been for Justin Teague. Teague, like Cal, worked at the stable . . . that is when he wasn't in jail for drunkenness or getting into a fight or some other misdemeanor.

"One of these days I'm going to just up and leave this place," Teague said, more than once. Generally the threat to leave would come right after Teague had had a run-in with Miller. "Then where will Miller be? Stuck with a fifteen-year-old, snot-nosed, whore's son, that's where."

"I'm sixteen," Cal said.

"You just have to wonder what's going on in his mind now," Smoke said.

Julia put her hand on his brow. "He's burning up with fever," she said. She picked up the wet cloth and laid it on his forehead.

"Fifteen, sixteen, it don't make no difference. If I left and you was the only one still a workin' here, Miller would be in a fix, now, wouldn't he? That's all I'm sayin'."

"I don't think he would like it much, if you was to leave," Cal said. "I'm sorry, Miz Sally. What I meant to say was, if you were to leave."

Teague made no reaction to Cal's grammatical correction, nor his mention of Miz Sally.

One day Cal was getting ready to take the week's receipts to the bank when Teague came into the office.

"How much money you got there?" Teague asked.

"One hundred and seven dollars."

"A hunnert and seven? This has been a good week."

"Yes, but don't forget, we rented a wagon and team for three days to the lumber mill."

"Oh, yeah, I do remember that. Anyway, give the money to me."

"Give it to you? Why?"

"Miller told me to make the deposit for him today," Teague said.

"I always make the deposit. Mr. Miller didn't tell me he wanted you to make the deposit."

"Why should he tell you? Give me the money."

"No, sir. Mr. Miller told me to make the deposit, and unless he tells me himself that he wants you to do it, then I aim to do what he told me. Mr. Miller is just out back. If you want to go with me to see him, and if he says for you to make the deposit, then I'll be glad to give you the money. But I'm not going to do that until he tells me."

Teague pulled his pistol from his holster. "Boy, if you don't hand that money over to me now, I'm goin' to shoot you dead 'n take it. Now, what's it goin' to be? You willin' to get yourself kilt over this little difference of opinion we're havin'?"

"I told you, Mr. Miller is just out back," Cal said. "Like I said, come with me, and we'll go ask him what he wants me to do."

"We ain't goin' to ask him nothin'," Teague said. "You're goin' to give me that money now." Teague pulled the hammer back on the pistol he was holding.

"All right," Cal said, handing the money over to him.

"Ha!" Teague said. "Thanks for the money, kid. Tell Miller I said good-bye."

"You mean you're stealin' the money?"

"Yeah," Teague said, with an evil laugh.

Teague turned to leave, but Cal, knowing that Miller kept a gun in the middle desk drawer, opened the drawer and picked up the gun.

"Mr. Teague," he called. "Drop your gun and bring the money back."

Teague whirled around and pointed his pistol at Cal, but Cal shot before Teague could. The bullet hit Teague in the heart, and he went down.

"Mr. Teague!" Cal shouted, moving to him quickly. He knelt beside him, the smoking gun still in his hand. "Mr. Teague!"

Miller came into the office then and saw Cal kneeling beside Teague's body, holding the gun in one hand and the money in the other.

"Boy, what have you done?" Miller shouted.

"He was trying to steal your money, Mr. Miller."

"I don't think so. You're the one holding the gun and the money. I think Teague caught you trying to steal the money, and you shot him."

"I shot him 'cause he was goin' to shoot me."

"Teague is a troublemaker, I'll admit. But he ain't never done nothin' to get him in real trouble. You stay right here, young man, until I come back with the sheriff. Maybe you can convince him."

"I didn't have no choice!" Cal called after him. "He was fixin' to shoot me!"

"I told you to stay right there," Miller called, holding his hand out as if by that action he could keep the boy in place.

Cal didn't know what to do. If Miller didn't believe him, he was sure the sheriff wouldn't. He waited only until Miller was out of sight, then he took the fastest horse in the stable and left.

When he was ten miles out of town he let the horse go, knowing it would return to the stable. He needed to get out of Kansas, so he hopped a freight train going west.

"As his body fights off the infection, he's going to have bouts of high temperature," Dr. Urban said as he removed a dressing on Cal's abdomen, exposing an oozing wound. "Young lady, you're going to have to keep this clean and change the dressings at least twice a day."

"I'm afraid of sepsis," Julia said.

"You are right to be afraid of it. I'm going to leave you some antiseptic. Has he been hallucinating?"

"You could say that," Smoke said. "He just told us he was sixteen."

"Running a fever like this, there will be periods of time when he is perfectly lucid, as well as times when he is hardly making any sense at all. But you are doing exactly the right thing by bathing him with cool water to keep the temperature down."

"We've been very lucky to have her," Smoke said.

"I would say that you are. I'll leave you a little

laudanum too, but only give it to him if he is in pain. And be very careful with it."

"Yes, sir, I will."

"Let me ask you this, Doctor. I need to go to Denver, but I don't want to leave if, well, if—"

Dr. Urban interrupted him. "Go ahead, Smoke. It will more than likely be several weeks before Cal is back on his feet. But I think I can assure you that there is no danger of any precipitous calamity."

Smoke nodded. "Thanks, Doc, I appreciate the reassurance."

Smoke followed Dr. Urban outside where Pearlie had brought the buggy around.

"Don't worry about Cal," Dr. Urban said. "I think he's going to pull through just fine, and that young lady you've got nursing him can do about as much for him as I can. She's quite a find."

"Yes, we think so as well," Smoke said.

Smoke and Pearlie watched the doctor drive away.

"Pearlie, I'm going to Denver tomorrow. I'm going after the people who did this to Cal, but I want to be legal, so I'm going to see the governor and have him give me an appointment as an officer of the law of the state."

"Take me with you."

"Not to Denver. But I promise that you will be with me when I go after Hannibal and his gang. I don't think I would want to take them all on by myself."

"You're sure you won't go off without me?" Pearlie asked.

Smoke smiled and put his hand on Pearlie's shoulder. "I'm sure," he said. "But now I need you to stay here and keep an eye on Cal. Knowing him, if he gets to feeling better, he'll be going out to curry Prince Dandy or something, and break everything open again."

"He won't get up," Pearlie said. "I promise you that."

Smoke stepped back into Cal's room. As she had been from the very beginning, Julia was sitting in a chair that was right next to his bed.

Cal was awake, and he and Julia were talking.

"No kidding," Cal said. "Pearlie 'n I once went to a rodeo 'n both of us won our events."

"I believe you, Cal. Why, I think you could probably do just about anything you wanted to do."

"I could. Before this," Cal said. "I don't know what's goin' to happen now."

"What's going to happen now is you're going to heal up and get back to work," Smoke said. "I'm not paying you to just lie around with some pretty girl looking after you," he teased.

"She is pretty, isn't she?" Cal said.

"She sure is. Listen, I'm going to be gone for a while, so I don't want you trying to do anything foolish, like showing off to Julia how good you are at busting broncos."

"You don't have to worry about that, Mr. Jensen," Julia said. "I won't let him get up."

"You're goin' after them, aren't you, Smoke?" Cal said. "You're going after the men that shot me."

"What makes you think I'm doing that?"

"Julia told me I wasn't the only one shot. There were a lot more shot, even some women."

"I'm going to Denver," Smoke said, without elaboration.

Suttle, Colorado

When Rexwell stepped into the sheriff's office, the deputy had his chair leaning back against the wall and his feet propped up on the desk. He was sound asleep and snoring loudly. Rexwell looked around the inside of the jail. The room was dimly lit by a low-burning kerosene lantern. Wanted posters filled the bulletin board. A pot of aromatic coffee sat on a small, wood-burning stove. The regulator clock on the wall swept its pendulum back and forth in a measured ticktock, the hands on the face pointing to ten minutes after two. Moving quietly, Rexwell walked over to the stove to pour himself a cup of coffee; then he stepped over to the jail cell to look inside. The two men in the cell, Amos and Amon Scraggs, twins, were sound asleep. They had recently been convicted of murder and were waiting only for the gallows to be completed before they were to be hanged.

Rexwell took a slurping drink of his coffee. "You fellas plannin' on sleepin' the rest of your life away?" he asked. He laughed. "I guess maybe so, seein' as you pro'bly don't have that long left to live."

"Who the hell are you?" the deputy asked, from behind him.

"I'm a friend of the condemned men," Rexwell said. "I've come to tell them good-bye."

"I didn't even hear you come in," the deputy said, gruffly. "You aren't supposed to be in here—not at this hour of the night."

"Deputy?" Amos called.

"Now, what the hell do you want?" the deputy asked, turning back toward the jail cell. He was surprised to see that both prisoners were grinning broadly.

"You should be nicer to our friend," Amos said, easily. "Like he said, he just came here to tell us good-bye, is all."

"Nobody is allowed in here in the middle of the ni—" That was as far as the deputy got before he felt a hand come around to clasp over his mouth. His first move was to try and pull the hand away, and when that didn't work, he reached for his pistol. That was when he felt something sharp at his throat. Rexwell's hand flashed quickly across his neck. There was a stinging sensation, then a wetness at his collar. Rexwell let go of him and stepped back. The deputy put his hand up to his neck, then pulled it away and looked at blood on his fingers. It wasn't until then that he fully realized what had just happened to him. He fell to the floor and tried to call out, but was unable to do so because his windpipe had been cut and he could make no sound at all save the silent scream that was in his head.

As he was losing consciousness he saw the big, bald-headed man opening the cell door to let the prisoners out.

"We appreciate this, Rexwell, but I'm surprised to see you. I never know'd we was such friends," Amon said.

"You're going to pay me for this," Rexwell said.

"Ha! How the hell are we supposed to pay you?"

"I'm on a recruiting mission," Rexwell said. "You should be honored. I have to round up eight men, and you were the first two."

CHAPTER FOURTEEN

Denver

"You will be my supernumerary," Hannibal had told Boots Cardigan when he hired him.

"My what?"

"My supernumerary," Hannibal repeated it. "I am holding the operational strength of the Ghost Riders to thirty. But you will be in excess of that number, because you won't be making field operations with us. You will be providing me with the intelligence we need."

"You're a hell of a lot smarter than I am," Cardigan said. "How do you expect me to provide you with intelligence?"

"It isn't that kind of intelligence," Hannibal said. "Perhaps I should have said information. I want you to stay in Denver. Keep your eyes and ears open for anything that you think might be of some use to me. I will pay you for all the useful intelligence— that is, information—that you provide."

"How much?"

"What difference does it make, how much?" Hannibal asked. "You will be making money, and you won't be at risk."

"Yeah," Cardigan said. "Yeah, that's right, ain't it? I mean, if all I'm doin' is providin' you with information, I ain't likely to get shot in one of your jobs, 'n I ain't likely to get in trouble with the law, neither, am I?"

"Exactly."

"All right, I'll do it. But on one condition."

"What condition is that?"

"I want one of them red bands."

Hannibal shook his head. "There's no need for you to have a red band. You aren't operational, therefore there is little need for identification."

"I know, but I just want one."

Hannibal was about to say no again, but he changed his mind, and he smiled instead. The very fact that Cardigan actually wanted a red band meant that there was pride in having one. His intention to generate an *esprit de corps* was working.

"All right, I'll provide you with a red band," he said. "But you must never wear it. If you were ever seen wearing it in public, it could get you into a lot of trouble. They might even try you for murder by association, and you could wind up on the gallows."

"I won't wear it," Cardigan said. "I'll just keep it in my pocket."

"All right. You can have one."

The Rangers, Hannibal had told him, were the only law enforcement department in the entire state who could possibly represent a threat to them.

"So far they haven't made a concerted effort to

come after us," Hannibal said. "But if the governor decides to set them on us, I would like to know in advance."

Governor's office

"Mr. Jensen, Governor Adams will see you now," the governor's personal secretary said.

"Thank you, Mr. Thomas."

Governor Alva Adams stood as Smoke entered his office, and smiling, extended his hand as he came around the ornately carved desk to greet him.

"Smoke Jensen," he said. "To what do I owe the honor of being visited by one of Colorado's most esteemed citizens?"

Smoke chuckled. "No wonder you got elected governor, Alva, with a line like that."

"Sit down, sit down," Governor Adams said, taking him over to a seating area to the side of his office. Smoke knew that this part of his office was reserved only for close friends or for important visitors when the governor wanted something. Otherwise, the desk separated the governor from his staff and petitioners.

"Coffee? Tea? A glass of wine, perhaps?" the governor offered.

"A glass of wine would be good, I think," Smoke said, seeing a corked bottle of red wine, half full.

"Wonderful, I was looking for an excuse to have a bit myself," the governor said. He pulled the cork, poured two glasses, then handed one of the glasses to Smoke.

"Here's to you," he said, holding up the glass.

Both took a sip before the governor spoke again. "Tell me, Smoke, what brings you to Denver?"

"Ghost Riders," Smoke said. "I know you know about them."

"Oh, yes, the newspapers are full of their heinous deeds. I believe I heard, also, that they started in Wyoming. It was our misfortune that when they left Wyoming, they chose Colorado."

"Do you have any plan for dealing with them?"

"I have considered sending the Rangers after them, but I think it would be a waste of manpower to commit the entire battalion just to run down one, outlaw gang. I would like to think that some sheriff somewhere will deal with them, but I don't have a lot of hope for that. What is your interest in them?"

"I was at Brown Spur to witness the hanging of two of the Ghost Riders."

"But the hanging didn't take place," Governor Adams said. "Yes, I know about that incident. The sheriff, the hangman, a parson, I believe, and a few others were killed. The two condemned men got away."

"Yes. And in the shooting my friend, Cal Wood, was shot three times and nearly killed."

"Oh, that's too bad. How is he doing?"

"He's not out of the woods yet. I have taken that personally, Alva, and I'm going to go after them."

"Smoke, your . . . exploits . . . are legion and well-known. But really, you need to think this through. I'm told there may be as many as two dozen men in this gang. Maybe even more, nobody knows for sure exactly how many."

"Yes, there are at least twenty-four," Smoke said.

"And you want to go after them?"

"I'm sure you know what happened at Laurette."

"Yes, the sheriff and his deputy were both killed there. I think there were what . . . twenty-three men and women killed?"

"Yes. That's another reason I want to go after them."

"Alone?"

"I won't be entirely alone. I'll have Pearlie with me."

"Who is Pearlie?"

"Pearlie is one of my men. He is extremely loyal, trustworthy, and he has been by my side in more adventures than I can count."

"And that's his name? Pearlie?"

"That's the name he goes by and has gone by ever since I've known him."

"He's pretty good? This man, Pearlie?"

"He's very good," Smoke said.

"Still, two of you against twenty-four."

"You sound like my friend Monte Carson."

"Ah, yes, he's your sheriff, I believe."

"He is."

"You should listen to him, Smoke."

"Governor, you know how these things turn out. It is highly unlikely that we would ever encounter all of them at one time. In fact, it would be foolish of me to do so. I will engage them tactically."

"Tactically." Governor Adams laughed as he repeated the word. "Well, I would certainly hope so. All right, Smoke, I know you didn't come to see me just to tell me what you planned to do. What do you want from me?"

"I want a commission in the Colorado Rangers for me and for Pearlie. But I don't want to actually be a part of the Rangers, I want the authority to be able to operate independently from the Rangers. And I want you to specifically assign us the mission of going after the man who calls himself Hannibal and putting an end to him and the Ghost Riders by whatever method it takes."

"What do you mean, when you say *by whatever method?*"

"I don't plan to bring any of them in for trial, Governor. I intend to kill them."

"And you want my authorization to just kill them outright?"

"What's the difference between me killing them, and a hangman killing them?" Smoke asked.

"A trial, for one thing. A judge and a jury."

"I will be the judge and the jury," Smoke said.

"You are serious about this, aren't you?" Governor Adams asked. "You really do want the authority to kill them, and you really do want to go after them alone."

"I'm very serious, and I won't be alone. I told you, Pearlie will be with me."

"All right," the governor said. "I suppose that, when you look at it, authorizing you to kill them on sight is really no different from a wanted, dead or alive, poster. I'll write out two commissions for you," the governor said. Drinking the rest of his wine, he walked over to his desk, then sat down and picked up a pen and a piece of stationary with his letterhead.

"If you don't mind, I'll just put both of your names on this same commission," he said.

"That'll be fine," Smoke replied.

The governor made a carbon-paper sandwich of two more copies.

"You have to have copies of everything now," he complained. "We are no longer the independent country we once were. Bureaucracy rules now."

The governor began to read aloud, as he wrote. "Know ye all that I, Alva Adams, Governor of the State of Colorado do, by these presence, confirm and command that," he looked up. "I know you only as Smoke."

"My first name is Kirby."

"Kirby Jensen and," again he looked up, "Pearlie?"

"Pearlie," Smoke said.

"Pearlie," Governor Adams continued, "are hereby commissioned as officers in the Colorado Rangers, with the authorization to operate in complete independence of the Rangers so that they may pursue the outlaw known as Hannibal, and all such outlaws as are affiliated with him, in the group known as the Ghost Riders. And, in performance of this duty, Kirby Jensen is further authorized to take the life of Hannibal, and/or any of his men, if he deems such action to be necessary.

"And to this document, I hereto affix my signature, signed, Alva Adams, Governor of the State of Colorado."

Governor Adams blew the ink dry, applied his seal, then handed the original document to Smoke.

"Here it is, Smoke, and I pray to God that I didn't just sign your death warrant."

Smoke smiled. "It is a death warrant, Governor. But it won't be mine."

"You're right. I've just issued you a license to kill. I hope history is kind to me."

After Smoke left the governor's office, the governor's secretary gave the two carbon copies of the order to Marvin Thigpen.

"File these, would you please, Mr. Thigpen? Put one in the Governor's personal file and one in the Colorado Rangers' file."

"Yes, sir," Thigpen said.

Thigpen filed one of the onionskins in the governor's file, but he kept one back, putting it in his pocket.

CHAPTER FIFTEEN

Sugarloaf Ranch

"How come the only thing you're giving me to eat is soup?" Cal asked Julia. "Only it's not even soup. It's . . . I don't know what it is. Flavored water, I guess, only there's not that much flavor to it."

"It's a clear broth," Julia said. "And it's the only thing you should be eating now. If you eat any solid food before your stomach heals, it could be dangerous."

"But I'm starvin' to death," Cal said. "I mean, here you say you're tryin' to save my life, but what's goin' to happen is, you 'n Miz Sally are goin' to come in here one day and find me lyin' here in bed, skinny as a rope, dead from starvation."

Julia laughed. "I think not," she said.

"Anyhow, I know that Miz Sally is cookin' some real food, 'cause I can smell it. How come you aren't lettin' me eat any of it?"

"Cal, even if it wasn't dangerous for you, you

would get a stomachache so bad that it wouldn't be worth it."

"All right, if you say so," Cal said.

Julia reached down to take Cal's hand in hers.

"I'm just trying to do what is best for you," she said.

Cal smiled. "You've been holdin' my hand a lot since you've been here, haven't you?"

"I'm sorry," Julia said, dropping his hand.

"No, no, I want you to hold it," he said. "It makes me feel better when you hold my hand."

Julia returned the smile. "Does it?"

"Yes, it does. You know, I've been having these . . . I don't know what you call them, dreams, thoughts, memories. . . . I don't know what's real and what's not real. The other day I saw my ma, plain as if she was right here in front of me, only it wasn't now, it was when I wasn't but a kid. But in all that, I could feel your hand holdin' mine. And it's like . . . well, I don't know how to explain it, really. But, it's kind of like, as long as I can feel your hand holdin' on to mine, I know that I'm connected to someone real. And even when the dreams . . . or whatever they are . . . get too bad, they don't scare me all that much, on account of 'cause I'm connected. And since you're the one I'm holdin' on to, that means I'm connected to you."

"Cal, that's the nicest thing anyone has said to me in a long, long time."

"I'm glad you came home with us."

"I'm glad too," Julia said.

Cal yawned. "I've sure been sleepin' a lot here lately, haven't I?"

"That's all right. You heal faster when you're sleeping."

"I do? Why?"

"Because when you are asleep, your body doesn't have to do anything but heal."

"You sure are smart," Cal said, though he barely got the words out as he drifted off.

Julia sat beside the bed looking at Cal as he slept. In the time she had spent here at Sugarloaf Ranch she had watched the interaction between Sally, Smoke, Pearlie, and some of the other ranch hands. There was a camaraderie among them that she had never seen before . . . not even among the girls at Bagby's, and she considered them her friends.

And, in the time she had been here, she had observed Cal very closely. He was good enough looking, but there was more to him than just good looks. He was, she was now convinced, a very decent man. Totally unlike the man she had married.

"Oh, Cal," she said quietly. "Why couldn't I have met you first?"

Julia knew that Cal was a cowboy, but she also recognized that he occupied a special place here. She found herself fantasizing that she was here to share that place with him.

She stayed with him until she knew he was asleep, and seeing that it wasn't a troubled sleep, she left the room. Going into the kitchen, she saw that Sally was preparing lunch.

"Is there anything I can do to help?" she asked.

"Oh, honey, you're helping more than you can possibly know by looking after Cal the way you are."

"He's asleep now." Julia poured herself a cup of

coffee. "How long do you think Mr. Jensen will be gone?"

Sally smiled a wistful smile. "With Smoke, I never know."

"He is sort of a . . . I don't know how to say this . . . but he is a famous man, isn't he?"

"I suppose he is."

"Do you ever wish that he wasn't?"

"That's a very good question. Because he is famous, I sometimes feel that I'm having to share him with the whole world, and a part of me resents that. But I love all that Smoke is, and I wouldn't change anything about him. So, the answer to your question is no."

"I think it is wonderful how much you two care about each other."

Sally had the feeling that Julia wanted to say more, but she didn't elaborate.

"Thank you," was all Sally said.

Ten Strike

Hannibal was reading an article in the *Brimstone News* that had caught his attention.

SILVER PRODUCTION CONTINUES IN DOUBLE DINKLE MINE

Since the discovery of a new vein of silver six months ago, the Double Dinkle Mine has caught the attention of investors from far and wide. With more than fifty men employed in working the mine, the monthly payroll has greatly increased the amount of money in circulation within our fair city. It is believed that the mine is now bringing as much revenue as all the neighboring ranchers and city businesses combined.

Brimstone is truly a city on the rise and may well become one of Colorado's greatest cities.

"Well, now," he said aloud as he tapped his finger on the story. "Brimstone might be worth a little more investigation."

He had been understrength when he raided Laurette, but despite that, the raid had been a great success. Before undertaking a similar operation at Brimstone, though, he wanted to be at full strength. He would wait until Rexwell had completed the recruiting campaign. That would also give him time to gather as much information as he might need about Brimstone.

Satank, Colorado

Behind the bar of the Silver Nugget Saloon in Satank, there was a sign that read NO CARD SHARKS ALLOWED. ALL GAMES MUST BE HONEST. CHEATERS WILL BE ASKED TO LEAVE THE PREMISES.

There was no gilt-edged mirror, but there were several large jars of pickled eggs and pigs feet on the bar, and towels, tied to rings, placed every few feet on the customer's side to provide the patrons with a means of wiping their hands.

The saloon had an upstairs section at the back, with a stairway going to a second-floor landing. When Bo Rexwell looked up, he saw that a heavily painted saloon girl was taking a cowboy up the stairs with her. He figured that after he finished his business here he might take one of the women up himself.

He could afford it. He had never had as much money in his life as he had now since joining with the Ghost Riders. That had been his principal draw in recruiting. Hannibal had sent him out to find eight men to make up for the riders they had lost to Smoke Jensen. So far he had signed up seven of them: the Scraggs twins in Suttle, Snake Eye Mason and Bart Jennings in Hermitage, Emerson Case in Livermore, and Jeb Jones and Hock Granger in La Porte.

Given the amount of money someone could make with the Ghost Riders, it wasn't hard to find people who would ride with them. But Hannibal had given him the assignment because he knew that Rexwell wouldn't settle for just anyone. Rexwell had exacting standards, and so far everyone he had recruited met those standards.

There was a man here that Rexwell knew. His name was Vince Oceans and Rexwell and Oceans had been in the army together. They had also deserted together. Over the intervening years they had gone their separate ways—but he recently heard that he could find Oceans here in Satank.

There were nearly a dozen tables full of drinking customers, three of which had card games in session.

Rexwell bellied up to the bar.

"What'll it be?" the barkeep asked as he moved down to Rexwell. He wiped up a spill with a wet, smelly rag.

"You got any good whiskey?"

"Got some Old Overholt."

"That's what you sell to wranglers and wagon drivers," Rexwell replied. "What do you keep for bankers and those as can afford it?"

"I've got some Irish whiskey, fifty cents for a shot."

"I'll take a bottle."

"That'll be ten dollars."

Rexwell slid the money across the bar to him. "I'm lookin' for an old friend of mine. I heard I could find 'im here."

"What's 'is name?"

"Oceans. Vince Oceans."

"He's a friend of yours?"

"Yeah, you have a problem with that?"

"Not a problem, just a wonder. Oceans isn't the kind of man who makes very many friends."

"Well, is he here or not?"

"Have a seat somewhere 'n enjoy your whiskey. He'll be in, by 'n by."

Rexwell turned to look out over the room. A bar girl sidled up to him then. She was heavily painted and showed the dissipation of her profession. There was no humor or life left to her eyes, and when she saw that Rexwell wasn't interested, she turned and walked back to sit by the piano player.

The piano player wore a small, round, derby hat and kept his sleeves up with garters. He was pounding away on the keyboard, but the music was practically lost amidst the noise of a dozen or more conversations.

"Barker!" someone shouted, and looking toward

the door he saw a man with a full, black beard. This was the man who had called out the name. "Barker, you son of a bitch! Are you in here?"

Rexwell smiled. He hadn't recognized Oceans at first, because of his beard. But he recognized his voice. He started to get up, when he saw another man stand.

"I don't want any trouble with you, Oceans," Barker said, holding out his hand.

"Well you got trouble, Mister. I heard what you said about me. Did you really think I wouldn't find out?"

"I take it back."

"It's too late."

"Come on, Oceans, I was just tryin' to look big. I didn't really mean nothin' by it."

"Draw," Oceans said.

"No, I ain't goin' to draw on you."

Oceans drew and fired, and there was a collective gasp in the room as they thought he had shot Barker. What he had actually done was clip one of Barker's earlobes, and now Barker was holding his hand to his ear, as blood streamed through his fingers.

"Draw," Oceans said again.

"No, I ain't goin' to draw on you!" Barker said.

Oceans fired again, this time hitting his other earlobe.

"Please! No more!" Barker shouted.

"The next one is going to be between your legs," Oceans said.

"Ahhhh!" Barker shouted, as he made a desperate grab for his pistol.

Oceans stood there with a triumphant smile. He waited until Barker got the pistol from his holster before he drew again. Then Oceans drew, fired, and put his pistol back in his holster before Barker was able to raise his gun. Barker fell facedown on the floor and lay there without moving.

So stunned was everyone in the saloon, that there was absolute silence in the place, no conversation and no piano playing.

"Vince," Rexwell called.

The black-bearded man looked toward the call.

Rexwell held up the bottle of expensive Irish whiskey. "Come over and have a drink with an old friend."

"I'll be damned if it ain't Bo Rexwell. I heard you was dead," Oceans said.

Within half an hour, Vince Oceans became Rexwell's eighth recruit and the newest member of the Ghost Riders.

Denver

Marvin Thigpen stepped into the Silver Palace Saloon and saw the man he was looking for. Boots Cardigan was sitting alone, at a table in the back. Thigpen started toward him.

"I've got some information that might interest you," Thigpen said.

Cardigan took a drink before he responded.

"What is it?" he asked in a low, gravelly voice.

"It's about Kirby Jensen," Thigpen said as he sat across the table from him.

"Kirby Jensen? I've never heard of him."

"Well, he must be pretty good, or Governor Adams would never have appointed him to this position."

"What position?"

"Colorado Rangers."

"Now why the hell would I be interested in the governor appointing someone to the Rangers? What's one more Ranger?"

"This is different," Thigpen said. "Jensen is going to be a Colorado Ranger, but separate from them. He has one job, and that's going after the Ghost Riders."

"One man plans to take on the Ghost Riders? All by himself?"

"Actually there will be two of them. Jensen and another man named Pearlie."

Thigpen took the copy from his pocket and gave it to Cardigan. Cardigan read it, then looked up.

"Where is he now? This Jensen fella?" Cardigan asked.

"I don't have any idea where he is."

Cardigan looked at the paper again, then handed it back to Thigpen, who folded it and returned it to his shirt pocket.

"Is Hannibal supposed to be afraid of this Jensen and someone named Pearlie?"

"They must be capable, or the governor would not have appointed them to this special commission."

"Oh yeah, I'm just quaking in my boots." Cardigan laughed. "Boots Cardigan quaking in his boots. That's a good one, don't you think?"

"Is what I told you worth ten dollars?" the clerk asked.

"A dollar, maybe," Cardigan said handing the informer a bill.

"A dollar? I risked my position to tell you about this and all it's worth is a dollar?"

"Look, if I was to go back there 'n tell them that they need to be careful because two men are after 'em, 'n one of 'em is named Pearlie, I'd more 'n likely be laughed plumb out of the state. What the hell kind of man calls hisself Pearlie? Take the dollar or don't take it."

"I'll take it," Thigpen said, reaching for the proffered bill.

"Yeah, I thought you might."

"Oh, oh, speak of the devil," Thigpen said.

"What do you mean?"

"That's him, that's Jensen! He just came in!"

The man Thigpen pointed out was a big man, with broad shoulders and a narrow waist. He was wearing a tooled-leather gunbelt around his waist, with cartridge-bullet-filled loops all the way around. His pistol, with a plain wooden grip, was holstered low and tied down on his right side. When he came into the saloon he moved immediately, but unobtrusively, to the side of the swinging batwing doors and putting his back to the wall, perused the saloon.

"Look at 'im," Cardigan said. "The dumb bastard doesn't have an idea in hell what is about to happen to him."

"What do you mean?"

"I'm goin' to call him out."

"I wouldn't do that if I were you."

"Yeah, well, you ain't me," Cardigan said.

"I'm leaving," Thigpen said.

"Don't leave. Stick around for the show. But I would advise you to get out of the way. You wouldn't want to be hit by a stray bullet now, would you?"

"No," Thigpen said. "No, I would not."

Thigpen got up from the table and walked away, but his morbid curiosity kept him from leaving. Instead, he chose a table in the farthest corner of the saloon, then sat there with his hands clasped in front of him.

CHAPTER SIXTEEN

Thigpen's quick departure from the table didn't go unnoticed by Smoke. Perhaps if he had gotten up and left the saloon, Smoke would have thought nothing of it. But he didn't leave the saloon, and he purposely chose a table as far away from where he had been sitting as he could. What made it even more intriguing was the fact that the table he chose was empty, and the table he left had a half-finished mug of beer in front of where he had been sitting.

Smoke looked at the man who was still sitting at the first table. And though the man pointedly looked away when Smoke glanced toward him, it was obvious to Smoke that the man had been studying him.

He was used to people recognizing him and then staring at him. He was a well-known personality, and people looked at him to satisfy their curiosity. But he also knew what it was like to be measured as a target, and that was exactly what was happening now.

Smoke had survived many gunfights over the years, not only because he could draw faster and shoot straighter than anyone who had ever tried him, but also because he had an innate sense about him, a gut instinct when someone was about to try to kill him. And he felt that now.

Smoke walked over to the bar, and though it may have looked to the casual observer, or even to Cardigan who was studying him, that he had no interest in him, nothing could be further from the truth. Smoke found the man in the mirror and, without being too obvious, kept his eye on him.

"Yes, sir, Mr. Jensen, what can I get for you? Same as last time?"

"Hello, Mr. Stallings, yes, a beer, thank you." Smoke had come into the Silver Palace for a beer when he first arrived in Denver.

"Yes, sir, I've been telling my customers that the great and famous Smoke Jensen had a beer here."

Smoke chuckled. "Isn't that laying it on a little thick?"

"Oh, no, it's good for business," Stallings insisted. He drew a mug of beer then set it on the bar in front of Smoke.

Smoke, purposely, didn't reach for the beer until Stallings was well out of the way. He had been keeping an eye on the man at the table, and the more he studied him, the more he was certain that he was going to make a play.

Smoke not only knew that the man was going to draw on him, he knew exactly when it would be. The man would wait until he had the maximum advantage, not only of surprise, but when Smoke's gunhand was occupied. What the man didn't know is that Smoke wouldn't be surprised, and it made no difference if his gunhand was occupied or not.

Smoke picked the beer mug up with his right hand.

"Draw, Jensen!" the man shouted, standing up from the table with the pistol already in his hand.

Smoke dropped the beer mug, drew, and fired before the mug even hit the floor.

The man fired as well, but his pulling of the trigger was nothing but a reflexive action, muscle memory in the finger of a dead man, and the bullet poked a hole in the bar. Boots Cardigan fell back into his chair even before the sound of the two gunshots had faded away. He sat there, his head slumped over, his lifeless arms hanging by his side, and the pistol still clutched in his hand.

Seeing what had just happened, Thigpen got up to leave. He was shocked when Smoke swung his still-smoking pistol toward him.

"Stay right where you are, Mister!" Smoke called out to him.

Thigpen stuck both hands in the air. "I'm not armed! I'm not armed!" he shouted, his voice breaking with terror.

"Put your hands down," Smoke said, holstering his pistol. "Get over here."

Nervously, Thigpen walked toward Smoke while the others, not yet over the shock of the sudden death that had taken place right before their eyes, now watched this side drama play out before them. What did Smoke Jensen want with this meek-looking man?

"Who was that man?" Smoke asked.

"I . . . I don't know," Thigpen said.

"You were at the table with him, but got up to move when I came in. You knew he was going to call me out, didn't you?"

"No."

"Don't lie to me, Mister. I can't stand a man who lies to me."

"I . . . uh . . . told him not to."

"Wait a minute," Smoke said. "I saw you a little while ago, didn't I? Yes, you were in the capitol building."

"I never go into the capitol building."

"That's a bald-faced lie, Thigpen," Stallings said. "You work there."

"Well, uh, I—" Thigpen stopped in midsentence, and Smoke saw the edge of an onionskin protruding from his shirt pocket.

"What do you have in your pocket?" he asked.

"I don't know what Thigpen has in his pocket," one of the other saloon patrons said. "But look what I just found in this feller's pocket." He held up a red armband.

"A red armband," someone said. "Ain't that what them Ghost Riders wear around their arm?"

Smoke reached over to Thigpen and grabbed the folded piece of paper from his pocket. When he unfolded it, he wasn't surprised to see that it was the copy of the commission the governor had written out for him.

"What are you doing with this?" Smoke asked.

"I'm a file clerk. I was going to file it," Thigpen said.

"After you showed it to him?"

"I didn't show it to him."

"You're lyin', Thigpen," one of the other men in the saloon said. "I seen you and that man talking a while ago, 'n I seen you show him that piece of paper."

By then a couple of Denver uniformed police officers had come into the saloon. "We heard shootin' in here," one of them said.

"Yes," Stallings said. "That fella over there," he pointed to Cardigan's body, which was still sitting in the chair, "drawed on Smoke Jensen. It was a fatally foolish thing for him to have done."

"Smoke Jensen is here?" one of the policemen asked.

"That's him," Stallings said, pointing to Smoke.

"Officer Givens, you might be interested in this," the patron who had discovered the red armband said. He held it up so the two policemen could see it.

"I'll be damned," Givens said.

"What was the man's name, Thigpen?" Smoke asked.

Thigpen didn't answer.

"If you've read that commission, you know that I have the authority to arrest you and put you in prison for accomplice to attempted murder," Smoke said.

"His name was Cardigan," Stallings said. "He's

been a regular here, but I sure didn't know he belonged to the Ghost Riders."

"I didn't know Cardigan was going to draw on you. I just thought he was going to tell Hannibal about it," Thigpen said. "Really, I didn't have any idea he was going to try 'n kill you."

"Do you know where I can find Hannibal? Are he and his gang here, in Denver?"

"No," Thigpen said. "At least I don't think so."

"Then, what was Cardigan doing here?"

"Cardigan wasn't actually a member of the gang. That is, he didn't ride with them."

"How do you know that?" Givens asked.

"Well, I know for a fact that he was here during the thing that happened at Laurette."

"That's true," Stallings said. "Cardigan was here then."

"Are you part of the gang?" the other policeman asked Thigpen.

"No!" Thigpen answered, sharply.

"Then what were you doing with Cardigan?" Smoke asked.

"I don't have anything to do with the gang itself, but from time to time I would deal with Cardigan. I gave him information, and he paid me for it."

"How much did you get for showing him this?" Smoke asked, holding out the piece of paper.

"He gave me a dollar for it," Thigpen said in a small, weak voice.

"So, what you are saying is, you made yourself an accessory to attempted murder for one dollar?"

"I didn't know he was going to try and kill you!

I swear I didn't know!" Thigpen said in a pleading voice.

"Mr. Jensen, you want to put him in jail?" Givens asked.

Smoke shook his head. "No. Let him go. He might be of some use to me, later."

"Thank you, thank you! And, yes, sir, whatever you want me to do, Mr. Jensen, I'll do it," Thigpen said. "Yes, sir, you can count on me."

"Where can I find Hannibal?"

"I don't know."

"Then tell me, Mr. Thigpen, what possible use are you to me, if you can't tell me where to find Hannibal?"

"I . . . I don't know where he is, but—"

"But what?"

"I think something is going to happen in Brimstone soon."

"What's going to happen there?"

"I don't know. But Cardigan wanted me to give him information about Brimstone."

"What sort of information was he looking for?"

"He wanted to know the population of the town and how many lawmen were there."

"Did you give him the information he asked for?"

"Yes, sir, I did."

"Why did he want the information?"

"He didn't actually say why he wanted it. But I figure the Ghost Riders have some plan in mind for it."

"Thanks. If you get any other information you think I can use, give it to Officer Givens. And

Givens, if you don't get any cooperation from him, put him in jail."

"Yes, sir, I will be glad to do that," Givens replied with a broad smile.

Smoke walked back over to the bar and, without being asked, the bartender put a new mug of beer before him. Smoke put a nickel on the bar, but it was pushed back.

"No, sir, this one is on the house," the bartender said with a broad smile.

Ten Strike

A knock on the door caused Hannibal to look up. "Yes?" he called.

"Hannibal, I've got the new men out here," Rexwell called.

"I'll be right there."

Hannibal stepped outside to meet his new recruits. "Tell me about them," he said as the eight men stood in front of him.

"These two are twins, Amos and Amon Scraggs," Rexwell said. "They robbed a bank in Suttle, killed the bank guard there. When I caught up with them they were in jail, waitin' to be hung."

"How were you caught?" Hannibal asked.

"We was run down by a posse. They was just too damn many of them," Amos said.

"This is Snake Eye Mason," Rexwell said, and looking at him, Hannibal could see how he got his name. A scar ran through one of his eyes, causing it to be in a perpetual squint.

"How'd you get that scar?" Hannibal asked.

"I got into a knife fight," Snake Eye said. "He left me with this permanent scar." He ran his finger across the scar; then he laughed. "I left him permanently dead."

Bart Jennings had always operated alone, and though he had never been caught, neither had he ever made a big score with any of his jobs.

Emerson Case had been teamed up with another man, and they had specialized in robbing stores, generally those that were remotely located. But the man he had worked with was killed in their last robbery, and Case was looking for another partner when he was approached by Rexwell.

Jeb Jones was a card cheat who had killed a man who caught him in the act. He was on the run when Rexwell offered him a way out. Hock Granger had escaped from Yuma Prison, killing a guard in the process.

Vince Oceans was the last of the new recruits. Oceans would kill anyone, if someone paid him enough.

"I'm told you are good with a gun," Hannibal said.

"I'm not just good, I'm the best," Oceans replied.

"You are the best, huh? That's quite a claim."

"It ain't a claim, it's a fact," Oceans said. "There ain't a man alive that can beat me."

"Have you ever heard of a man named Smoke Jensen?" Hannibal asked.

"Smoke Jensen? Hell yes, who hasn't heard of him?"

"Do you think you are better than he is?"

"I *know* that I'm better than he is."

"But you have never gone up against him, have you?"

"No. And you'll pardon me for sayin' this, but that is a dumb question."

"Mr. Oceans, if I decide to let you ride with the Ghost Riders, you will treat me with absolute respect, and that means I will not allow you to be insubordinate. But, your response has aroused my curiosity. I asked you if you had ever gone up against Smoke Jensen, and you said that was a dumb question. Why do you say that?"

"It's a dumb question because if I had gone up against him, he would be dead now."

"I see."

Hannibal addressed the new men.

"Men, you are about to embark upon a new adventure, an adventure that will make you more money than you have ever even dreamed possible."

The men looked at each other as wide grins spread across their faces.

"But, in order for this to happen, you must adhere to a strict code of obedience."

"Obedience?" Snake Eye asked.

"Yes, obedience to the men who are appointed over you."

"Who would those men be?" Oceans asked.

"I am your commanding officer, and Rexwell is my executive officer."

"Hold it," Oceans said. "What is this *officer* thing?

I was in the army for a while, and I didn't like it. And I especially didn't like the officers."

"How much did you make while you were in the army?" Hannibal asked.

"I made twelve dollars a month."

"With me, there will be no month in which you make less than two hundred dollars," Hannibal said.

Oceans smiled. "Two hundred dollars a month? I like that."

"Does that mean you will stay?"

"Yeah."

"Yes, sir," Hannibal demanded.

"Yes, sir."

"Hold up your right hand."

The men did as they were directed.

"Repeat after me: I solemnly swear that I will obey all orders given me by Hannibal, Rexwell, or whomever they may appoint over me."

The men repeated the oath, and Hannibal nodded. "You are now duly installed as a Ghost Rider."

When the men were dismissed, Hannibal asked that Smith, Collins, and Oceans be brought to him. When they came to the house he was using for his headquarters, he gave them their orders.

"I want you men to go to Brimstone. Spend several days there blending in. Do nothing to call attention to yourselves, but find out as much about the town as you can."

"What for?" Collins asked.

"Because in two weeks, I plan to make Brimstone our next target. And in the words of Sun Tzu, "if you know the enemy as you know yourself, you need not fear the result of a hundred battles."

"Hey, Collins," Oceans asked as he, Collins, and Smith rode toward Brimstone. "Who do you think the Sunsue fella is, Hannibal is always talkin' about?"

"Beats the hell out of me," Collins replied. "But he must have made some kind of impression on Hannibal."

CHAPTER SEVENTEEN

Sugarloaf Ranch

When Sally stepped into Cal's room, she saw that he was twitching around on the bed and Julia was sitting on the side of the bed, holding his hand.

"Since you didn't come to breakfast, I brought breakfast to you," Sally said, holding a small plate with a sausage biscuit.

"Oh, thank you," Julia said reaching for it.

"And I'll join you. How is our patient?"

"He was sleeping peacefully when I first came in, but he's been restless for the last few minutes. I think he's having another one of his dreams. He told me the other day that he could see his mother, as she was when he was a child. And I got the idea that was an unpleasant experience for him."

"Cal has never spoken much of his past, and I think the reason he hasn't is because I gather it was rather difficult for him," Sally said. "Neither Smoke nor I have ever asked him about it because we've always figured that if he wanted us to know, he would tell us. Maybe his dreams are acting as a catharsis for his old memories."

"Catharsis?"

"It's just another way of saying that you are getting something off your chest," Sally said.

"You are a very smart woman," Julia said.

"Coming from you, I take that as a huge compliment," Sally said with a smile. "Dr. Urban said that if it hadn't been for you, Cal would have died before Smoke got him home. You are a very good nurse."

"The only thing I know, I learned from my father," Julia said.

"Yes, you said he was a doctor. Did you ever think about going to school to become a doctor?" Sally asked.

"No, I'm not that smart." Julia smiled. "But I do know how to set a table for a group of officers' wives."

"Officers' wives?" Sally asked, surprised by the comment.

"I'm . . . that is, I was once married to an army officer."

The expression on Julia's face as she mentioned it signaled to Sally that she really didn't want to talk about it. But she was saved from exploring the subject any further when Cal spoke from his sleep.

"I'm starvin' to death. I've got to do something," Cal said.

"Bless his heart, even in his sleep he complains about only having bouillon," Sally said.

"No, I don't think so," Julia said.

"You don't?"

"No. I think he's reliving another part of his past." Julia leaned over to take Cal's hand in hers.

"You may be right," Sally said, impressed with Julia's empathy with Cal.

Cal's experiences

Three months after Cal left Eagle Tail, he found himself in the town of Big Rock, Colorado. He tried to get a job at the stable, only to learn that there was nothing available. He tried at Guthrie's Lumber Yard, nothing there, and nothing at the blacksmith shop either. He hadn't eaten in two days and he had to do something. He was starving. That was when he saw a pretty woman coming out of the dress shop.

He crossed the street then walked past the Dunn Hotel and the Bank of Big Rock, keeping his hand on the gun that he had stuck down in his waistband. It was the same gun he had used to shoot Teague. Cal stepped up to the woman as she climbed into the buckboard.

"Ma'am, I hate to do this, but I'm goin' to have to ask you for all your money," he said.

"All of it?" she replied.

"Well, maybe not all of it. I just need enough so's I can get out of town."

"And if I don't give you all my money, are you going to shoot me?"

"Yes, ma'am, I've come too far now. I reckon I would have to."

"What are you going to shoot me with?"

"As you can see, I've got a gun in my waist," Cal said.

Then, in a draw that was so fast that Cal almost couldn't believe he had seen it, the pretty woman pulled a pistol from her holster.

"And as you can see, I've got a gun in my hand," she said.

Cal was quiet for a moment. "Yes, ma'am, I reckon you do," he said.

"Use your thumb and your forefinger to take the gun from your waistband and hand it to me," she said.

Cal did as he was instructed.

"You goin' to take me to jail?" Cal asked.

"Do you think that's where you belong?"

"Yes, ma'am, I expect that is where I belong. At least I'd get somethin' to eat there."

"How old are you?"

"I'm twenty-one."

"Don't lie to me, boy. How old are you?"

"I'm sixteen."

"When is the last time you had a meal?"

"I had me a biscuit 'n a piece of bacon day before yesterday."

"You mean to tell me that you haven't eaten for two days?"

"Yes, ma'am, well, sometimes I'll go two or three days without eatin'. I'm pretty much gettin' used to it now."

"Are you?"

"Yes, ma'am. Well, I mean, I got no choice in it, so I may as well get used to it."

"What is your name?"

"It's Cal, ma'am. Cal Wood."

"My name is Sally Jensen." Sally put her gun away, and scooted over on the seat. "Climb up here beside me, Cal. I'm going to take you home and give you a meal."

"Ma'am, you don't have to do that."

"I told you my name and it isn't ma'am."

"Miz Sally. You don't have to feed me."

Sally laughed. "You were willing to take money from me at gunpoint, but now you aren't willing to take food from me?"

"Yes, ma'am, now that you mention it, I reckon that is some foolish, ain't it?"

"Isn't it."

"Yes, ma'am."

"No, you said *ain't it*, I corrected you. *Ain't* is not a word I will permit you to use. Now, are you going to come home with me and let me feed you, or not?"

"Yes, ma'am. If you don't mind, I will let you feed me. And I'll be most grateful for it. And I'll be glad to work for it."

Sally tried to carry on a conversation with Cal during the time it took to go from town to the ranch, but, though he replied in general terms, he told her nothing about himself. When they turned under an arched sign, with the name SUGARLOAF in wrought-iron letters, Cal let out a low whistle.

"Lord a'mighty, Miz Sally. This here is where you live?"

"This is where I live. This here is grammatically incorrect."

"Yes, ma'am, you seem to be big on grammar. I'll try 'n remember that."

As they drove up the long drive, Cal saw a big, two-story house, a large barn, a long bunkhouse, and a few other buildings. Every building was well kept and had a fresh paint job.

"Lord have mercy, I ain't never seen no place this big," Cal said.

"Cal, if you are going to stay here and live with us, you are going to have to learn proper English. I insist upon it."

"What do you mean, live here with you?"

"We'll discuss it later. For now, I want you to tell me what you said wrong."

"*Ain't*," Cal said with a smile. "I said *ain't* again, 'n I'm sorry for that. I mean I haven't never—"

"Ever," Sally corrected.

"Ever seen a place this big."

"Thank you, that is much better."

"But, what did you mean when you said, live here with you?"

"I told you, we'll discuss it later."

As Cal was eating his third helping of chicken and dumplings, Sally came into the room with a big, powerful-looking man.

"I hear you tried to hold up my wife," he said.

Cal dropped the fork. "Yes, sir," he said in a small

voice, as a piece of dumpling dribbled from his mouth.

"Have you ever held up anyone before?"

"I'm not going to lie to you, Mister, I've stolen a few things, but I ain't never—" He looked at Sally, then corrected himself. "That is, I haven't never held no one up before."

"You mean you haven't *ever* held up *anyone* before."

"No ma'am, it's like I said, I haven't never done it before."

Sally sighed. "It's going to take a while."

"Why did you try to hold up my wife?" Smoke asked.

"I was hungry."

"If you were hungry, why didn't you take a job?"

"I was looking for a job, but I couldn't find one."

"If I hire you, you aren't going to try and steal anything from me, are you?"

"If you hire me? You mean, after what I did, you would hire me?"

"Yes, but I'll keep you on only as long as you are a good worker and an honest hand."

"Mr. Jensen, I'll work myself to the bone for you, and I swear to you, I'll never take a thing that doesn't belong to me again."

"Come on, I want you to meet Pearlie."

"Pearlie?"

"You don't like the name?"

"I think Pearlie is a fine name," Cal said. "Oh, 'n Miz Sally, I wouldn't have really shot you."

"That's good to know," Sally replied. "But just so

you understand what a dangerous game you were playing, Cal, I *would* have shot you."

"Miz Sally, I wouldn't have really shot you," Cal said aloud.

Julia gasped. "Heavens! What kind of dream is he having now, that he says he wouldn't have really shot you?"

Sally chuckled. "I never really thought he would."

"You never thought he would?" Julia asked, now totally confused.

"Sally! What's for breakfast?" The shout came from outside the house before Sally could explain her odd comment.

"Oh, Smoke is back!" Sally said happily, not responding to Julia's implied question. She reached for the empty saucer that had held the sausage biscuit she had given Julia. "I'll take that. I'd better get in there, I can tell you right now that Smoke Jensen is not going to be content with one biscuit and one piece of sausage."

Carrying the two empty plates, Sally hurried into the kitchen, meeting Smoke just as he stepped inside. He didn't even give her the opportunity to set the plates down before he pulled her to him for a long, homecoming kiss.

"Oh, my," Sally teased. "If I'm going to get kissed like that, you'll have to go away more often."

"Or, you could just welcome me home every now and then without me ever actually having been gone," Smoke suggested.

Sally laughed. "I suppose I could."

"How is Cal?"

"I think he is still hallucinating, reliving things from his past. How was your trip to Denver?"

"I got what I went for," Smoke said. He didn't mention the incident with Boots Cardigan. "Are you going to make me some breakfast, or what?"

"Julia and I have already had our breakfast. You should have eaten in town. Now you're going to have to wait until lunch."

"What?"

Sally laughed. "I'm teasing, I'll fix something for you. As a matter of fact, Julia thinks that Cal could start on solid food today as long as it isn't too hard to digest. I think scrambled eggs would be all right for him."

"I'll ask him if he wants to have breakfast with me," Smoke said.

"You know, when I wake up and I see you still sitting here, so pretty and all, why, sometimes I think I'm still dreaming and you're just an angel in my dreams. But—" Cal stopped in mid-sentence when he saw Smoke.

"Smoke!" he said, sitting up in the bed.

"Hold on, don't break everything loose now," Smoke said, holding out his hand.

"It's all right, I've been up lots of times, haven't I, Julia?"

"Yes, I would say he's coming along just fine now."

"How would you like to have breakfast with me?" Smoke asked.

"More bouillon?"

"Well, I was thinking more along the lines of scrambled eggs, maybe even with a little cheese."

"Ha! For you, maybe. Miz Sally won't let me eat anything but bouillon. I swear, I never had any idea how mean that woman could be."

Julia laughed. "Cal, don't you be talking like that," she said. "You know she is just doing what is best for you."

"And she just told me you could have eggs," Smoke said.

"She did? All right!" Cal said excitedly, and throwing the sheet aside he started to get out of bed until he realized that he was wearing his underdrawers. "Oh!" he said, throwing the sheet back across himself.

"Oh pooh, Cal," Julia said. "In all the time I've spent here with you, you don't think I've seen you in your drawers?"

"I reckon maybe you did," Cal said. "But not while I was lookin' at you, you didn't."

"All right, I'll leave the room until you're dressed."

When Smoke and Cal went into the dining room a few minutes later, Pearlie was already there, sitting at the table.

"I saw you ride in," Pearlie said. "Did you get what you went for?"

"I sure did. You and I are now officers of the Colorado Rangers, with the dedicated mission of going after Hannibal and the Ghost Riders."

"Wait a minute," Cal said. "You mean to say that you are going after them without me?"

"Oh yeah, you'd be a big help," Pearlie teased.

"You could wait until I get better. I mean, I'm the reason you're going after him, aren't I?"

"Sort of," Smoke said.

"What do you mean, sort of?"

"A few weeks ago Hannibal and the Ghost Riders robbed a bank in Laurette," Smoke said. "They killed twenty-three people before they rode out of town."

"Twenty-three? There were that many in the bank?"

"They shot up the whole town, killing indiscriminately. Apparently they thought that the more they killed, the better their chances would be of getting away."

"Wow, that's in addition to the ones they killed at Brown Spur," Cal said. "They have to be stopped, Smoke, and they have to be stopped soon. I really do wish I could go with you, but you are right. This isn't something that can wait."

"When do we leave?" Pearlie asked.

"As soon as I finish breakfast."

"I'll put a couple of changes of clothes in your saddlebag," Sally said.

"Yeah, maybe I'd better do that too," Pearlie said. "Uh, after breakfast. I'll just wait here with you and Cal."

Sally chuckled. "Pearlie, would you like some scrambled eggs?"

"Yes, ma'am. And, uh, if you're goin' to fry up

some more sausage I'll have a patty of that too. Do you have any biscuits? Are you going to make some gravy?"

"Pearlie, didn't you eat breakfast in the cook-house with the others this morning?"

"Well, yes, ma'am, I did. But it wouldn't be polite for me to just sit here with Smoke 'n Cal 'n not join them."

"Good point," Sally said. "All right, I'll make gravy as well."

CHAPTER EIGHTEEN

Sally, Cal, and Julia walked out onto the porch to tell Smoke and Pearlie good-bye. They stayed there until the two men passed under the arched gate.

"I was surprised that Sally didn't try and talk Smoke out of going," Julia said, later, when she and Cal returned to his room. "Or at least try and talk him into waiting a little while."

"She would never do that," Cal said.

"Why not?"

"In the first place, she knows that Smoke is right, those people have to be stopped. And she knows that he would go, no matter what she said to him. So why should she make his job any harder by making him think that she may not be behind him when he does this?"

"I guess you're right. It's just that I don't know if I could let my man go into such danger without trying to stop him."

"Yes you would," Cal said. "You would be just like

Miz Sally. You would know how important it is for me to go, and you wouldn't try to stop me."

Julia laughed. "I wouldn't try to stop you?"

"Oh, yeah," Cal said. "I uh, was just sort of giving an example, you know."

"Maybe you have a point."

Smoke and Pearlie had been on the road for three days, and the steady clip-clop of the horses' hooves had a calming effect as they continued on their journey. A rabbit jumped up from a bush, ran in quick, long hops in front of them, then darted off the road and into some dry shrubbery. Carefully concealed, it watched the mounted men with big, curious eyes as they rode past.

It was late afternoon when Smoke and Pearlie approached the little town, and they paused on top of a small hill to look down at the buildings and even a few tents. The long, golden rays of the setting sun caused the buildings in the valley below them to glow orange and red, almost as if they were ablaze. As they approached, they saw that the name on the welcome sign was appropriate to the gleaming red of the town.

BRIMSTONE
Population 623
A Growing Community

Smoke removed his canteen from the saddle pommel, took a swallow, then offered it to Pearlie who declined. Recorking the canteen, he put it back, then slapped his legs against the side of his horse to head Seven on down the long slope of the ridge.

"The sign says six hundred and twenty-three. Do you think there are that many people living here now?" Pearlie asked.

"Could be," Smoke answered. "There are quite a few houses, and they have a pretty good-looking downtown."

There were private homes at the outer edge of the town, as well as along some of the streets that bisected the main road. As the two men rode farther, they passed by three young girls who were playing hopscotch on squares marked out in the dirt and a couple of boys who were sitting nearby playing mumbly-peg.

Then they rode into the business section. Both sides were lined with rather substantial-looking stores and shops, most with false fronts. There was a three-story hotel, and a nice-looking, white church with a towering steeple right in the center of town.

A wagon was backed up to the general store and a couple of men were listlessly unloading it. They looked over at Smoke and Pearlie, perhaps curious as to who they were and what brought them to town, though, in the heat, neither of them was ambitious enough to speak.

Inside the saloon, just ahead of Smoke and Pearlie, a drama was playing out before the curious and concerned customers. It was taking place between a large, rough-looking man in his early thirties and a much younger, well-dressed man who was barely old enough to drink.

"I'll ask you again," the ruffian said. "I want to know what you were doin' with my girl?"

"Oh, Mr. Oceans, for heaven's sake," the bar girl in question said, speaking up then. "I'm not *your* girl. I belong to anyone who is willing to buy me a drink. You know that."

"Ain't I bought you drinks?" Oceans asked.

"Well, yes, but—"

"And let me ask you this. Has anyone else bought you as many drinks as I have since I been here?"

"Well, no, but—"

"There ain't no buts to it," Oceans said. "You're my woman, and I want this little fancy-dressed shit to admit it."

"Manny," the bartender said to the younger man. "Tell him that Nell is his woman and stop this thing now, before it gets out of hand."

Manny nodded. "All right, Oceans, Nell is your girl."

A humorless smile spread across Oceans's face. "That ain't good enough."

"What do you mean?"

"I want you to get down on your knees and beg me to take her."

"I'm not going to do that," Manny said.

"Yeah, you are. You are going to get down on your knees, and you are going to say, 'I'm sorry, Mr. Oceans. Nell is your girl, and I beg you to take her.' Then, after you say that, I want you to beg me to forgive you."

"No," Manny said. "I told you Nell is your girl, but that is as far as I'm going to go."

The humorless smile on Oceans's face grew even larger.

Outside, totally unaware of the confrontation between Oceans and Manny, Smoke and Pearlie continued on deeper into the town.

"What do you say we settle some of this trail dust with a beer?" Smoke suggested.

"Sounds good to me. Almost as good as something to eat," Pearlie replied.

"Maybe we can get both in the same place."

It wasn't hard to find the saloon. It was painted gray, with a high false front. A golden mug of beer was on one side of the false front, then painted in red and black was the name of the saloon: DEVIL'S DEN. On the opposite side of the front from the mug of beer, was the painting of a horned devil's head, also in red and black, except for the eyes, which were yellow.

Just as they were tying their horses off in front of the Devil's Den they heard a pistol shot coming from inside. In a reflexive action, both Smoke and Pearlie drew their pistols, the Colts appearing in their hands with lightning speed.

When it appeared that they were in no immediate danger, they holstered their pistols, stepped up onto the porch, pushed through the batwing doors, and went inside. Smoke moved to the left of the doors, Pearlie to the right, both men backing up against the front wall for just a moment.

There was a man lying on his back on the floor. His right arm was thrown out beside him, with a pistol nearby his open hand. A man was standing over him, a smoking gun still in his hand.

"You had no call to be doin' that, Oceans," the bartender said to the man who was holding the gun.

"You want some of the same?"

The bartender put up his hands. "I'm just a bartender, and I ain't armed. All I'm sayin' is, you pushed that boy into drawing on you."

"I give him a way out," the gunman replied.

"Some way out. You wanted him to get on his knees and beg you."

"Yeah, well if he had done what I ask, he'd still be alive now, wouldn't he? I tell you what, give ever'one in the place a drink, on me."

"All right!" one of the patrons shouted, and everyone rushed to the bar to take the gunman up on his offer.

Smoke and Pearlie hung back until the crowd had been served; then they stepped up.

"Two beers," Smoke said, putting a dime on the bar.

"You don't have to pay for it, the man over there is buying for the house," the bartender said, sliding the dime back toward Smoke.

"Thank you, but we'll pay for our own beers," Smoke replied, pushing the money back toward the bartender.

The gunman had seen the exchange, and he called out to Smoke. "What's the matter, Mister? My money not good enough for you?"

"Your money's fine, but we prefer to buy our own beers," Smoke said.

"You tryin' to pick a fight with me, Mister?"

"Not particularly. It's just that my friend and I are particular who we drink with, and we'd rather not drink with a loud-mouthed blowhard."

The gunman smiled. "I see that there are two of you. Is that what is giving you your false courage? Because it's two of you to one?"

"Do you have a name?" Smoke asked.

"Yeah, I got a name. It's Oceans. Vince Oceans." He grinned. "I reckon you've heard of Vince Oceans, ain't you?"

"I can't say that I have."

"Where you from? Back East somewhere? Ever'body in Colorado has heard of Vince Oceans. Now that you know who I am, why I reckon you'd be right proud to drink with me."

"Not particularly," Smoke said. "Let it go, Mr. Oceans. My friend and I have had a long, hot ride, and we want to drink our beer in peace, maybe get something to eat, then find someplace to sleep."

At that moment a lawman came into the room. "Damn," he said when he recognized the body that was lying on the floor. "That's Manny Parker. What happened?"

"He drew on me," Oceans said.

"Is that true, Mark?" the lawman asked the bartender.

Smoke saw Oceans stare hard at the bartender, who blinked a couple of times before he responded.

"What are you askin' the bartender for?" another man asked. Smoke noticed that this man, like Oceans, was wearing his holster low and tied down. And like Oceans, he had a killer's eyes. "The man that's lyin' there dead, draw'd first. Oceans warn't doin' nothin' but defendin' hisself."

"What's your name?" the marshal asked.

"Collins. The name is Spike Collins."

"You two rode into town together, didn't you, Collins?" the marshal asked.

"So, what if we did?"

"It's just that if the two of you come here together, well, you're bound to back up what he says."

"Are you callin' me a liar?" Collins asked.

"No, I wouldn't say that. But I would like to hear what happened from someone else. Did any of the rest of you see it?" the marshal asked.

"They're both tellin' the truth, Marshal Hardegree. Manny draw'd first," one of the others said. "But this feller Oceans kinda egged him on."

"I didn't exactly egg him on, Marshal," Oceans said. "Me 'n him got into an argument 'n started throwin' words back 'n forth. One thing led to another, 'n the fool pulled his gun on me. What was I s'posed to do? Just stand here 'n let 'im shoot me? I was defendin' myself, that's all I was doin'."

"Can I get him out of here, Stan?" the bartender asked. "Havin' his body lyin' here ain't good for business."

"Yeah, I've seen enough. You can get 'im taken down to the undertaker's."

"Half a dollar apiece to anyone who'll get him out of here," Mark said, and two men stepped up to take the job.

With the body removed and his curiosity as to what happened satisfied, the marshal left the saloon, and everything returned to normal.

"I've seen you before, Mister," Oceans said to Smoke.

"Could be," Smoke agreed. "I've been to a lot of places."

Oceans stroked his chin. "It'll come to me."

Collins had turned away, apparently no longer interested in baiting him.

"What are the chances of getting something to eat in this place?" Smoke asked the bartender.

"We've got ham, biscuits, and the cook can fry you up some taters."

"Sounds good," Smoke said. "We'll be over—"

"Smoke!" Pearlie shouted, and even as he was calling the warning, he pulled his pistol and fired at Collins, who had already drawn and was aiming at Smoke. Collins fell back, belly-side-up across a table with his head hanging down on the far side while blood dripped from the hole in his forehead to form a puddle below him. His gun fell from his lifeless hand and clattered to the floor.

"What the hell? Mister, you just killed my partner!" Oceans shouted, angrily.

"Yeah, I did," Pearlie said.

"Yes, and now I'm goin' to kill you," Oceans said.

"There's really no need for you to want to kill me," Pearlie said, easily. He took in Collins with a sweep of his hand. "You aren't the one who was about to shoot my friend, so I've got nothing against you. You and I don't have a fight."

"The hell we don't. Collins was my friend, and you made it my fight when you kilt him. Now I reckon I'm goin' to have to kill you."

"Well, I guess you have to do whatever you feel you have to do," Pearlie said, his voice still calm and controlled.

"Which one of us are you planning on killing?" Smoke asked.

"What do you mean, which one of you? He's the one that killed Collins."

"Well, yes, but you have to think about this," Smoke said. "If you kill Pearlie, I'm going to be very upset, and I'll have to kill you. So, why don't we just skip one step and I go ahead and kill you now so we can get this over with?"

"That's not fair," Pearlie said. "Come on, I'm the one he challenged, so I'm the one who should get to kill him."

"Yes, but wasn't the fella you killed, about to shoot me?"

"Yes."

"All right then that makes this my fight, can't you see that? And anyway, you've already killed one of them. It's my turn now."

Smoke and Pearlie were discussing this as calmly as if they were discussing who should pay for a beer.

"I guess you do have a point there. All right, I'll go get us a table while you kill—" Pearlie looked toward Oceans. "What did you say your name was again? Oceans, was it?"

"You know damn well what my name is. It's Vince

Oceans, and folks tell me I'm the fastest gun in Colorado."

"Is that a fact? Well, folks are wrong. All right, Smoke, you kill Oceans while I get us a table."

"Smoke? Did you call him Smoke?"

"Yes, Smoke Jensen," Pearlie said. "Have you ever heard of him?"

An evil smile spread across Oceans's face. "Yeah," he said. "Yeah, I've heard of Smoke Jensen. I've waited a long time to run across you," he said.

"Have you now? Well, Oceans, it could be that you and I just got off on the wrong foot, and all because we wanted to pay for our own beer. So I tell you what. Why don't you just pay for our supper? That way, we can call it even," Smoke said.

Smoke turned away from Oceans and started toward the table Pearlie had picked out for them.

"Draw, Jensen!" Oceans shouted, though he had already drawn his own pistol even before he issued the shout.

Smoke whirled, drew, and fired in the same movement, shooting Oceans before he was even able to pull the trigger. The bullet hit Oceans in the chest, and he slapped his hand over the wound and stared at Smoke in total shock as he realized what had just happened.

"I thought . . . I thought I could beat you. I'll be damned," Oceans said, but by now the words were little more than a death rattle. He took one step forward, held out his bloody hand, then fell facedown onto the floor where he lay as still as the one Pearlie had shot just a moment earlier.

"Did he already have the gun in his hand?" someone asked.

"You mean Oceans? Yeah, he had the gun in his hand before he yelled out."

"No, I mean the other fella, Jensen. Did he already have the gun in his hand? 'Cause I never even seen him draw."

"I didn't either, but I did see the gun in his holster when he turned away."

CHAPTER NINETEEN

Shortly after Oceans shot Manny Parker, Bill Smith had taken one of the bar girls upstairs. She was willing enough to go with him because the shooting had frightened her, and she would just as soon be as far away as she could.

But Smith hadn't even gotten undressed yet when he heard another shot.

"What was that?" the girl asked in a frightened tone of voice.

Smith held his hand out to keep her on the bed. "I'll take a look," he said.

Smith stepped out and looked down on the main room of the saloon. There, he saw Collins lying belly up and obviously dead on one of the tables. He also saw Oceans challenging two men.

For a moment he thought of Hannibal's motto of one for all, and all for one, and he thought that he should go down to help Oceans. Then he thought that it wouldn't be necessary for him to go down, he could help Oceans from up here.

He reached for his gun, just as he heard Oceans shout "Draw, Jensen!"

But before he could get the gun from his holster, the man Oceans had challenged whirled and fired with a speed unlike anything Smith had ever seen before.

Smith dropped the pistol back into his holster. There was no way he was going to get involved in this now. The one for all, and all for one didn't matter if the person you were going to help was already dead. Smith went back into the room and saw the girl cowering under the sheet.

"You can come out now," he said. "The shootin' is all over."

"I . . . can I give you your money back?" the girl asked. "I don't want to do anything now."

"I don't care whether you want to do anything or not," Smith said. "I paid for it, so we're goin' to do it."

It wasn't just that he wanted to get what he paid for, it was also that he had heard Smoke Jensen give his name.

During the raid at Brown Spur, there had been a brief moment when he and Smoke Jensen had come face-to-face. He feared that Jensen might recognize him and he didn't want to give him that opportunity.

Marshal Hardegree came back into the saloon. "Damn!" he said, seeing Oceans lying on the floor and Collins spread out across the table. "What the hell is goin' on in here, Mark? A war?"

"Marshal, I can tell you right now that them two is the ones that started it," the bartender said, pointing to the two dead men. "Only this time, Oceans picked a fight with the wrong man. He was dumb enough to brace Smoke Jensen."

"Smoke Jensen is here? In my town?"

"That's him, right over there," Mark Worley said, pointing to the table where Smoke and Pearlie sat, waiting for their supper.

The marshal walked over to them. "You're Smoke Jensen?"

"Yes."

"I'm Marshal Stan Hardegree. Did you kill these two men?"

"He didn't kill both of them, Marshal, 'cause I shot the one that's lyin' across the table," Pearlie said.

"Why did you shoot him?"

"I shot him because he was about to shoot Smoke."

"And I shot the one on the floor, because he was also trying to shoot me," Smoke said.

"You know, if I was the kind of man that worried about such things, I'd wonder why both of them wanted to shoot you, but neither one of them was interested in shooting me," Pearlie said. "Why do you think that is? Damn, aren't I worth shooting?"

"What's your name?" the marshal asked.

"My name is Pearlie," Pearlie replied with a broad smile. He stuck out his hand. "I'm pleased to meet you, Sheriff."

Pearlie's spontaneous offer of his hand caught

the marshal by surprise, and he accepted it and shook hands with him.

"It's marshal, not sheriff," Hardegree said.

"Sorry, I mean marshal."

"I've heard of you, Smoke Jensen," the marshal said.

"What have you heard?"

"I've heard that you are deadly with a gun."

"Well, Marshal Hardegree, I never use a gun unless I am forced to use it. But, as you are a lawman, I'm sure you realize that if you ever do find yourself backed into a gunfight, then it's good to be proficient with the weapon."

"No, I don't suppose I can argue with that," Hardegree said.

"I'll be damned, Marshal, look at this!" one of the patrons of the saloon said. When the marshal, Smoke, Pearlie, and everyone else looked toward the man who had called out, they saw that he was holding a red armband in his hand.

"Where did you get that?" Marshal Hardegree asked.

"When we moved this fella off the table, it fell out of his pocket."

"Check Oceans's pocket," Hardegree said.

"Yeah, he's got one too," another patron said, holding up a red armband.

"Damn! They must have been riding with the Ghost Riders! What the hell were they doing here?" the bartender asked.

"Maybe scoutin' the bank," someone said. "I'm sure you heard what they done in Laurette. They cleaned that bank out."

"And left just a whole passel of dead behind 'em," another man said. "Includin' women and kids."

"You reckon maybe they're plannin' on robbin' our bank?" the bartender asked.

"I don't know," Hardegree said. "It could be, I suppose."

"What do you think Hannibal is goin' to do when he finds out we killed two of his men?" someone asked.

"We didn't do it," another said. "These two did." He pointed to Smoke and Pearlie.

"Maybe we should ask these two to move on."

"Don't be foolish," Marshal Hardegree said. "As far as Hannibal is concerned, it doesn't make any difference who killed his men. If he decides he wants to punish the town it won't matter whether these two men are still here or have ridden on. And if Hannibal does decide to attack the town then who better to have on our side than Smoke Jensen?"

"Whoa, what about me?" Pearlie asked. "I mean, I killed one of them."

"Yeah, I'm glad you're both here. But, why are you here, anyway? I mean, what would bring someone like you two to Brimstone?"

"The Ghost Riders," Smoke replied.

"Ghost Riders? You came to Brimstone, looking for the Ghost Riders?"

"In a matter of speaking, I did."

"Why? What made you think they would be here?"

"I heard from a source that they were interested in Brimstone, for some reason."

"Damn, it *is* our bank," Marshal Hardegree said.

"This is a pretty small town. Do you think there's enough money in the bank here, to attract them?"

"We have a couple of big ranches nearby, but the biggest thing now is the Double Dinkle Mine. It's been producing a goodly amount of silver lately. The mine owners bring in the payroll ever' two weeks, so, yes, I expect we do have enough money to interest someone like Hannibal and his gang."

Ten minutes later, Smith was dressed and walking down the stairs. Everyone was talking about the shooting, and he was stopped short when he saw two red armbands lying on the end of the bar. Hannibal had given them specific orders that when they came into town that they weren't supposed to show their armbands. He felt in his pocket, just to make certain it hadn't fallen out when he was in the whore's room, and was satisfied to see it was still there.

He stepped up to the bar to order a drink.

"Who shot them two?" he asked.

"Smoke Jensen shot Oceans, and the man with him shot Collins," the bartender replied.

"Collins and Oceans? That was their names?"

"Yeah. Are you tellin' me you didn't know them? You rode in with these two, didn't you? I thought maybe they were friends of yours."

Smith shook his head. "I never saw 'em before today. We rode in at the same time, but we didn't exactly ride in together."

The bartender returned with a mug of beer, and Smith drank it as he watched Smoke Jensen talk to the star packer. He wanted to leave the saloon, but he couldn't do so now, without walking past Smoke Jensen and maybe being recognized.

"Mr. Jensen, we held your food up in the kitchen so it wouldn't get cold," the bartender said. "Would you like it brought out now?"

"Would that be all right, Marshal?" Smoke asked.

"Yes, go ahead and eat," Marshal Hardegree said.

When Smith saw Smoke Jensen and Pearlie go across the floor to a table, it provided him with the opportunity to leave without being noticed. He finished the beer, then walked out, keeping his head turned in such a way as to not give Smoke a good, clean look at him.

Smith, Collins, and Oceans had tied their horses up three buildings down from the saloon. They had come this morning and hadn't yet gone into the bank to scout it out. They had planned to do that tomorrow, then ride back to Ten Strike. And everything would have been fine if Oceans hadn't picked a fight with the kid. He was just a well-dressed kid, and something about that irritated Oceans. He wouldn't leave it alone, and he goaded the kid into a fight. It all went downhill from there.

Smith thought about going into the bank to check it out, but decided it would be better for him to get back to Ten Strike to tell Hannibal what happened.

Before he left, though, he took the saddlebags from Collins's and Oceans's horses. He told himself he was doing it so the law couldn't find anything in them that might lead to Ten Strike. But he also knew that each of them had over a hundred dollars in their saddlebags. There was no sense letting the law have that money.

And there was no sense in turning it back in to the Ghost Riders' treasury, either. In this case the one for all, and all for one was strictly all for one. He giggled. Collins and Oceans were all, and he was one.

He rode out of town at a brisk trot, staring straight ahead. When he crossed over the Grand River, he tossed both pair of saddlebags into the water.

"Collins and Oceans are both dead?" Hannibal asked, after Smith returned.

"Yes, sir."

"Then tell me, Smith, why is it that you are still alive?"

"There warn't nothin' I could do about it, Hannibal. I wasn't even there in the saloon at the time."

"Where were you?"

"Well, I had walked down to take a look at the bank, when I heard the shootin'. And since it come from the saloon, I went back down to see what had happened. That's when I saw both of 'em lyin' on the floor, dead. I figured the smartest thing I could do then, would be to come back here 'n tell you about it."

"Who killed them?"

"Yeah, well, you ain't goin' to like this," Smith said. "But from what I heard, the man that kilt them was Smoke Jensen."

"Smoke Jensen," Hannibal said. "He has, indeed, become an irritant. Collins and Oceans now make a total of nine of my men he has killed. We need to kill him before this goes any further."

"This Jensen feller wasn't alone," Smith said. "There was another man with him, and from what I hear, he's the one that kilt Collins."

"What is the other man's name?" Hannibal asked.

"Pearlie."

"Pearlie?"

"That's the only name I heard."

"Taylor, is he the one that was with Jensen when you and Moss were brought in?"

"No, sir. That was a fella by the name of Cal, something. I don't know what his last name is, 'cause I never heard it spoke."

"But you would recognize Smoke Jensen on sight, wouldn't you?"

"Oh, yes, sir, you better believe that. I'll never forget what that son of a bitch looks like."

"Good. When we conduct our raid on Brimstone, I want you to be looking for Smoke Jensen. If you see him, point him out to me. I intend to make him a special target."

"When are we going to hit Brimstone?" Rexwell asked.

"When I give the order," Hannibal replied.

"But with Oceans and Collins both dead 'n Smith not in town no more, we won't have nobody in town waitin' on us," Rexwell said.

"I have planned the operation and we will not deviate from it," Hannibal said.

"You think that bank will have as much money as the one in Laurette had?" Moss asked.

"Because of the Double Dinkle Mine nearby, I

expect it will have even more money than did the bank in Laurette," Hannibal said. "But, no matter how much they have, we will take every cent."

"Hannibal, may I make a suggestion?" Rexwell asked.

"What is it?"

"Well, sir, just rememberin' what Jensen done at the ranch 'n then what he done at Brown Spur when we went to get Taylor 'n Moss back, do we really want to hit the town while he's there? Don't forget, like you said, he's done kilt nine of us."

"What is your suggestion?"

"More 'n likely he will be spendin' tonight in town. I say we find out what room he's stayin' in 'n we sneak up to the room 'n kill 'im in his sleep."

"You have someone in mind for the job?"

"Yes, sir, I do. Advendingo is half-injun, 'n he can walk so light that he don't even leave tracks in the dew. He could get into Jensen's room and slit his throat before Jensen ever know'd he was there."

"Yes, that's a good idea. We'll send him in there tonight."

CHAPTER TWENTY

Sugarloaf Ranch

Sally and Julia were in the parlor, listening to the rich, resonating tones of the large, mahogany music box. Cal was back in his room, sleeping peacefully.

"How old is Cal?" Julia asked.

"He's twenty-five, but I swear sometimes I think he's still a kid."

"Is he always this nice?" Julia asked. "I mean, he has the best manners of about anyone I have ever met."

"Cal is exactly what you see," Sally said. "I don't think he has an insincere bone in his body."

"Does he have any . . . uh—"

Sally's chuckle interrupted the sentence. "Lady friends?"

"Yes. Does he—" Julia stopped in midsentence, then, to Sally's surprise, her eyes welled with tears.

"Why am I even talking about this? I mean, someone like me."

"Julia, I'm curious. Your father was a doctor, and you are quite a skilled nurse. How—"

"Did I become a whore?"

"I wasn't going to be quite as blunt," Sally said.

"That's all right. Those of us who are on the line have a saying, you know. Show me a whore and I'll show you a girl with a tragic tale to tell. I guess I'm no different.

"Sometimes, when I'm sitting there in the bedroom, looking at Cal, realizing what a fine young man he is and what fine people you and Mr. Jensen are, I feel so ashamed of myself.

"You can see now, why I had no right to even ask whether or not Cal has any lady friends."

Sally walked over to Julia, pulled her to her feet, then gave her a hug.

"Thanks," Julia said. "I needed that." She laughed, self-deprecatingly.

"I don't deserve it, but I needed it."

"Julia, don't be so hard on yourself. In all the time Smoke, Cal, and I have known you, you have been nothing but a sweet, caring, and helpful young woman. As far as any of us are concerned, your history started the moment you began taking care of Cal."

"Where's my angel?" Cal called from his room.

"You'd better go see what he wants," Sally said. "When he's calling for his angel, he isn't talking about me."

"Do you think I can get through the door without damaging my wings?" Julia asked with a little laugh.

Brimstone

It was dark when Emilio Advendingo stepped into the lobby of the Del Rey Hotel. A lantern burned dimly on the front desk, while the desk clerk was asleep in a chair that was tilted back against the wall.

Advendingo checked the registration book and found the name Kirby Jensen. He didn't know who Kirby was, but this was the only Jensen registered. He was in room 309. Behind the desk there was a big board, with keys hanging from hooks. Some of the hooks had two keys, some had only one key. There were numbers above the hooks, and hook number 309 had only one key.

Advendingo left the desk, then walked up the stairs, moving so quietly that the desk clerk was not even aware that he was there. The hall on the third floor ran in both directions from the stairs, but it was illuminated by mounted lanterns so he was able to read the door numbers. It took him but a moment to determine that he needed to go right.

He walked softly down the carpet until he found the room he wanted, which was the last room and on the right side. He pulled a knife from its sheath, then put the key into the lock and turned it, doing so, so skillfully that it didn't make a sound. He opened the door, then stepped inside.

It was Advendingo's plan to cut Jensen's throat. He smiled as he thought of what a sight it would make in the morning when Jensen's body was discovered lying in a pool of his own blood. He started toward the bed.

Smoke heard nothing, but even in his sleep, he sensed a slight change in the air. His window was raised about six inches, and when the door was opened, the flow of air increased. It was that increase in the flow of air that awakened him.

Smoke opened his eyes. That was when he saw the shadow pass in front of the window. Someone was in his room!

Smoke rolled off the bed, just as the intruder made a slashing motion with his knife. Smoke heard the blade cut through cloth, and he reached out, quickly, to grab the wrist of the man who had attacked him.

The man jerked his arm back, trying to free his knife hand, but Smoke didn't let go. On his feet now, Smoke struggled with the intruder as they shuffled across the floor, knocking over the table. The glass lantern fell and broke on the floor. There was no flame, but the smell of kerosene assailed Smoke's nostrils.

They continued to struggle until they were next to the window. Then, the intruder made one mighty jerk to get free, and when he did, he lost his balance and fell backward through the window, the crash of glass drowned out by his scream as he tumbled out, falling headfirst. His scream stopped in midscreech.

Smoke leaned out the window to look down, but it was too dark to see anything.

"Smoke!" Pearlie shouted, running from his adjacent room into this one. Pearlie was in his long johns, with his gun in his hand.

"I'm here," Smoke said. "Watch your feet, there's broken glass on the floor."

"What happened?"

"I had an unwelcome visitor but he fell through the window. Let's get dressed, I'm going to go down and see if he is still here."

Smoke dressed quickly, as Pearlie hurried back to his room to do the same. A moment later both men were dressed and walking down the lighted hall.

Nobody in any of the other rooms showed any curiosity, either because they didn't hear anything or perhaps they did hear something, but were afraid to investigate. As they walked through the lobby they noticed that the desk clerk was asleep. Smoke went over to pick up the kerosene lantern.

Once outside, Smoke turned up the lantern so that it cast a golden bubble of light around them. Using the light, they walked in between the hotel and the leather goods store, which was next door. As they approached, the outer limit of the golden circle of light picked up a body, lying motionless. They walked all the way up to him, but it didn't require much investigation to determine that he was dead.

"Who was he? A burglar, do you think?" Pearlie asked.

Smoke shook his head. "Not unless he planned to kill me first. He had a knife, and if I hadn't moved when I did, he would have cut my throat."

"Hmm, so he intended to kill you?"

"I would say so. Look at this." Smoke pulled a red armband from the dead man's pocket.

"I'll be damned."

"Let's take him over to the marshal's office."

Smoke and Pearlie made a rather macabre sight as they carried the dead body across the street in the middle of the night . . . Smoke at the man's head and Pearlie at his feet.

The door to the marshal's office was locked.

"What do we do with him now, Smoke?"

"Let's just put him down here, in front of the door," Smoke said. "That way the marshal can't possibly miss him. I'll leave him a note that says it's from us."

Marshal Hardegree came into the restaurant the next morning when Smoke and Pearlie were having their breakfast.

"I found what you left for me," he said. "And the note."

"Join us for breakfast?"

"Don't mind if I do," Hardegree said, joining them at the table.

"Here's something I didn't leave with you." Smoke pulled the red armband from his pocket.

"Damn," Hardegree said. "Another Ghost Rider?"

"So it would appear," Smoke said.

"I don't like it that there have been so many of them here. It makes me think you're right. They really are planning something. Maybe like Laurette."

"We'll be ready for them," Smoke said.

"What do you mean when you say that we will be ready for them? Unless you are volunteering to be my deputies."

"No need to deputize us," Smoke said. "Pearlie and I are both Colorado Rangers on special assignment."

"You are a Colorado Ranger? I've heard of you, Smoke. Just about everyone in the state has heard of you, I expect. But in all the stories I've heard, I never knew that you were a Colorado Ranger."

"We have only recently been given the commission," Smoke said. "And it is a dedicated commission, to be used only to find and deal with the Ghost Riders."

"Deal with? What do you mean, deal with?"

"Deal with," Smoke said without further amplification.

"All right." Hardegree knew that was all the explanation he was going to get from Smoke. "So, what do we do now?"

"I want you to call a town meeting. Pick a place large enough that it can handle the most people. But post a guard outside, and let nobody in who you don't know," Smoke suggested.

"Why keep anyone out just because we don't know them?" Hardegree asked.

"Because it might be someone from the Ghost Riders checking us out."

"Yeah, I didn't think of that. The problem is, most of the Ghost Riders aren't like the regular criminals we deal with. There are no wanted posters out on them . . . or if there are wanted posters, they aren't linked with the Ghost Riders. I know the leader has written some letters to some of the newspapers and he signs them as Hannibal. But nobody knows if that is his first name or his last name."

"Or if it is his name at all," Smoke said.

"What do you mean? You don't think it's his name?" Hardegree asked.

"I have a friend who has a pretty good theory about his name. He thinks this man, whoever he is, is a frustrated, would-be army officer and he has taken his name from a famous general in the past."

"Yeah," Hardegree said. "Now that you point that out, it all makes sense."

Ten Strike

"Advendingo didn't come back," Rexwell said.

"Then that means he was discovered and is now either dead or is in jail," Hannibal said.

"Yeah, that's what I was thinking too."

"I hope he is dead," Hannibal said.

"Why would you say that?"

"Because if he is alive and in jail, our entire operation could be compromised."

"Could be what?"

"They might learn from him where we are head-quartered."

"Oh, uh, yeah."

"We have to find out whether he is dead or in jail."

"Are we going to break him out of jail?"

"If we can, we will. If we can't break him out of jail, then we need to kill him."

"Are you serious? You want to kill him?"

"Yes."

"What about one for all, and all for one?" Rexwell asked.

"In this case, it would be one for all," Hannibal

replied. "Advendingo's life will be forfeited for the good of all."

"Yeah," Rexwell said. "Yeah, I see what you mean."

"We must send someone into Brimstone to find out whether or not Advendingo is still alive. And to find out what's going on in that town."

"What about Smith?" Rexwell suggested.

"No, he failed on his first mission into Brimstone. Bring Pugh to me."

Five minutes later, a thin man with a handlebar moustache and a pockmarked face stood in front of Hannibal.

"Do you understand what I want you to do, Pugh?"

"Yes, sir, you want me to find out what happened to Advendingo."

"And if he is alive and in jail, I want you to kill him."

"How will I do that?"

"Damn, Pugh, are you telling me you don't know how to kill someone?" Rexwell asked.

"Well, yeah, I know how to kill someone. But what I mean is, I can't just walk into the jail and kill 'im in front of everyone. Not without I get myself kilt too."

"There is more than likely a back window to the jail," Hannibal said. "Go into the alley behind the jail and call his name. Advendingo will trust you because he has no reason to expect you are there to kill him. When he comes to the window, shoot him."

"All right," Pugh said, hesitantly.

"I know it sounds harsh. But it is for the good

of the whole. And if you do this, I will give you Advendingo's share of the next job."

A huge smile spread across Pugh's face. "Well, hell, why didn't you say that in the first place? I'll be glad to kill the son of a bitch for you."

"While you are in town, take a look around and see if there is anything we need to know before we undertake our mission."

CHAPTER TWENTY-ONE

Brimstone

Marshal Hardegree, Smoke, and Pearlie went down to the church that stood in the middle of town.

"Pastor Owen, are you in here?" Hardegree called as they stepped through the arched, front doors.

A middle-aged, gray-haired man stepped out of a room at the front of the church.

"I'm here, Marshal," he said, wiping his glasses as he came toward them. "I was just working on Sunday's sermon."

"Pastor, do you think you could get over two hundred people in here?" Hardegree asked.

A wide smile spread across Pastor Owen's face. "Oh, my, that has long been my dream. Yes, I'm sure I could. And I know exactly what sermon I would preach on such—"

"Not for a church service, Pastor," Hardegree said, holding up his hand.

Owen got a confused look on his face. "Then, I

don't understand. Why else would there be two hundred people in my church?"

"We want to hold a town meeting," Hardegree said. "A very important town meeting, one that might save many lives. And this church is the only place I know that could hold that many people. That is, if you will agree to let us use it."

"Well, yes, of course I will, if you are serious about the meeting saving lives."

"Good, I'm going to try and round up as many as I can by ten o'clock. But, and this is the important thing, I don't want to let anyone in the church who isn't a resident of Brimstone."

"Oh, but Marshal, the church is open to all of God's children," Pastor Owen replied.

"Not for this meeting. The only *God's children* who will be allowed in are the ones who live here. Like I said, Pastor, it is a matter of public safety."

"Well, all right," Owen said. "I don't like turning anyone away from God's house but if that is the way it has to be, I'll go along with it."

"Good," Hardegree said. "Now, when people start coming, I want you to stand out front and turn away anyone who isn't a resident."

"Oh, I'm afraid I don't know every resident," Pastor Owen said. "If they aren't a member of my church, I wouldn't know them."

"You won't have to do it by yourself. I'll be out there with you and so will Mark Worley."

"Mark Worley? But, Marshal, he is a purveyor of spirits."

"He's the bartender at Devil's Den, yes. But he knows a lot of people in this town, and I figure that between the three of us, we can determine who is and who isn't a resident."

"There are more than two hundred people in town, and I truly don't think we could accommodate everyone," Pastor Owen said.

"No, I don't think so either. But if we get enough people in here, they can carry the word to everyone else. I'm pretty sure everyone in town will know what we have planned before it is all over."

Just before ten o'clock, Pearlie climbed up into the church bell tower, which was the highest point in town. From here, he could see at least a mile beyond the outer limits of the town in all directions. He was there to see if a large body of riders approached the town.

By ten o'clock, a huge crowd was gathered in front of the church.

"Hey, Stan, this ain't some trick to get me into a church, is it?" one man called out. "I mean, we ain't goin' to have to listen to a sermon or anything, are we?"

"No," Hardegree replied. "Mark Worley is here too, but we won't be serving liquor, either."

Finally everyone was in the church and they were about to close the doors when one more man came up. He was a thin man with a handlebar moustache and a pockmarked face. Mark Worley stuck out his hand to stop him.

"Pastor, do you know this man?" Worley asked. "'Cause I don't know 'im."

"No, I don't believe I've ever seen him before," the pastor said.

At that moment Smoke and the marshal came out of the church. "We're about to get started," Hardegree said.

"Do you know this man, Marshal?" Worley asked, pointing to the pockmarked man.

Hardegree looked toward the man, then shook his head. "I can't say as I do."

"Move on, then," Worley said. "This meeting is only for townspeople."

"I just happened to be here in town, 'n I want to see what this meeting is all about," the man said. "If it's a public meeting, you got no right to keep me out."

"Marshal, check his pockets," Smoke said. "See if he has a red armband. If he doesn't, you can let him in."

"Hold on here! You ain't got no right to be goin' through my pockets," the man said.

"That's true," Hardegree replied. "But you can't come in unless we check your pockets."

Hardegree started toward him, but the man pushed him away, then started for his gun.

"No! Don't do that!" Smoke shouted.

Despite Smoke's warning, the man continued to draw and he had his gun in his hand before Smoke drew and fired. Smoke's bullet struck home, and the man fell backward.

"Heavens!" Pastor Owen shouted.

"He had no choice, Pastor," Hardegree said. "This man would have killed one of us."

"I have seen men and women pass peacefully to

their Maker, but I have never seen anyone killed before."

Hearing the gunshot, a few of the people started to come back outside.

"Go on back in, folks," Hardegree said, holding his hands out to stop them. "It's all over."

"What's goin' on, Marshal?" one of the men said. "What was the shootin'?" He saw the body then. "Damn, is that man dead?"

"I'm sure he is," Hardegree said.

"Why was he killed? 'N what's this meetin' about?"

"Please, Mr. Phillips, go on back in and get everyone settled down. We'll be in there in just a minute, and we'll tell you what this is all about."

"All right, but you'd better have some answers for us, and they better be good answers," Phillips said as he turned and went back into the church.

Hardegree shut the door behind him.

"Marshal, check that man's pockets," Smoke said.

Hardegree knelt beside the man and searched through his pockets. He pulled out a red armband.

"You were right," Hardegree said, holding up the band.

"I thought he might be one of them."

"How did you know?"

"I just had a feeling."

"We had better go in, they're getting a little restless," Hardegree said.

"Do you intend to leave this poor soul's body lying here?" Owen asked.

"The pastor's right," Smoke said. "We should at least pull him around the corner so the people won't have to look at him when they come out."

Hardegree nodded and he and Worley moved the man's body to the side of the church, out of sight of the people when they left.

When the three of them went inside a few minutes later, the church was buzzing with agitated conversation.

"What is it?"

"Why did you call us all here?"

"And why was that man killed? In front of a church of all places?"

"There needs to be a good reason for killing anyone, anywhere, but in front of a church?" one of the women asked.

Hardegree walked up to the front of the church and held up his arms, calling for quiet. Finally the conversation halted.

"I want to show you something," he said, and reaching into his pocket he pulled out four pieces of red cloth.

"Marshal, what are you doin' with those armbands?" someone asked.

"In the last two days there have been four men killed in this town, all four of whom, including the man who was just killed a few moments ago, had these red armbands in their pockets."

"They wasn't kilt just 'cause they had them red armbands, was they?"

"No. All four of the killings were cases of justifiable homicide. They were killed in self-defense. I don't know how many of you are aware of it, but Ghost Riders wear these red bands around their arms. It is the way they are able to identify each other when they're making a raid. I'm sure you have all heard of the Ghost Riders, haven't you?"

"Ain't they the group that robbed the bank in Laurette 'n kilt all them people?" someone asked.

"Yes, they are the ones."

"What were four Ghost Riders doing in our town?" another asked.

"I'm going to let Ranger Smoke Jensen speak to you about that, and I expect he can handle your questions better than I can."

At the name Smoke Jensen, there was a murmur of excitement throughout the church. Everyone had heard of Smoke Jensen, but there weren't that many who knew that he was in town. And until this very moment, no one but Marshal Hardegree knew that he was a Colorado Ranger.

"You ask what four Ghost Riders were doing in Brimstone," Smoke said. "I think they were here to scout out the town and the bank. I believe it is their intention to rob the bank, and they wanted to see what sort of protection the town has."

"I've got three hunnert dollars in that bank," someone said. "If that money gets stole, it's goin' to work a big hardship on me."

"I got my whole life savin's there," another said.

"The bank isn't going to be robbed," Smoke said. "As long as we know what their plans are, we can prevent it."

"But we don't know what their plans are, do we? I mean, we don't even really know if they intend to rob the bank," someone said.

"Maybe not, George, but don't you think it would be better to plan for it as if they are going to rob the bank, and it not happen, than not have any plan at all and have the bank get robbed?" Joel Montgomery asked. Montgomery was president of Brimstone Bank and Trust.

"Yeah," George agreed. "I guess you're right."

"Let me tell you why I called for this meeting," Smoke continued. "If the Ghost Riders use the same tactics to rob the bank here that they used in Laurette, they will ride in shooting at everyone they see."

"Oh, heavens!" one of the women gasped. "We can't let that happen here."

"They won't do it here," Smoke said. "Laurette was caught completely off guard. Nobody expected a bank robbery, and even if they feared a bank robbery, nobody had any idea that they would come in shooting everyone as they did. But we are expecting it, and we can be ready for them."

"How can you be ready for something like that?" Montgomery asked.

"Right now, my partner is up in the church bell tower," Smoke said. "That is the highest structure in town, and from there you can see in all four directions. Pearlie!" he shouted.

"Yeah, Smoke?" a disembodied voice replied.

"Do you see anything?"

"No, I don't see anything at all. It's all clear," Pearlie called back down.

"Marshal Hardegree and I will work out a watch schedule," Smoke said. "We will have someone up in the bell tower from dawn 'til dusk. We'll have two-hour shifts. From the belfry you can see far enough to give a warning in plenty of time for everyone to get to a safe place. And if the lookout sees a group of riders approaching the town, he'll ring the bell."

"What place is safe, if they're shooting everyone?" another woman asked.

"I want you to do two things for me," Smoke said. "Obviously we weren't able to get the entire town in here for the meeting. So when you leave, I want you to find two of your neighbors who weren't at this meeting and tell them what you have heard today. If you have a root cellar, get in it when you hear the bell. If you don't have one, go to the room that is the farthest from the street. Move a chest, a dresser, or maybe turn up a table, anything you can use to make yourself a sheltered place. If it is in the back room, the walls of the house will probably stop any bullets before they reach you, but that one additional piece of cover will surely do so."

"How soon do we need to do this?"

"I would say that we start immediately," Smoke said. "When you leave here, find a safe place to be. And men, those of you who have rifles, make certain they are loaded, and put them someplace where you can get to them quickly."

"But not so as to be a danger to any children," Marshal Hardegree put in.

"Good point," Smoke said. "Once you hear the bell ringing, women, children, and any men who won't actually be in the fighting, get to a place of safety. I want every man who can, to grab your rifle, get on the roof or find some advantageous position, and start shooting as soon as the group rides in."

"Shouldn't we wait until they shoot first?" someone asked.

"Why? We know what they did in Laurette, in Brown Spur, and other places. These men are murderers. You don't give a murderer any advantage," Montgomery said.

Smoke sat down then, and Hardegree stood.

"All right, unless anyone else has a question, this meeting is over. Go back home, spread the word to others, and do what Smoke told you to do. If the Ghost Riders come to Brimstone, we have the opportunity to make certain this is the last town they will ever attack."

CHAPTER TWENTY-TWO

"If Smoke Jensen doesn't leave town, I'm going to have to hire more men," the undertaker said when the latest body was brought to him. "I've got four men to bury now."

"Mr. Prufrock, I want you to do something for me," Marshal Hardegree said.

"Anything for the law," Prufrock replied.

"I want you to display all four of these men for twenty-four hours, and I want them all to be wearing one of these red armbands."

"What for?"

"Just do it," Hardegree said.

"All right, Marshal, if you say so."

LETTER TO THE EDITOR

Dear Editor:

It is no longer necessary for me to address these dispatches to any specific editor, as it has been brought to my attention that these reports I am sending from the battlefield are being published by several other newspapers across the state.

That is very good, because news of the exploits of the Ghost Riders should be known to all. I have no doubt but that, someday, historians will write of these campaigns and will mention with awe, the brilliance of the man who leads them.

Some of you may know that my ranks were somewhat depleted after the Brown Spur operation. Losses, of course, do occur in battle. But the most important thing is the mission. Our mission at Brown Spur was to rescue two of my men, and as I indicated in an earlier letter, that mission was accomplished.

And now I am equally happy to say that we have recruited reinforcements so that the Ghost Riders are once again at full strength.

I am in the midst of planning my next campaign and, upon its completion, will send out another dispatch so that you may follow us.

I am Hannibal,
Commandant of the Ghost Riders.

He wasn't at full strength; he had lost four men in the last week. But he was reminded of another saying by Sun Tzu: "It is a paradox of warfare that it is sometimes good to make your enemy think your strength is greater than it really is, and it is sometimes good to make your enemy think your strength is less than it really is."

Sugarloaf Ranch

Cal was sitting at the dining room table eating solid food.

"It's almost solid food, anyway," Sally said. "It's a vegetable soup, but it has potatoes, carrots, and I made some noodles to go in it."

"Miz Sally, this couldn't taste any better to me if it was a Christmas goose with all the trimmings," Cal said. "It is delicious . . . and, Julia, I thank you for talking her out of starving me to death."

"Oh, I did no such thing!" Julia said.

"You mean she just took it on herself to have mercy on me?"

"She must have. I was perfectly willing to let you starve," Julia said, laughing and returning Cal's teases.

"Wait a minute. I've never heard of a mean angel," Cal said.

"There is something she did talk me into," Sally said.

"What's that?"

"She thought you might like a few of these."

"Bear claws!" Cal said excitedly.

Sally put one in front of Cal and one in front of Julia, then she took the pan away.

"Where are you going with them?" Cal asked.

"Don't you think the boys in the bunkhouse would like a few?" Sally replied. "Besides, it's probably not good for you to eat too many of them. And if I know you, you could eat this whole pan. Just be thankful for the one you've got."

"Yes, ma'am," Cal said.

"I'll just take these out," Sally said.

"Why don't you let me do it, Miz Sally? I need to get out and walk around some. I want to see Prince Dandy anyway. I haven't seen him in so long that he probably thinks I've deserted him." He reached for the pan. "I'll take those."

"No you won't," Sally said. "I can't trust you not to eat more on your way out to the bunkhouse."

"What makes you think I would do that?"

"Cal, I know you, remember? Julia, you go with him to keep him honest."

"I'll be happy to go with him."

When they reached the bunkhouse, Cal held his hand out. "Better let me take 'em in. They might not be all dressed."

"Promise me you won't take one of them?"

"I promise."

There were only two cowboys in the bunkhouse when Cal stepped in.

"Well, I'll be damned. Look what the cat's drug in. How are you doin', Cal?" one of them asked.

"I'm doin' just real fine," Cal replied. "Miz Sally made these 'n thought you boys might like them."

"Oh, yeah," one of them said, and both men grabbed a pastry.

"Now, don't you two eat all of 'em. Save some for the others when they get in."

Cal reached for one, lifted it up as if to take a bite, then put it back down.

"Why are you doin' that? Somethin' wrong with 'em?"

"No," Cal replied. "It's just that I promised I wouldn't."

"Yeah? Well, I didn't make no promise," one of them said as he reached for another bun.

"I'm really proud of you for not eating one of them," Julia said when Cal stepped back outside.

"How do you know I didn't? Were you looking?"

"No, but I could hear you."

Cal took Julia out to Prince Dandy's stall.

"There he is," Cal said. "Have you ever seen a more handsome bull? He won best bull at a show in Denver, you know."

Prince Dandy, seeing Cal, came over to the side of the stall and stuck his head out. Cal began rubbing him behind his ears.

"He likes this," Cal said.

"It looks like he likes you."

"Yeah, he does. He likes me a lot. I feel guilty."

"What do you feel guilty about?"

"Well, I'm real sorry the Condons got killed. But I'm glad we still have Prince Dandy. And I feel guilty about that."

"Nonsense. There was nothing you could have done."

They walked back up to the house.

"Do you want to sit in the swing for a bit?" Cal invited.

"Yes, I think that would be nice."

"Miz Sally had Pearlie and me hang this porch swing for her. She likes to sit in it."

"She really thinks a lot of you," Julia said.

"I think a lot of her, too."

"When I first came here, I thought she was your mother."

"Well, she's like a mother. I mean, seein' as my own ma is dead."

"Oh, I'm sorry to hear that. You dreamed about her, you know."

"What?"

"The effects of the laudanum stayed with you for a while, and you had a lot of dreams."

"Yeah," Cal said. "I sort of remember them."

"You called for your ma a couple of times. I thought you were calling for Sally, until she told me she wasn't your mother."

"What else did I say?" Cal asked.

"You said you wouldn't really have shot Sally."

Cal chuckled. "I said that, did I?"

"Yes."

"Well, that's right, I wouldn't have shot her."

"But I don't understand, why would you have even considered it?"

Cal shared with Julia the story of how he met Sally and how, as a result of that meeting, he came to work for Smoke.

"It's the best thing that ever happened to me," Cal said.

"I can see why you would think so."

Cal was silent for a long moment before he spoke again.

"She was a whore."

"What?" Julia gasped.

"My ma. She was a whore, but she did the best she could by me. Some folks might have held it against her because of that, but I didn't then, and I don't now. She was a good woman at heart, and I loved her as much as any son could love his mother."

"So, you don't hold it against someone if circumstances make them turn to prostitution?"

"Julia, I've killed. I've never killed anyone who wasn't either trying to kill me or someone I care for, but still, taking a life is a terrible thing. Now if some woman is earning her living by going to bed with men . . . how can that possibly compare with killing someone?

"So the answer is no, I don't hold it against you because you were working as a bar girl when I first saw you."

"You . . . you remember that? How can you remember that? You were unconscious when Mr. Jensen brought you in."

"Do you know what I remember most?"

"What?"

"I remember the angel who lay on the mattress with me to keep me from bouncing around. And I remember the angel who held my hand while I was having nightmares." He reached over to take Julia's hand. He couldn't take her other hand, because she was using it to wipe the tears from her eyes.

At that moment Sally stepped out onto the porch.

"All the boys were just real thankful for the bear claws," Cal said.

"And did all of them make it to the bunkhouse?" Sally asked.

"Yes, ma'am, I didn't take a one."

Sally saw that Julia had tears in her eyes. "Is something wrong?" she asked.

"No," Cal replied. "Why would you think something is wrong?"

Sally didn't answer, but she nodded toward Julia.

"I'm sorry," Julia said, smiling through her tears. "It's just something that Cal said."

"Cal! How could you possibly say something to hurt Julia, after all she has done for you?"

"I didn't say anything to hurt her," Cal said. "Or if I did, I sure didn't mean to."

"It's not because he said something that hurt me," Julia said. "It's because he said something that was so sweet."

Ten Strike

"What's going on in that town?" Hannibal asked. "Advendingo didn't come back, and when I sent Pugh in to check on him, he didn't come back either."

"Would you like for me to go in and have a look around?" Rexwell asked.

"I don't want to lose you, you're my second-in-command," Hannibal said.

"I've got more sense than Pugh or Advendingo," Rexwell said. "I plan to just ride in, have a look around, then come back."

"All right, go on in," Hannibal said. "But be careful, don't do anything to get yourself noticed."

Rexwell smiled, showing a mouth full of crooked, yellow teeth. "You don't have to worry none about that. I plan to be no more 'n a shadow while I'm in town."

When Bo Rexwell rode into Brimstone it seemed no different from any other town he had ever been in. There was a scattering of private houses at the end of town, then the downtown part, which consisted of the stores and businesses and a bank. Seeing the bank he stopped, dismounted, and went in.

The bank was small, with a counter between the customers and the teller, the counter made higher by a pane of frosted glass that ran from one side to the other, with a single teller's window in the middle.

Rexwell stepped up to the teller's window.

"Yes, sir, may I help you?" the teller asked.

Rexwell presented a twenty-dollar bill. "I wonder if I could have twenty, one-dollar bills. Sometimes at a bar or café you can't always get 'em to make change for you, if you want to use a bill this big."

"Indeed you can't, sir," the teller said. "I'll be glad to make change for you."

"I was surprised to see that a town this small even had a bank. Then, when I saw that there was one here, I wasn't sure you even had enough money to bust a twenty for me." Rexwell laughed. "I'm teasing of course, you probably have as much as two or three thousand dollars cash on hand."

"Oh, sir, we may be a small bank, but we serve not only the town, but the ranchers, farmers, and miners around us. Why, it might surprise you to know that we have almost ten thousand dollars in available cash," the teller said proudly.

"Ten thousand dollars? My, that is somethin'," Rexwell said, counting the one-dollar bills as the teller laid them before him. "Thanks," he added as he picked up the money.

They had sent five men into town and only Smith returned, but without the information he had just learned. Brimstone was smaller than Laurette, but if the teller was telling the truth, the bank had more money.

As Rexwell rode on down the main street, he saw a group of people gathered in front of one of the buildings. Curious about it, he dismounted, tied off his horse, then walked on down to see what they found so interesting.

When he saw what it was, it gave him a start. There were four coffins standing up in front of the building. Inside the coffins were Collins, Oceans, Advendingo, and Pugh. And all four had a red armband around their left arm.

What the hell? he thought. Were they so damn dumb that they were wearing their armbands when they came into town?

There was a painted sign posted on the wall above the men.

**THIS IS WHAT HAPPENS
TO GHOST RIDERS
WHO COME TO BRIMSTONE**

CHAPTER TWENTY-THREE

Bo Rexwell walked back to the Devil's Den Saloon. There were at least two dozen men inside, and they were all talking animatedly.

"They goin' to be some surprised, is all I got to say," one of the men said. "When we get rifles, and take up positions on the roof of ever' buildin' in town, we're goin' to rain hell down on 'em. Some of us was in the war, and battle ain't nothin' new to us."

"Yeah," another agreed. "I'm sure you've all heard 'bout what happened to Jesse James 'n his gang when they tried to hold up that bank up in Minnesota."

"I ain't heard nothin' 'bout that. What happened?"

"Northfield, it was. What happened was, damn near the whole town got guns 'n purt' nigh wiped out the whole gang. 'N the James gang? Well, sir, they wound up without gettin' no money a-tall from the bank."

"Yeah, we could do that here. Soon as we get word that the Ghost Riders is comin' into town, we can get all the kids and womenfolk into someplace that's safe 'n shoot 'em down."

"Ha! After what they done in Laurette, it'll be a fine comeuppance for 'em, won't it? More 'n likely after this happens, we'll be as famous as that town where Jesse James got all shot up."

Mark Worley set down the glass he had been wiping, then moved down to Rexwell, who had turned his back to the bar and was listening to the conversation.

"Yes, sir, what can I get for you?"

"I'll take a beer," Rexwell said.

"That'll be a nickel," Worley said a moment later, as he put the mug of beer before Rexwell.

Rexwell put a nickel on the bar, then picked up the beer mug and walked over to join the men who were doing all the talking.

"You're new in town, ain't ya?" one of the men asked. "Don't believe I've seen you before."

"I was just passin' by, saw the town 'n got thirsty," Rexwell said, holding up his beer mug. "Say, as I rode by, I seen them four bodies standin' up down the street a bit. Don't you folks bury your dead in this town?"

"They're a little different from most," one of the men said. "Maybe you didn't notice, but they was all wearin' red armbands."

"Yeah, I did notice it, but didn't take no mind of it. What was they wearin' 'em for?"

"Mister, are you tellin' me you ain't never heard of the Ghost Riders?"

"Can't say as I have."

"Well, it's a band of outlaws, is what it is. Up until recently, they was pretty much keepin' to Wyomin', but for some reason they left Wyomin' 'n come down here to Colorado. And what they do is, they all wear those red armbands, only nobody really knows why.

"Anyway, we put those red armbands on the four corpses you saw, because we intend to send a message to any of the Ghost Ridin' bastards that might happen to town."

"What makes you think they'll be comin' to town?" Rexwell asked.

"We're pretty sure they're plannin' on hittin' our bank, 'n when they do, well, sir, we will damn sure be ready for 'em."

"That's what you men was all talkin' about a minute or so ago, when you said you was goin' to get rifles and be ready for them?"

"Yes, sir. If the Ghost Riders hit this town, they are goin' to be in for quite a surprise."

"What makes you think these outlaws you are talkin' about, the Ghost Riders you're callin' 'em, plan to hit Brimstone?"

"Well, seein' as you said you ain't never heard of 'em, then mayhap you ain't heard about what happened in Laurette neither," one of the saloon patrons said. "What happened there was, the Ghost Riders come into town, more 'n twenty of 'em, and they commenced shootin' at ever'body, women and kids, it didn't make no never mind to 'em. 'N they cleaned out the bank. And there warn't a one o' them bastards kilt. Well, that ain't a goin' to happen here. Fact is, as you've done seen with them corpses standin' up in front of the undertaker's shop, we've done kilt four of 'em, 'n we plan to kill a lot more."

"You keep saying you are goin' to surprise 'em, but how do you plan to do that? I mean it seems to me like the advantage would be with them. They know when they plan to come in, but you don't."

"First of all, they won't be surprisin' us, on account of because we're goin' to have us a lookout up in the church bell tower. From up there, you can see near 'bout two miles in ever' direction, all around the town. Soon as our lookout sees riders comin' he'll ring the bell, 'n that'll be our signal."

"Sounds like you've got it all worked out," Rexwell said.

"You mighty damn right, we do. I tell you the truth, I hope they do come to town. By damn, we could near'bout kill ever' one of 'em if they do."

"Hell, Cecil, if you stop to think about it, Smoke Jensen has near'bout already done that all by his ownself," one of the others said. "Them four bodies that's standin' up in front of the undertaker's was all kilt by him."

"No, he only kilt three of 'em," Cecil said. "It was Pearlie, the fella that's with him, that kilt one of 'em."

"Oh, yeah, I'd near forgot that."

Rexwell finished his beer, ran the back of his hand across his mouth, then set the mug back on the bar.

"Well, it's been interestin' talkin' to you," he said.

"I wish you lots of luck, but I need to be ridin' on. I've got a long way to ride yet, today."

"Where is it that you're a goin'?"

"Oh, I got no particular place in mind," Rexwell said.

After Rexwell left, Worley called Cecil up to the bar.

"What were you and that bald-headed fella talkin' about?" Worley asked.

"We was tellin' 'im how we're gettin' set to welcome the Ghost Riders when they come into town," Cecil said.

"Do you think that was smart?"

"What do you mean?"

"Well think about it. None of us know that man. How do we know he isn't a Ghost Rider come into town just to scout us out?"

"Damn!" Cecil said. "I never thought about that."

"Cecil, why don't you go find Smoke 'n ask him to stop in for a free beer?"

"Do I get a free beer for goin' to fetch 'im?" Cecil asked.

"I don't see why not," Worley said.

Cecil didn't have to go very far because Smoke, Pearlie, and Marshal Hardegree were all standing out in the middle of the street, right in front of the saloon.

"I think we could put four men up there," Smoke said, pointing to the false front of the saloon. "One man on each end, and one man on each side of the step up."

"Yes, and we could do the same thing with the apothecary," Pearlie said.

"Mr. Jensen, Mark Worley needs to talk to you. He said he'd give you a free beer if you would come in," Cecil said. He smiled. "And he'll give me one too, for comin' to get you."

"All right," Smoke said. "I'm always ready for a free beer. Pearlie, you and the marshal find a few more good spots."

"What about my free beer?" Pearlie asked.

"I'll buy you one after we get through here," Marshal Hardegree said.

"I'll take you up on that."

Smoke followed Cecil into the saloon and, without being asked, Worley drew two beers and set them on the bar.

"He was right out front, so I didn't have to go far," Cecil said.

"Did you see him leave the saloon?" Worley asked.

"See who?"

"Ugly looking man, bald-headed, looked like he didn't even have a neck, had a purple scar right here," Worley described, using his finger to trace the path of the scar.

"No, we just came out from the marshal's office a moment before Cecil came for me. But I've seen someone who looks like the one you described before. He's one of the Ghost Riders," Smoke said. "He was here, you say?"

"Yes sir, he was."

"It's more than likely that he was just checking on the men that have been killed here."

"Oh damn, I should have realized that," Cecil said. "I probably shouldn't have said anything, should I?"

"I don't know," Smoke said. "What did you say?"

"I told him we was ready for the Ghost Riders when they come, that we have a surprise waitin' on 'em."

"Well, that may make it less likely now, that they will come into town. So, in the long run, you may have done just the right thing."

Ten Strike

"What did you find out in Brimstone?" Hannibal asked, when Rexwell returned to the outlaw encampment.

"For one thing, I learned that they have over ten thousand dollars in the Brimstone bank," Rexwell said.

Hannibal smiled. "Ten thousand? I knew it. I knew that with a working silver mine nearby, the bank would have a sizeable amount of money there, just waiting for us. Yes, this will certainly be a bank worth hitting."

"Yeah, that's what I thought too, when I first got there," Rexwell said. "But now, I ain't so sure."

"What do you mean, you aren't sure?"

"Well, for one thing, I know where Advendingo and Pugh are."

"Oh? Where are they?"

"They're in coffins that's stood up right in the middle of town so that ever'one can see 'em,"

Rexwell said. "And Collins 'n Oceans is standin' right beside them."

Hannibal nodded and stroked his chin. "Yes," he said. "I was pretty sure something like that had happened to them. Smoke Jensen killed all four of them."

"Well, three anyway. Remember, Smith told us that the fella that was with Jensen is the one who killed Oceans."

"Whether it was Jensen himself or merely someone who was with him, it makes no difference, it all comes back to Smoke Jensen. And that's eleven men we've lost because of him," Hannibal said. "Over one third of my command lost to one man!"

"We need to stay away from him," Rexwell said.

"No, what we need to do is kill him," Hannibal said.

"And here's another thing. All four of 'em has a red armband around their left arm." Rexwell said.

"You don't say?"

"Yes. And they're waitin' for us, Hannibal. They know we're plannin' on robbin' the bank there. I went into the saloon to have a drink 'n see if I could tell what was goin' on, 'n I learned a lot. They're goin' to put a man with a rifle on top of ever' roof."

"No doubt this is a plan worked out by Smoke Jensen," Hannibal said.

"I don't know whether it was or not. But whatever it is, it's pretty obvious to me that we won't be able to do this job without gettin' a lot more of our men killed."

"We're going to do the job," Hannibal said. "But first, we are going to kill Jensen."

"How are we goin' to do that? I don't think we have anyone who can stand up to him, or any two men who could. Not without gettin' kilt their own selves."

"I've been thinking about this, and I've got an idea how we can do it and not lose one of our men."

"How?"

"You just leave that to me. We'll put off the raid on Brimstone for a little while, until I can put my plan into effect."

"All right."

"In the meantime I've got a diversion worked out. I'm going to be gone for a few days, and while I'm gone, I want you to break down four tactical teams of four men each. We are going to rob four stagecoaches at the same time."

"How much do you think we'll get from four stagecoaches?" Rexwell asked.

"I don't know, and it doesn't matter."

"What do you mean, it doesn't matter? What if they aren't carrying money boxes?"

"The chances are that at least one will. Take what you can from the passengers if there is no strongbox. The whole operation is to be a diversionary tactic anyway."

"You mean to take their minds off Brimstone?"

"Yes."

Rexwell laughed. "Yeah, that's a good idea. Where'd you come up with that?"

"It is a classic military tactic," Hannibal replied. "While I'm gone, let no more than four men at a time go into Sorento, and make certain that they are well-behaved. We don't want to do anything that will call attention to us."

"I'll take care of it. What about the stagecoaches? Have you worked out a plan which ones we should hit?"

"Yes. Three days from now, I want you to hit the Bordenville, Hutchins, Rocky, and Florissant coaches. I'll show you the map and where to put the men. I've chosen them because we can hit all four of them at exactly two o'clock in the afternoon. A coordinated strike like that will not only be disruptive to the law, it will also be a tactical coup for the Ghost Riders."

CHAPTER TWENTY-FOUR

Puxico, New Mexico

When Hannibal presented himself to the desk clerk of the Homestead Hotel, he was wearing the uniform of a Lieutenant Colonel.

"Yes, sir, Cap'n, can I help you?" the desk clerk asked.

"My rank is Lieutenant Colonel," Hannibal said. "I am Colonel Elmer Peabody, here on special assignment from the Department of War."

"I'm sorry, Colonel, never having been in the army, I don't know nothin' about rank and all that. What can I do for you?"

"I require a room. A suite if you have it."

"Yes sir, we've got a real nice suite."

"I may not need it, I expect I will be given quarters out at Fort Union in the senior officers' batchelor officers' quarters. If so, I will pay you for the suite, anyway."

"Very good, sir. The Homestead Hotel will do all it can to make your stay here a pleasant one."

"Indeed," Hannibal said. "Is there a messenger service with Fort Union?"

"Yes, sir, they have a soldier who comes into town twice a day, bringing messages and delivering them."

"I shall require this message to be delivered to the commanding officer with the next messenger. Can you arrange that for me?"

Hannibal handed the desk clerk a dollar bill.

"Yes, sir," the desk clerk replied with a huge smile.

To Major Phillip Garneau
Commandant of Fort Union:
   In accordance with War Department orders, I
am here to inspect the prisoners being held in your
post stockade. Please arrange for transportation for
me from the Homestead Hotel.

Elmer Peabody
Lt. Col. Judge Advocate Corps

Hannibal was in his room an hour later when there was a knock on his door. When he answered the door, he saw a young second lieutenant on the other side. The lieutenant came to attention and saluted.

"Sir, Lieutenant Kirby with your transportation to Fort Union."

"Thank you, Lieutenant," Hannibal said, returning the salute.

Major Garneau had sent the ambulance for him, the ambulance being the best sprung and most comfortable of all the army vehicles. It took but half an hour to reach the post and when the ambulance stopped in front of the headquarters building, Major Garneau was there to meet him. He saluted.

"Sir, welcome to Fort Union."

Hannibal returned the salute. "Thank you, Major. I take it that you have reports drawn up on all your prisoners for me. How many do you have, by the way?"

"We have eight, sir. But—"

"But what?"

"Colonel, I was totally unaware you would be here for such an inspection."

"Surely not, Major, I personally authorized that the message be sent."

"No, sir, I received no such message."

"Then I apologize, Major. I don't know how I could have possibly beaten the letter here, when we both came from Washington, D.C. Then, I take it you have not prepared reports on your prisoners?"

"No, sir. I can do so, if you'll forgive the delay."

"Ahh, I see no need for actual written reports. Suppose you just give me a verbal report on each of the men you are currently holding . . . over dinner at the open mess?"

"Sir, I insist that you be my guest tonight. Mrs. Garneau enjoys having guests."

"I wouldn't want to put her out."

"Believe me, it would be a pleasure."

Over dinner that evening, they told stories about their times at West Point and discussed a few officers that both of them knew. Because of Hannibal's military history, he was able to be quite convincing

as a colonel sent out from the War Department in
order to conduct an on-site inspection.

After dinner, they retired to the parlor where
Hannibal asked the major to give him a report on
the prisoners.

"Three of them are in the stockade for minor vi-
olations, improper uniform, insubordination, that
sort of thing. But five of them are of a more serious
nature. Three of the five will, no doubt, receive dishonorable discharges, and two, I'm quite certain,
will be hanged."

"Tell me about the five," Hannibal said.

"Three of them robbed a liquor store." Major
Garneau laughed. "Then they got drunk on the
liquor they stole, passed out, and the sheriff picked
them up and brought them out here."

"You said you had two who would probably be
hanged. Tell me about them."

"Malloy and Keefer. They stopped a stagecoach,
while in uniform, claimed they had been sent to
escort the coach into town, but killed the shotgun
guard and two of the passengers, then stole the
money box."

"How were they caught?"

"There were supposed to be three of them in on
the job, but at the last minute one soldier backed
out. He told us where to find them, and Lieutenant
Emerson took a patrol out and brought them in."

"Ah," Hannibal said. "Those are the two men I
want to interview tomorrow. Could you find a private room for me?"

"Yes, sir, but how private?"

"Very private. I want to gain their confidence."

"Colonel, these are very dangerous men."

"Oh, I'm quite aware of that, Major. I will request to have two armed guards posted right outside the room while I am interviewing them."

"All right, sir, yes, we can do that."

On the Bordenville Road in Colorado

Taylor was in charge of the four men who had been detailed to rob the Bordenville coach, and he, the Scraggs twins, and Carl Moss had prepared a tree so that it would take very little to drop it across the road in front of the stagecoach when it came by.

"How much money do you think they'll be carryin'?" Amos Scraggs asked.

"Accordin' to Rexwell, it don't matter none," Taylor replied.

"What do you mean, it don't matter none?"

"From what I understand, Hannibal's got it all figured out. Somehow if we rob four stagecoaches at the same time, no matter whether they've got any money or not, it will make it easier for us to hold up the bank in Brimstone. And that bank is just full of money."

"Yeah, well, when Rexwell got me 'n my brother to come in with you, he was tellin' us about how much money we would be makin', but I ain't seen none of it yet. That's why I was wonderin' about whether or not this coach would be carryin' anything."

"In just two of our jobs we got over six hunnert dollars apiece from one, and three hunnert from the other," Taylor said. "Believe me, there is a lot of money to be made as long as we all stick together."

"Taylor! Coach is comin'!" Moss called.

"All right, ever'body back off the road. Moss, tell us when to bring the tree down!"

"All right."

Taylor picked up the axe. The tree had already been wedged so that it would take no more than two or three strikes to finish it.

"Now!" Moss called.

Two more blows of the axe and the tree began to move. They all pushed on it, and it fell across the road less than twenty yards in front of the approaching coach.

"Whoa!" the driver called.

The guard stood up to look around.

"Shoot 'im," Taylor said, and three shots rang out.

The guard grabbed his stomach, then fell over the wheel, landing hard on the ground. From inside the coach, a woman screamed.

Taylor and the others, their red bands prominently displayed, stepped out into the road.

"You people inside," Taylor called. "Come out now." Amon Scraggs jerked open the door to the coach.

Taylor looked toward the driver who was sitting on the seat with his hands up. "You, throw down the money box."

The driver did as he was ordered, and Taylor shot the lock off. Opening it, he found a stack of bound bills, and showing it to the others, he stuck it in between the buttons on his shirt.

"Take what they have," he ordered.

Moss and the Scraggs twins stepped up to the passengers. Amos and Amon took money from the men, and Amon snatched a silver watch from the vest pocket of one of them.

"Well now, ain't you a purty one?" Moss said to the young woman. He reached for the gold locket she was wearing, then jerked it off her neck.

"No, please, that belonged to my mama," the young woman said.

"Is that a fact? Well, it belongs to me now."

"All right, you folks can climb back into the coach now," Taylor said as soon as the collection was made.

When the passengers were loaded, Taylor called up to the driver.

"You can go on now."

"What about my shotgun guard? Can I take him back with us?"

"Why bother? He's dead," Taylor said.

"Which means he won't be no trouble to you."

Taylor looked at Moss and the Scraggs twins. "Pick 'im up and drop 'im in the box boot."

The three men picked up the guard, then dropped him into the front boot, just beside the driver's legs.

"Go ahead!" Taylor called.

Taylor and the others watched as the driver pulled the coach off the road to maneuver, carefully, around the fallen tree.

"All right, men, let's go," Taylor said, after the coach had gone some distance.

When Taylor and the men with him returned to

Ten Strike, the other three teams were back as well. They had robbed four stagecoaches at the same time and had taken in seventeen hundred dollars, total.

Fort Union, New Mexico

"Which one are you?" Hannibal asked the next morning when the first of the two prisoners to be interviewed was brought to him.

"Keefer's the name. I don't see as you need to know my first name."

"You're right, I don't need to know it. As far as I'm concerned, your first name is Prisoner. How much money did you get from the stagecoach hold up?"

"Who says we held up a stagecoach?"

"Keefer, you are facing the gallows. They don't hang people for uniform infractions. Now, how much money was in the strongbox?"

Keefer was quiet for a moment. "Two hundred dollars," he finally said.

"And there were two of you, so what you are saying is, the army is about to hang you and all you got out of it was one hundred dollars."

"Yeah," Keefer said.

"That doesn't seem like such a smart move, does it?"

"I reckon not."

"What if you were associated with a group of men who are well led, and who have averaged at least two hundred dollars per month, for the last two years?"

Keefer got a confused look on his face.

"Colonel, I don't know what you are talking about," he said.

"Let me put this as succinctly as I possibly can. Suppose someone arranged for your release from the stockade and from the army. If that someone was in charge of this group of men that I mentioned, would you serve him loyally and without question?"

"You're damn right I would," Keefer said.

"Keep our conversation confidential."

"What does that mean?"

"It means do not mention one word of what we have talked about this morning, and especially not to any of the other prisoners. Your future depends on it."

"My future? Colonel, the way I look at it, I ain't got much of a future."

"If you do as I say, you may have a most lucrative future."

After a similar discussion with Malloy, Hannibal returned to the headquarters building to speak again with Major Garneau.

"Major, I am going to take Keefer and Malloy off your hands."

"I don't understand, sir, what do you mean you are going to take them off my hands?"

"I will be transporting them to Fort Seldon. There, they will appear before a board of inquiry—army officers from the War Department who are specially trained to interview these men to find out what motivated them to commit such a heinous crime. By what they learn from the inquiry, we hope to reduce these incidents in the future."

"How will you get them there?" Major Garneau asked.

"Ahh, I will require your assistance for that, Major. I will want you to provide two armed guards to accompany me . . . and five mounts. The guards can bring the three mounts back from Fort Seldon after the prisoners are delivered."

"Colonel, I will do as you order, of course. But since I have received no orders from the War Department requiring me to release these men, would you be so kind as to provide me with written orders directing me to do so?"

Hannibal smiled. "Of course I can do that," he said.

"Thank you, sir."

After leaving Major Garneau, Hannibal asked to speak with Keefer and Malloy again, this time requesting to see both of them together.

When the two men were brought to him, again in a private meeting, he turned to Malloy.

"Malloy, what did Keefer and I talk about this morning?"

Malloy had a confused look on his face. "What did you and Keefer talk about? I don't know, Colonel, he never told me."

"Keefer, I shall ask you the same question. What did Malloy and I talk about?"

"Colonel, that beats the hell out of me."

Hannibal got up and walked to the door. When he opened it, he saw that the armed guard was sitting some distance away, drinking coffee and reading a newspaper. Closing the door he returned to the two men.

"I told both of you the same thing, this morning. Now that I have you together, I will elaborate. If you two men will volunteer to serve me loyally, I will get you away from the hanging that you face and enlist you in an elite military-style organization where you will make at least two hundred dollars per month. Are you interested in such an opportunity?"

"Hell yes, we are, Colonel," Keefer said. "At least I am. But I don't understand, what army regiment has such a deal?"

"I said military-style organization," Hannibal said. "It has nothing to do with the army, but I will require discipline and absolute adherence to my orders. Are you willing to do that?"

"You're damn right we are," Malloy said with a broad smile.

CHAPTER TWENTY-FIVE

Hannibal was invited to lunch at the Officers' Open Mess, which he shared with Major Garneau, Garneau's executive officer, and the six company commanders.

"I really see no need to have some board of inquiry question these men. Keefer and Malloy were both in my company, and I can tell you now, they are the very dregs of the earth. To tell you the truth, Colonel, I don't understand how they managed to get into the army in the first place."

"I can," one of the other captains said. "Ken, you know yourself that our ranks are filled with men who are running away from something, be it as severe as a murder charge somewhere, or as benign as a sweetheart who found someone else. But few of our recruits are serving out of a sense of duty to country. The enlisted ranks are filled with such men."

"Unfortunately Captain Greenly, it isn't just the enlisted ranks," Major Garneau said. "We have some officers who are just as bad."

"Oh, sir, I hardly think so," Captain Greenly replied. "Most of our officer corps comes from the academy. And West Point values honor above all."

"The officer I am thinking of is a West Point graduate. His name is Enid Prescott, and he was selling army rifles to a civilian, who was in turn selling those rifles to Indians. And for his crime Prescott was court-martialed, had his commission withdrawn, then was ceremoniously stripped of all rank and accoutrements, and drummed out of the service."

"Did you know this officer?" Captain Greenly asked.

"No, but I do know Colonel Rector. He wrote to me, telling in great detail of the events surrounding the incident."

"I knew the officer," Hannibal said.

"You did?"

"Indeed."

"What kind of officer was he?"

"Captain Prescott was . . . is a brilliant man," Hannibal said. "He had superb leadership skills, which the army failed to recognize. I do believe that if his skills and ability had been recognized and had he been promoted, as he should have been, none of that would have happened."

"Where is Captain Prescott now?" Captain Greenly asked.

"Wherever he is, he isn't a captain," Major Garneau said.

"Good point, Major. Indeed he is not," Hannibal replied. "And to answer your question, I have no idea where he is. I haven't seen him since Jefferson Barracks."

Half an hour later, a small detachment consisting of Hannibal, the prisoners Keefer and Malloy, as well as the two armed guards supplied by Major Garneau, rode through the gate of Fort Union. Hannibal returned the salute of the gate guard.

When they were about three miles away from the fort, Hannibal, who was riding behind the two guards, pulled his pistol and shot both of the guards in the back.

"What the hell?" Malloy asked. "Colonel?"

"I am not a colonel, I'm not even in the army," Hannibal said with a broad smile. "And now, neither are either of you. You are now part of the best led group of outlaws in the United States. You are Ghost Riders, and no military unit has more esprit de corps."

Hannibal laughed. "And no military unit makes nearly as much money."

"What do we call you, if it ain't colonel?" Malloy asked.

"You will obey me as if I were a colonel. But you can call me Hannibal."

"Hannibal? That's it? We call you Hannibal?"

"Yes. Will that be a problem for you?"

"Hell, no. No problem at all."

"Sir," Hannibal said.

"I beg your pardon?"

"I told you, this operation will be run as a military

unit. And we must have discipline. You will call me *sir*."

"Yes, sir, if this outfit is all that you claim it to be, I'll call you *sir* and wave flags while I'm doin' it," Keefer said with a laugh.

Sugarloaf Ranch

"Miz Sally, where is Julia?" Cal asked, coming into the parlor where Sally was reading a book.

"She's taking a bath right now."

Cal nodded. "That's good, it'll give us an opportunity for you and me to talk. That is, if you don't mind."

Sally closed the book and put it on the table beside her.

"All right," she said.

"I know that Smoke was married once before."

"Yes, to Nicole."

"He told me once that even though he loves you, he also loves Nicole, even though she's dead now."

"I'm sure that he does."

"Does that bother you any? I mean, him still lovin' Nicole 'n all."

"No, of course not. Why should it bother me?"

"I don't know. I was just sort of wonderin' about it, is all."

"Cal, are you asking if I am jealous of Nicole? Quite the contrary, I love Nicole, even though I never met her."

"I don't understand. How can you love her if you never met her?"

"I love Nicole because she's a part of Smoke's

history. You might even say that she taught him to love, and I am now the beneficiary of that."

"That's good to know," Cal said.

"Cal, this isn't about Nicole, is it?"

"No, ma'am, it isn't."

"Let me guess. It's about Katrina Byrd."

"Yes, ma'am. I loved her a lot."

"I know."

"When Keno took Katrina's life, I thought it was the same as him taking the rest of my life from me. Katrina and I would have married, and we would have had kids and grandkids, and they would have had kids and grandkids. It was the same as him killing a hundred years of what would have been.*

"Only now, well—" Cal let the incomplete sentence hang.

"Are you in love with Julia?"

"Yes ma'am, I kind of think I am."

"You *think* you are?"

"Yes, ma'am."

"It's no surprise that you are feeling something for her. After all, she saved your life, and for the last few weeks, she has, quite literally, been your connection to reality. Are you sure that what you are feeling isn't just a sense of gratitude?"

"No, ma'am, I think it's more than that."

"Have you told her how you feel?"

"I haven't said anything to her. I guess I wasn't sure whether I should tell her or not. I mean, I still love Katrina. I would say that you probably think that doesn't make sense, but since you know that Smoke

---

* *Terror of the Mountain Man.*

still loves Nicole, then you would understand. But, I don't know if Julia could understand that like you do. And, I don't want to be unfair to her or to Katrina."

"Cal, what would be unfair to Julia and equally unfair to your memory of Katrina, would be for you to never allow yourself to fall in love again. If this is going to happen, let it happen. Don't step into it, but don't step away from it, either. If it is meant to be, it will be."

Cal smiled. "I knew that if I talked to you about it, you'd be able to tell me what to do. For something like this, I'd rather talk to you than to Smoke or Pearlie. This is the kind of thing a man would need to talk to his ma about. And, right now, you're sort of my ma. I mean, if you don't mind me thinking of you like that."

"Of course I don't mind, Cal. I'm very flattered that you think of me in such a fashion."

Julia came into the parlor then. "Good, Cal, I'm glad you're in here and not running around outside somewhere, getting in trouble."

"Now, just what kind of trouble do you think I would be getting into?" Cal asked.

"I don't know. Maybe trying to ride or wrestling with a steer or something. Didn't you tell me that you and Pearlie did that for a rodeo once?"

"Oh," Cal said, putting his hand over his stomach. "Don't say anything like that, Julia. That's giving me a bellyache, just thinking about it.

"You put somethin' on to make you smell good, didn't you?" Cal asked, sniffing audibly.

"It's Essence of Lilac," Julia said. She held the inside of her wrist up to Cal's nose. "Do you like it?"

"I like it a lot," Cal said with a wide smile.

"Cal, why don't you have one of the boys hitch up the buggy, and you take Julia out to dinner tonight?" Sally said.

"Great idea! I'll take her to Lamberts."

"No, with all the biscuits and the extras they bring around there, you would eat too much. I would say take her to Delmonico's. It has a much nicer ambience."

"A nicer what?" Cal asked.

"Let's just say that if you are going to take a young lady out for a nice evening, Delmonico's would be the best place to go."

"Yes, ma'am, now that I think about it," Cal said, "I believe it would be at that."

"Julia, can I trust you to make certain that Cal doesn't overdo it?"

"I'll watch him like a hawk," Julia promised.

"Cal!" Tim Murchison said when Cal and Julia stepped into Delmonico's. Tim was sitting at a table with his wife and two children, but upon seeing Cal come through the front door, he hurried over to greet him.

"It's good to see you up and around," Tim said. "Half the town thinks you're at death's door."

"I would be, if it weren't for Julia," Cal said. "Julia, this is my friend, Tim Murchison. That special tooled saddle I've got? He made it. Oh, wait, I guess you haven't seen it yet."

"I'm pleased to meet you, Mr. Murchison," Julia said, extending her hand.

"You must be that nurse that Doc Urban and Smoke have been carryin' on about," Tim said.

"I didn't know anyone was carrying on about me," Julia said, her smile causing the dimple to appear. "But I have been looking after Cal."

"Well, I think I can speak for the entire town when I say thank you. Cal is a good man; it would have caused a big hole in Big Rock if we had lost him."

"Cal," Dale York said, coming to greet him. Dale owned Delmonico's. "I have a nice table for you and your lady friend back here. Come with me."

A moment later, Cal and Julia sat at a table in the corner of the restaurant, separated somewhat from the main dining room by an L shape in the floor plan. They were examining the menus, a single candle lighting the distance between them.

"I'm going to have a huge, T-bone steak," Cal said.

"Why don't you have a Hamburg steak?" Julia suggested. "It will have been tenderized for you. I think it will be easier for you to digest."

"No, I want—" Cal started to reply, then he smiled. "All right, whatever you say. You can order for me."

A few minutes later, as they were eating the dinner, Cal said, "Julia, did you know that Smoke was married to someone before he married Miz Sally?"

"No, Sally has never mentioned it, but then, why would she?"

"You know, when you were taking your bath today, Miz Sally and I were talking about that. His first wife was named Nicole. And here's the thing. Smoke is still in love with Nicole."

"What?"

"Oh, it's all right," Cal said, reaching across the table to put his hand on Julia's. "You see, Nicole is dead."

"Dead?"

"Yes, she was killed. Then, sometime after she was killed, why Smoke met Miz Sally, and now he loves her more than anything. But, see, he's still in love with Nicole, and Sally is all right with that. And even though she never met Nicole, Miz Sally loves her too, because she says that Nicole taught Smoke how to love. And you know that's true, because you can see how much Miz Sally and Smoke love each other. You can see that, can't you?"

"Yes, it's very obvious."

"Good. I'm glad you can see that."

"Why are you telling me all this, Cal?"

"I'm telling you that because of Katrina."

Now the expression on Julia's face became even more confused.

"Katrina?"

"Yes. She was a schoolteacher, just like Miz Sally. And I'm still in love with her."

"Oh, I see," Julia said, the expression on her face now somewhat disappointed.

"Only thing is, Katrina was killed a couple of years ago. So, I still love her, the same way Smoke still loves Nicole."

A wide smile spread across Cal's face. "I love you, just the way Smoke loves Miz Sally. And I plan to get around to asking you to marry me, soon as I get up the courage."

"Oh, Cal," Julia said, her eyes welling with tears. "I want to marry you more than anything in the world."

"Then why are you crying?"

"I'm crying because I can't marry you," she said. "I'm already married, and I don't even know where my husband is."

CHAPTER TWENTY-SIX

Ten Strike

When Hannibal returned to Ten Strike, he learned that there was a total of seventeen hundred dollars taken from the four stagecoaches. That came to sixty-two dollars per man, counting the two new men, Keefer and Malloy.

"Why are they getting anything?" Snake Eye Mason asked. "They ain't done nothin' to earn their share yet."

"Remember our motto, Mason. It is one for all, and all for one. You haven't forgotten that, have you?"

"No, but—"

"I beg your pardon?" Hannibal asked, sharply.

"No, sir, I ain't forgot," Mason said.

"Good. And as for whether or not these two men have earned their cut, they are about to earn it and more."

"What do you mean, and more?" Amos Scraggs asked.

"I am giving them an additional one hundred dollars apiece to go into Brimstone and kill Smoke Jensen and the man he has brought with him."

"Would you give me 'n my brother a hunnert dollars apiece to go with them . . . I mean, just to make sure the job is done?"

"That might not be a bad idea, Hannibal," Rexwell said. "Besides which, there is no way Jensen is liable to recognize any of them, 'cause he ain't never seen none of 'em before."

"Very well," Hannibal said. "The offer goes for all four of you."

"When do we get the money?"

"When the job is done and you come back."

"Make sure none of you have your red armbands," Rexwell cautioned. "In fact, don't even take them with you."

"Yes, thank you, Rexwell, that is a good idea," Hannibal said.

Hannibal watched the four men ride off; then he went into his quarters and picked up a copy of the *Sorento Sun Times*. It was carrying the latest letter he had written to the newspapers. He continued to address the letters to the editor of the *Commerce Commercial Press* knowing that now, every newspaper in the state was carrying the letters. Also, by sending the letters to the *Commercial Press*, it might give the illusion that he was close to Commerce, which was in reality all the way across the state from Sorento.

He had sent every letter from a different location

so that they wouldn't be able to trace him by the postmark.

LETTER TO THE EDITOR

Dear Editor:

Recently the Ghost Riders did something that has never been done before. We robbed four stagecoaches simultaneously, even though the coaches were all separated by distances ranging from ten to thirty miles. It was a brilliant military maneuver, one that may in fact become an object of study for army officers at some future date.

We were able to accomplish this task because of training, planning, discipline, courage, and leadership.

There is no group, short of an entire army regiment, who will ever be able to stop us.

I am Hannibal,
Commandant of the Ghost Riders.

Brimstone

"If that son of a bitch's head gets any bigger, there won't be a hat made that is big enough to fit him," Hardegree said, after reading Hannibal's latest letter.

"He does seem to be awfully full of himself," Smoke said.

"I tell you the truth, I'm beginning to think that the Ghost Riders won't be coming here at all," Hardegree said.

"I think you're right," Worley said.

"So, Smoke, what do we do now?" Pearlie asked. "I mean if they don't come here, we'll lose our lead on them, won't we?"

"They'll be coming here," Smoke said.

"Why do you say that? They haven't come yet, and like you said, if that bald-headed fella that showed up is who you think he is, then he found out what we've got planned for them," Pearlie said.

"I'm just going by the letters this man, Hannibal, has written," Smoke said. "Marshal Hardegree is right. Hannibal, is one arrogant bastard. It has become a challenge to him. He'll come all right, but not as much for the money as it is just to prove to everyone that he can do it."

"You may be right," Hardegree said.

"I'm sure I'm right," Smoke said.

"But what about the stagecoaches he held up?" Worley asked. "Don't you think that might mean that he's changed his mind?"

"Not at all. I think he had two reasons for robbing four stagecoaches at the same time, neither of which was for the money. One reason, clearly, is that he wanted to do something no one else had ever done before just so he could send us another letter bragging about how good he is. And I believe that the second reason he did it, is because he wants to use them as a diversion, to get our guard down here. But I don't think we should let our guard down. I think we should keep the watch going."

"We may as well," Hardegree said. "It doesn't

appear to be causing a great disservice to anyone. Business is pretty much going along as normal."

When the Scraggs twins, Keefer, and Malloy rode into town, their horses were proceeding at a leisurely enough pace that nobody noticed them, even though it was relatively unusual to have four men come into town together. And nobody was surprised when they stopped in front of Devil's Den, since that was first stop for many when they first arrived in town.

Once inside they found an empty table and waited until one of the bar girls approached.

"Let's see," the bar girl said. "I would say that you gentlemen prefer Kentucky bourbon to Irish or Scotch."

"Beer," Malloy said.

"That was going to be my next guess," the bar girl, whose name was Frieda said, recovering quickly. "I'll bring four to your table."

"Girl," Keefer said when she returned. "I heard that Smoke Jensen was here, and these three said he wasn't. We've got a dollar bet goin'. Who wins the bet?"

"It depends on what the bet is," Frieda replied. "If the bet is whether or not Mr. Jensen is in town, you win. But if the bet is that he is here in the saloon, you lose because he's not in here now."

Malloy watched Frieda walk away.

"How much you think she would charge me to take her upstairs?" Malloy asked.

"We don't have time for anything like that," Amos Scraggs said. "We're here to do a job."

"Yeah, well who is to say I couldn't take her upstairs first and then we do the job."

"Look, we've been around Hannibal longer than you two have," Amon Scraggs said. "And I'm here to tell you, right now, Hannibal ain't the kind of man you want to piss off."

"I think they're right, Malloy," Keefer said. "You seen how he handled them two soldiers that was guardin' us. He kilt 'em both without blinkin' an eye. I say we do the job first; then you can take the girl upstairs."

"Now that's a dumb thing to say, Keefer. Do you think, after we kill Jensen 'n the other fella that's with him, that I can just hang around town for a while?"

Keefer laughed. "No, I reckon that wouldn't be all that smart."

Frieda came back to the table then, carrying four beer mugs, grasping the handles, two in each hand.

"That'll be twenty cents," she said as she put the beer before them.

The four men came up with a nickel apiece.

Frieda picked up the money, then glanced toward the front door just as Smoke and Pearlie came in. "Well, what do you know? The man you asked about, Smoke Jensen? That's him and Pearlie by the door. They just came in."

"Which one is Smoke Jensen?" Keefer asked.

"He is the one on the right," Frieda replied. "Shall I ask him to come to your table?"

"No, that ain't necessary. We don't want to bother him none."

"Oh, it wouldn't be any bother at all. He is such a nice man."

"I said no!" Keefer snapped.

The unexpected sharpness of Keefer's response surprised her, and she stepped back away from the table.

"Enjoy your beer," she said.

After she walked away, Malloy looked at the other three.

"All right, we know what he looks like. Anybody have any ideas on what to do now?"

"I'd say we go back outside and mount up," Amon said.

"Why do we want to do that?" Keefer asked.

"So that after we kill him we can make our getaway."

"Yeah, well, we have to kill him first," Malloy said.

"Let's not talk about it in here," Amos Scraggs said.

"Yeah, good idea," Keefer agreed.

The four men got up and walked outside, leaving the four beer mugs on the table behind them. All four mugs were full.

"All right, Amos, you and Amon ride down that way about fifty yards, me 'n Keefer will go this way about fifty yards. When they come out of the saloon, start gallopin' back from your direction and we'll come from the other way. We'll shoot 'em down on the porch before they even know what's goin' on. Once they're down, keep on gallopin' and make your way back to the camp.

"You ready?"

"Yeah, we're ready," Amos said.

The four riders moved down the street and got into position.

"That's funny," Frieda said to the bartender.

"What's funny?" Mark asked.

Frieda pointed to the table the four men had just vacated. "Those four men just walked out without drinking their beer."

"Smoke, taste the beer," Mark said. "I just tapped a new keg, maybe it's flat."

Smoke took a taste. "Tastes fine to me," he said.

"I wouldn't think it was flat or they would have complained. But I have to admit, they were acting funny," Frieda said.

"Acting funny how?" Smoke asked.

"Well, they seemed awfully interested in you, and they had me point you out to them. I did that; then I asked them if they would like me to have you come over and meet them, and they said no."

"Smoke, do you think—?" Pearlie asked.

"Yeah, I do," Smoke replied, answering Pearlie's question even before it was fully articulated.

"Frieda, what did the men look like?"

"Funny you would ask that," Frieda said. "Because two of them looked just alike, like they were brothers or something. They had dark eyes and sort of narrow, pointy noses. The other two . . . to be honest, I didn't look at them all that close. I wouldn't have noticed the first two if they hadn't looked so much alike. Oh, but I can tell you what the other two were wearin'. Their trousers looked like army uniform trousers. One was wearin' a red shirt and the other gray."

"Thanks, you've been very helpful," Smoke said.

"What do you think we should do?" Pearlie asked.

"They just placed the bet. I think we should call," Smoke said as he turned away from the bar. "Let's go out the back door. If they're out there waiting for us, they'll be watching the front door."

Smoke and Pearlie went out the back door, then walked between the buildings until they reached the street.

"Smoke, there are two men, mounted, about thirty yards down to the left," Pearlie said. "One on either side of the street. Damn, they've both got guns in their hands."

"Yeah," Smoke said. "And there are the other two—army trousers, one with a red shirt, one with a gray shirt. They're holding guns too."

"How do we play this hand?" Pearlie asked.

"Let's go down the alley for one building. If they are looking for us to come out of the saloon, we can probably get into the middle of the street before they even notice us. Then we'll let them make the first play," Smoke said.

CHAPTER TWENTY-SEVEN

Smoke was right. Because they didn't come through the front door of the saloon, the door that their four assailants were watching, they managed to get all the way to the center of the street before anyone noticed them.

"Son of a bitch, Scraggs! There they are!" The shout came from one of the men who was wearing army trousers.

All four riders moved into the middle of the street, then started galloping toward Smoke and Pearlie.

"Back-to-back, Pearlie!" Smoke shouted, and the two pressed their backs together as they waited for the approaching gallopers.

The citizens of Brimstone who were out and about this morning were witness to a strange sight. They saw Smoke and Pearlie standing back-to-back in the middle of the street as four riders came toward them at a gallop. The riders had pistols in their extended hands, and they began firing.

Bullets were whizzing by Smoke's head and kicking up dirt around him. Smoke lifted his pistol, aimed, and fired twice. Two shots were all it took. Behind him, he heard Pearlie shooting as well.

The two men Smoke shot fell into the dirt and the horses they had been riding thundered by, their saddles now empty.

The two horses that had been coming toward Pearlie galloped by as well. Both saddles were empty, but the foot of one of the riders had hung up in the stirrup, and he was being dragged through the dirt. The horse dragged him for another forty feet or so; then his foot came loose and he lay still in the street, as it turned out, no more than ten feet from the two men Smoke had shot

The people who had been going about their normal daily business had been shocked by events that had played out so quickly that none of them had time to react. For a long moment there was absolute silence, the only sound being the drum of hooves as the horses continued galloping on out of town.

Because one of the assailants had been dragged for some distance, there were three men on Smoke's side of the street and only one on Pearlie's side.

"Go check him out, Pearlie, but be careful," Smoke ordered.

"Right," Pearlie said.

Smoke held his pistol ready as he approached, but he was pretty sure there would be no need for it. He knew he had hit them well when he shot, and now they were lying absolutely still.

Frieda had done a good job of describing them.

The two he had shot were both wearing army trousers, and the third man, the one who had been dragged to his side of the street when his foot hung up in the stirrup, could be described as having a pointy nose.

"I think I can identify the two of them that look alike," Hardegree said a few minutes later. He was standing alongside Smoke and Pearlie looking down at the four bodies that had been taken from the street and brought to the undertaker's. "I've got dodgers on those two. That's the Scraggs brothers, twins actually. They escaped from the Suttle jail a while ago, and they killed the jailer in the process. I have no idea who the other two might be, but none of them were carrying red armbands with them, so I don't think they are part of the Ghost Riders."

"They could be Ghost Riders, but just left their armbands behind," Smoke said. "Wherever *behind* might be."

"Yeah, you could be right. But apparently they were here just to kill you."

"That's true. And, long before I ever heard of the Ghost Riders or Hannibal, I've had people try to kill me."

"But, you think this is related to the Ghost Riders, don't you?" Hardegree said.

"Yes, I do."

"Which means they aren't through with us yet."

"No, I don't think so," Smoke answered. "It's like I said, from the letters he wrote I think this Hannibal character looks at this as a challenge now. I don't think there is any way he is going to pass you by."

Sorento

Rexwell was having breakfast at the Coffee Cup Café in Sorento.

"How is the mine doing?" the owner asked as he refilled Rexwell's cup.

"We haven't produced anything yet," Rexwell said. "But the owners are convinced there is still an untapped vein of silver there."

"They must be, because it seems to me they're spending an awful lot of money. How many men are working out there, anyway?"

"Oh, we've got about two dozen, I guess," Rexwell replied. "Why so many questions, Don?"

"I'm a worrier. Sorento was about to dry up and blow away until the mine reopened. I guess we just want to keep you men out there and keep the good times going."

"Yeah," Rexwell said. "So do we."

"Some of us were thinking about taking a trip out there, you know, sort of a courtesy trip, just to have a look around."

"No, don't do that."

"No? Why not?"

"You're liable to get shot if you do."

"What do you mean?"

"The owners are very particular, and they've given us word," Rexwell said. "If any of you was to show up, you'd either be run off or shot."

"Oh, my goodness. Well, we certainly don't want that."

"Everyone in town is making money from the mine being open, aren't they?" Rexwell asked.

"Yes, we are. You and all the other workers have been most generous with your spending."

"Then why would you want to spoil a good thing?"

"Why indeed?" Don replied.

The café owner walked away, leaving Rexwell with his breakfast and reading the newspaper. One article in particular caught his attention.

SHOOTOUT IN BRIMSTONE

On the 12th instant, Smoke Jensen and one of his employees were crossing the street in front of the Devil's Den Saloon, when they were set upon by four mounted gunmen.

According to those who witnessed the event, two armed riders approached from the north end of the street, while two others approached from the south end. The riders were at a gallop with pistols in hand. Jensen and Pearlie stood back-to-back, awaiting the charge. Shots were exchanged, and when the smoke had cleared the four mounted assailants lay dead in the street. Smoke Jensen and his friend were unscathed. Safe, too, were all the residents of the town

It is not known why the attack took place, nor is the identity known of two of the mounted gunmen. However, two have been identified, they being Amos and Amon Scraggs. Twins, the Scraggs brothers were awaiting execution in Suttle, Colorado, when, by a means unknown, they managed to escape jail, killing the jailer in the process. There have been some previous shooting incidents in town, which upon further investigation, proved to involve members of the infamous Ghost Rider gang.

As no red armbands were found on their persons, it is believed that these men were not affiliated with that band of outlaws.

Ten Strike

"I know what happened to the men we sent after Jensen," Rexwell said, handing the newspaper to Hannibal.

Hannibal read the newspaper story, then with an angry shout, threw the paper against the wall.

"That's fifteen!" he said. He pointed to the paper. "That son of a bitch has been responsible for killing fifteen of my men!"

"It says here that there were two of them," Rexwell said.

"Yes, but Jensen was obviously in command," Rexwell said. "That makes him responsible."

"But look at the good side," Rexwell said. "If Jensen is still in Brimstone, that means they still expect us to attack there. We can go somewhere else and they won't be expecting us."

"No," Hannibal said. "By now they are expecting us to go somewhere else. That's exactly why we will attack Brimstone."

"Hannibal, I told you what their plans are. They will put men on the roofs of every building. They could have as many as one hundred men waiting for us."

"Euripides once said that ten men, wisely led, are worth one hundred, without a head," Hannibal said.

"You rip a what? I don't think I ever heard of the fella. Where'd you meet him?"

"He was a Greek tragedian who lived well over two thousand years ago. The point is, I am in command of the Ghost Riders. You aren't only wisely led, you are brilliantly led.

"Not so with the town. The town will be nothing but a gathering of armed men with no direction, and they won't even have time to get into position. The essence of my battle plan is the shock effect of our attack. We will be on them before they have time to react."

"How will we be able to do that? They're going to have a lookout up in the bell tower of the church. From there, they can see for a long way off. And soon as they see us comin', they're goin' to ring the church bell. When that happens they're goin' to clear the streets of all them that won't be fightin' and men with guns will be on ever' roof. I don't see any way how we will be able to surprise 'em neither."

"Rexwell, one of the principles of warfare I learned at West Point was this—render your enemy blind, and you can work your way with him," Hannibal said.

"What are you talkin' about? I don't know what you mean."

"You said yourself that the entire element of their defense depends upon their lookout seeing us before we get to town and then sounding the warning, right?"

"Well, yeah, I reckon it does."

"If their lookout doesn't see us, there will be no

warning. That means we can still hit the town with shock and surprise."

"How do we do that?"

"I will just have to figure out a way," Hannibal said.

"All right," Rexwell said. "You're the boss."

"No, I'm the commander," Hannibal replied.

"Yes, sir," Rexwell said. Turning, he left the mine manager's house. After he was gone, Hannibal lay down on the bunk with his hands laced behind his head. He stared up at the ceiling trying to decide what to do about his planned raid on the town of Brimstone. His mission had been compromised. And mission was exactly how he thought about it. Every operation he had conducted since having been cashiered from the army was a mission.

Unbidden, the memory of his shame returned.

CHAPTER TWENTY-EIGHT

Fort Laramie, Wyoming, two years earlier

Colonel David Twiggs sat behind the desk in the commandant's office in the Post Headquarters Building. He was examining a sheet of paper that Sheriff Dailey had given him.

"And you say this man . . . what's his name?"

"Hall. Jesse Hall."

"You say he can identify one of my officers as the person he was dealing with?"

"He says he can, and that's the name he gave me. I brought him out here so your officer can confront him, face-to-face. This is a pretty serious charge to be makin'. I mean I know you've had some enlisted men go bad from time to time. Hell, half of 'em is runnin' from somethin' anyway, or they wouldn't be in the army in the first place. But I always thought that officers were somethin' different."

"And indeed, they should be," Colonel Twiggs said. "If you will wait for a while, we can get this matter taken care of. And I thank you, Sheriff, for bringing this to my attention."

Captain Enid Prescott stood in front of the mirror, shaving. He hadn't yet put on his tunic, and the hanging yellow galluses made a loop across the yellow stripe that ran down each side of the light blue trousers.

He was the commanding officer of D Troop of the Second Dragoons. He felt he should be a major by now, and he blamed his lack of promotion on his wife. Clearly, she had no idea of all the social responsibilities of being an officer's wife.

When he finished shaving, he put on his tunic, then went into the dining room of the post quarters and sat down for breakfast. When his wife set a plate down in front of him, he looked at it critically. The yellow of one of the eggs had broken and was fried hard.

"What is this?" he demanded. "You know I like my eggs over easy! Why are you serving me this garbage?"

"I'm sorry, Enid, but the yellow broke as soon as I dropped it into the skillet."

"Then why didn't you cook another one for me? You know I can't eat this!"

"I know that you prefer them over easy, but I was hoping you could make an exception this once. These were the last two eggs we had. I went to the Suttler's Store yesterday, but they didn't have any and they said they probably wouldn't get any more until today. I gave you the two eggs we have, I'm just having a biscuit."

"And I'm supposed to think, what, that you are sacrificing for me?"

"No, I don't look at it as a sacrifice. I know that you are under a lot of stress now, and I wanted you to face the day with a full stomach. I'm sorry the egg broke, if we had another one I would have prepared it for you."

"How many times have I told you to plan ahead?" Prescott shouted. Standing up so quickly that the chair turned over, he picked up the plate of bacon and eggs and threw it at her.

"Ahh!" she screamed, as the plate hit her in the face so hard that it cut her lip.

"Scream, why don't you?" Prescott said, angrily. "That way you can bring everyone in the officers' quarters to look into our private business. Better yet, scream loudly enough and maybe even the NCOs and the cows they are married to can come over here to be entertained."

"Enid, you have no right to treat me like this."

"I have every right to treat you anyway I want. You are my wife. When we were married you took an oath to obey me. Or have you forgotten that?"

"Oh, believe me, I can never forget that. You won't let me forget it."

"Don't get smart with me!"

Prescott slapped her so hard across the face that a redness instantly appeared around her left eye.

She cried out, put her hand over her eye, and took several steps away from him so that she was out of his reach.

"That eye is probably going to get black," Prescott said. "I don't want you to go outside until it goes away."

"I need to go to the Suttler's today."

"Oh, you would love that, wouldn't you? You could display your black eye as a badge of honor."

She didn't say anything.

"Get this mess cleaned up. I'll take breakfast in the Officers' Open Mess. As a matter of fact, I'll take all my meals in the officers' mess until you can be seen in public again." Prescott grabbed his hat and left his quarters.

There were three officers in the mess, but they all got up to leave when Prescott arrived.

"Where are you off to in such a hurry?" he asked.

"Duty officer," one of them called. Neither of the other two responded.

When Prescott looked over at the table, he saw that none of them had finished their breakfast. He found that rather odd. It was almost as if they wanted to avoid him.

Prescott ate his breakfast, then walked across the quadrangle to his company orderly room. When he stepped inside, his first sergeant saluted him.

"Sir, Colonel Twiggs asked you to report to him as soon as you came in this morning."

"What's it about?"

"I don't know, sir. The colonel didn't say."

"You are my first sergeant, Waters. How difficult would it have been for you to find out what this is all about?"

"I'm sorry, sir."

"You're sorry, all right. You are about the sorriest

NCO I've ever been around. All I'm looking for now is an excuse to bust you down to private. And it doesn't have to be all that much of an excuse. All right, tell Lieutenant Spalding to get all the training and work details started while I am gone."

"Yes sir," First Sergeant Waters replied, snapping a sharp salute.

Prescott, showing his disdain for his first sergeant, made a mere gesture as a return salute.

As he walked toward the post headquarters he returned the salutes of a sergeant and a second lieutenant.

When his first sergeant told him that he was to report to the post commandant he was, at first, a little concerned. But as he thought about it, he began to consider the possibility that he was being summoned to be told of his promotion. He had served enough time to be a major, and he knew that many of his classmates had already attained that rank.

He smiled. As major he would move up to a command staff position.

When Prescott stepped into the headquarters building, he saw Colonel Twiggs and Lieutenant Colonel Rector, who was Twiggs' executive officer. Prescott's smile grew wider. Of course both of them would be there to congratulate him on his promotion.

But Major Royal, the provost marshal, was there as well, and so were two enlisted men, bearing arms, standing nearby at parade rest. This was most unusual, and the smile faded. There could only be one reason why they were there, and he felt a weakness in his knees and a sinking sensation in his stomach.

He saluted. "Sir, Captain Prescott reporting to the post commandant as ordered."

Colonel Twiggs didn't return the salute and that, too, troubled him. He held the salute for a moment, then let his arm drop.

"Sheriff Dailey, bring the prisoner in, please," Colonel Twiggs said.

From another room the sheriff came in, responding to Colonel Twiggs's call. When Prescott saw the civilian who was with him, he recognized him immediately. All the breath left his body, and he got very light-headed. He was afraid, for a moment, that he might pass out.

"Mr. Hall, do you know this officer?" Colonel Twiggs asked, addressing the civilian who was with the sheriff.

"Yeah, I know 'im," Hall said.

"What is your relationship with him?"

"What is my what?" Hall asked.

"How do you know him?"

"All them army rifles I got caught with? I bought 'em off Captain Prescott here."

"Do you have anything to say for yourself, Prescott?" Colonel Twiggs asked.

Prescott noticed that when Colonel Twiggs addressed him, he didn't use his military rank. Colonel Twiggs was a very formal person, and he never addressed one of his soldiers, be it officer or enlisted man, by his last name only.

"I have nothing to say, sir."

"Major Royal, escort this . . . person . . . to the stockade," Colonel Twiggs said, purposely omitting use of the word *officer*.

"Sir, is there any way I could be placed on arrest in quarters? As a brother officer, can't you spare me the humiliation of being confined to the stockade with the enlisted men?"

"At the moment, Prescott, there is not an enlisted man on this post that I don't hold in higher regard than you, and I have a feeling that you won't be an officer much longer. Colonel Rector, if you would, sir, please inform Lieutenant Spalding that he is now the commanding officer of D Troop."

"Yes, sir," Colonel Rector said.

"Guards," Major Royal ordered. "Escort this prisoner to the stockade."

Although Major Royal was the provost marshal, the stockade was run by Provost Sergeant Schuler. Prescott had once dressed Sergeant Schuler down in front of several lower-ranking enlisted men because one button was open on his tunic.

When Sergeant Schuler saw who his new prisoner was, a broad smile spread across his face.

"Come along, Captain," Sergeant Schuler said. "I've got a nice room all ready for you."

The court-martial was little more than a pro forma proceeding. The prosecutor heard testimony from Sheriff Austin Dailey and Jesse Hall. Lieutenant Spalding acted as Prescott's defense council. He made no effort to prove Prescott's innocence, pleading only that Prescott be spared spending time in prison.

Two weeks later, the men of the Second Dragoons were in dismounted formation on the parade grounds, with Colonel David E. Twiggs in command. Each troop had its commander standing out front, captains all but one. D Troop, formerly commanded by Captain Enid Prescott, was now commanded by First Lieutenant Charles Spalding.

Captain Prescott, in full-dress uniform, stood in front of the assembled troops, flanked on either side by an armed private. His request to be guarded by officers had been refused.

"Colonel Rector, if you would, sir, please read the findings of the general court-martial," Colonel Twiggs ordered.

In a loud and commanding voice, Lieutenant Colonel Wharton Rector began to read from a paper he held in his hand:

"Having been found by a general court-martial, guilty of the crime of stealing and selling army equipment and supplies, Captain Enid Prescott is hereby sentenced to be reduced to the rank of private, stripped of all rank insignia and accoutrements, thereafter to be dishonorably discharged, and, under guard, to be marched through the front gate and barred henceforth from ever setting foot on any army post. By order of David E. Twiggs, Colonel, Second Dragoons, commanding."

After reading the order, Lieutenant Colonel Rector stepped up to Captain Prescott and, one at a time, ripped off his shoulder boards, each board bearing the twin bars denoting the rank of captain. After the shoulder boards were removed, he used a knife to cut each of the brass buttons from his tunic, dropping them on the ground where the shoulder boards lay. Then, using the same knife, he cut the stitching at the top of the gold stripes running down each pants leg and ripped them off. That done, he removed Prescott's sword and broke it across his knee, the blade having earlier been prepared to allow him to do so.

The broken sword was the last item to join the pile of uniform accoutrements that lay in the dirt alongside the disgraced officer.

Prescott, his face burning in shame, glanced toward the post civilians who had gathered to watch his humiliation. He saw his wife in the front row, the black eye now gray green as it healed. He was sure that, secretly, she was enjoying this.

Prescott had not spoken a word to her from the day he had been arrested, because he had been taken directly from the headquarters building of the Second Dragoons, to the Fort Laramie Post Stockade. She had not been present for his court-martial, and in the two weeks since he had been placed in custody she had not come to the stockade one time to see him

"First Sergeant Waters, front!" Rector called.

Waters, the First Sergeant of the company that Prescott had once commanded, marched up to Lieutenant Colonel Rector and saluted.

"First Sergeant Waters, escort Private Prescott to the front gate; then remove him from this post and from the army."

"Yes, sir," Sergeant Waters replied.

"Regimental Band Director, have your drummers

play the cadence," Lieutenant Colonel Rector ordered.

The drummers began playing a staccato cadence.

"Guards, right shoulder, arms," First Sergeant Waters ordered.

In perfect synchronization, the two privates brought their Springfield carbines, caliber .45-.70, to their shoulders.

"Prisoner and guard detail, forward march," First Sergeant Waters ordered.

As the small formation approached the gate, the gates were swung open.

"Prisoner and detail, halt! Guards, post!"

The two guards, with their carbines still across their shoulders, moved three steps to either side of Private Prescott, then turned to face him.

"Port arms."

The guards brought their rifles down sharply, holding them diagonally across their chests.

First Sergeant Waters then stepped up behind Prescott, and lifting his leg, put the sole of his boot on Prescott's backside. He then pushed him so hard that Prescott was unable to keep his balance, and he fell into the dirt on the outside of the gate. Once he left the gate he was no longer Captain Prescott, or even Private Prescott. He was a dishonorably discharged civilian.

"Dragoons, dismissed!" Colonel Twiggs shouted, and as the men were dismissed, they laughed and shouted catcalls at the disgraced former officer, who walked away from the front gate with his head down.

"Oh, Enid," his wife said.

Looking up, Prescott saw her standing outside the post, her luggage on the ground beside her. There was no luggage for him, he had only army uniforms, and he was no longer authorized to wear the uniform.

"I suppose you are happy now," Prescott said.

"No, of course not. I'm sorry for you, Enid. But you had to—"

Prescott slapped her in the face, hitting her so hard that it knocked her down.

"Get up," he said. He looked back toward the soldiers who were still standing in the open gate to the fort. "Get up, we're leaving this place."

She got up onto her hands and knees, but didn't stand. "No, Enid. I'm not going with you."

Prescott kicked her. "I said get up!"

"Prescott, you son of a bitch! If you touch that woman again I'll kill you where you stand!" the guard at the gate said, pointing his rifle at him.

"Go," Prescott said, with a dismissive wave of his hand to his wife. "You've been nothing but a burden to me from the time we got married. I don't care if I ever see you again."

"That's not anything you'll ever have to worry about," she said, as she stood.

"Disabuse yourself of any idea that I will ever give you a divorce, my dear." Prescott smiled at her, but there was no humor in his smile. "No, madam, you are doomed to a lifetime of marriage. Marriage to a man who despises you. And as long as you are married to me, you'll never be able to marry another."

She smiled at him. "Enid, if what I have been

through with you is any indication of what marriage is like, I don't ever want to be married again."

Prescott drew his hand back.

"I mean it, Prescott," the gate guard said. "You take one more step toward that lady and you are a dead man!"

Prescott made a dismissive wave with his hand, then turned and walked away. He had no money and no clothes, other than the stripped-down uniform he was wearing, and no weapon. Behind him, he heard the jeers of troopers who had once been obedient to him, had saluted him, and had given him the respect an officer was due.

Prescott, you son of a bitch! If you touch that woman again I'll kill you where you stand!

He had called him Prescott . . . not Captain Prescott, but Prescott. Never in the entire time he had been in the army, had an enlisted man addressed him so. And it was that—the shame of having an enlisted man refer to him simply as Prescott that bothered him more than the threat of being shot.

Chapter Twenty-nine

Millersburg, Wyoming

Prescott walked from Fort Laramie to Millersburg, a distance of about ten miles. Night had fallen by the time he reached the town, and he was tired, hungry, and thirsty. As he walked by a saloon, he could hear the laughter and happy conversation coming from within, and he hated everyone there. He hated them because they had food, and he hated them because they had a beer, and he hated them because they had not gone through the humiliation he had just suffered.

"Damn, I gotta pee," someone said from within the saloon.

"Well, pee in the toilet," a woman's voice said. "I don't know why all you men think you have to pee on the back of the building."

"You want to come hold it for me, Betty Lou?"

"Oh my, honey, do you mean you can't even find it by yourself?" Betty Lou quipped.

There was a loud guffaw of men's laughter.

That was when Prescott knew what he was going to do. Picking up a rock that was about the size of his fist, he ran into the gap between the saloon and the building next door. Shaded from the moon and with no ambient light, it was so dark here that he couldn't see his hand in front of his face.

He moved to the back of the saloon and, from here, could see the toilet because there was a lantern hanging just outside. He saw the man go inside; then he moved up to the toilet and waited. As soon as the man came out, Prescott bashed in the side of his head with a rock. When the man went down, Prescott dragged him into the dark between the two buildings. There, he stripped him; then, getting out of the remnants of his uniform, he put on the clothes of the man he had just killed. He also took the man's gun and holster. He found two dollars in the pocket of the denim trousers he had just put on.

Stepping back into the toilet, he dropped his uniform down through the hole.

Now wearing nondistinctive clothes and with a little money in his pocket, he went to the other saloon in town, where he bought a supper of ham and fried potatoes, washed down with a beer.

"They're making a ton of money," he heard someone say. The conversation was taking place at the next table over. "I mean, who would have thought that a general store, out in the country like that, would make so much money? You'd think they would have to be in town, wouldn't you?"

"No. I mean it's out there on the Hartville Road, halfway between Millersburg and Hartville, so it serves all the people who don't want to go into town."

After his supper, Prescott stole a horse and rode toward Hartville. When he saw the store, he camped out near it; then, the next morning, right after the store opened but before they had any customers, he went inside, his entry announced by the jingle of a bell that was attached to the front door.

"My," the store owner said. "Aren't you the early riser though?"

Prescott pointed his pistol at the man.

"They say the early bird gets the worm," he said. "Or in this case, the money. Hand it over. All of it."

With shaking hands, the man opened his cash drawer and pulled out a stack of money. He started to scoop out the coins.

"You can keep the coins," Prescott said.

"Jack, what is it? What's going on here?" a woman said, coming over to the counter.

When Prescott turned to look at the woman, Jack grabbed a gun that he kept under the counter. Whirling back toward him, Prescott fired. Then, when the woman screamed, he shot her too.

When he left the store a moment later, he had eighty-seven dollars in his pocket, two new pair of jeans and two new shirts, bacon, beans, sugar, and coffee. Jack and Mary Henderson lay dead on the floor in the store behind him. Prescott had killed for the first time in his life, and he felt not the slightest contrition.

Within a month, Prescott, who was now calling himself Hannibal, had put together a gang of some five men, using the principles of leadership he had learned at the U.S. Military Academy at West Point. Within another two months he had a gang of ten men, including Bo Rexwell, a former sergeant who had deserted the army. It was then that he came up with the idea of calling his command the Ghost Riders and having his men wear red armbands. It fostered a degree of camaraderie among the men, and it also subconsciously inculcated in them a degree of obedience to their leader.

Prescott discovered that the leadership skills he had learned at the academy, as well as his practical experience, proved to be very beneficial in his newly chosen profession. He commanded the Ghost Riders as if it were an army company in combat, and he became very successful. The Ghost Riders raised havoc all over Wyoming, and as the head of the outfit, Hannibal accumulated more money in less than six months than the sum total of every dollar he had drawn in his entire army career.

He worked Wyoming until he was sure that there were no more targets of opportunity remaining. Then, and with his command now numbering over twenty riders, he moved to Colorado.

"Damn! Another ringer! You got to be cheatin'! There can't nobody throw six ringers in a row!"

"How can you cheat at horseshoes?"

"I don't know, I ain't figured it out yet."

The noise of the horseshoe tossing game outside his window brought Hannibal back from his memories, and he knew it was time to start working on his plan for robbing the bank in Brimstone.

Sugarloaf Ranch

As Cal and Julia were sitting out on the porch swing, a meteor zipped across the night sky.

"Oh, a falling star!" Julia said. "I would like to see one when it landed. They must be as beautiful as a diamond."

"They're not pretty at all," Cal said. "They just look like a rock that's been in a fire is all. Pearlie and I found one, once. We saw it fall, and it was still smoking when we got to it. It's out in the bunkhouse, if you would like for me to go get it and show it to you."

"No, if it isn't as beautiful as a diamond, I don't think I would want to see it. I prefer to keep thinking of them as beautiful. And they are beautiful when you see them falling."

"I suppose they are," Cal said.

They were quiet for another long moment; then Cal reached over and took Julia's hand in his.

"Do you want to tell me about it?" he asked.

"You mean, me being married?"

"Yes."

"I fell in love with a West Point cadet. He was so handsome, so dashing."

Julia told the story in halting words and troubled

sighs. But despite the difficulty of telling it, she put into it so much feeling and such intensity that Cal was transported from the front porch of the Jensen house and was now reliving the experience with the beautiful and troubled young woman who was sitting beside him.

And, as she had gripped his hand to keep him grounded in reality when he was having his dreams, so too did he hold her hand now to let her know that no matter how painful the memories might be, he was here for her.

West Point, New York

Julia's father was a doctor at West Point, not the military academy, but the town of West Point. She had grown up around the academy and from the time she was a young girl had thrilled to the sight of the cadets marching so sharply in long rows of gray.

Then, when she was seventeen, she was invited to attend a dance, called a *hop* by the cadets, and to her surprise, her father let her attend. There, she was assigned to a handsome young first classman who showed her about the grounds.

"I've lived here all my life," she said. "But this is the first time I've ever actually been here, to the academy."

"Well, as you can see, this is a most historic place," her date said.

"These plaques," she said. "They all have names

of generals on them. But I know they aren't all buried here."

"No. Well, some are buried here, General Anderson, General Buford, Custer, of course. But most of these are just names of generals who graduated from here, and they represent all the wars from the Revolutionary War up to the Civil War. My name will be here, some day," he said confidently.

"You mean you think you will make general?"

"I know I will."

"Oh, here's one that doesn't have a name. It just says MAJOR GENERAL, BORN 1740. That's rather odd."

"That would be Benedict Arnold."

"But he was a traitor," Julia said.

"He was a traitor, yes. But despite that, he is regarded as a brilliant tactician."

"Was he the most brilliant of all the generals?"

"No."

"Who was?"

"The most brilliant general's name won't be here, because he lived long before there was a West Point, long before there was an America, even. That would be Hannibal Barca. He was a Punic Carthaginian military commander and the greatest military commander in history."

"I know, you think he's very handsome," Dr. McKnight said to his daughter two months later. "But cadet or not, there is something about him that bothers me."

"Papa, he has asked me to marry him in the West

Point Chapel as soon as he graduates and receives his commission," Julia said. "That's just two weeks from now, and I have said yes."

"Well if you have said yes, what are you coming to me for?" Dr. McKnight asked. "Apparently you have already made up your mind, with no input from me. No, I take that back. You have had plenty of input from me, and all of it negative. But it didn't seem to matter."

"Oh, Papa, it does matter," Julia said. "But you don't know him as I do. I think the reason you are against the marriage is because he is going to be posted out West and you don't want to see me go."

"I don't want to see you go, that is true. But that isn't the reason. Sweetheart, I just don't see him as the man for you. I wish I had set up my practice in Philadelphia or Boston or Chicago . . . anywhere but here and that blasted military academy. I know that all the young women in town are enamored of the West Point cadets. And no doubt, there have been some wonderful gentlemen who have graduated from that academy. I just wish I felt better about the man you have chosen."

"Papa, please say that you will come to my wedding."

"I will come," Dr. McKnight said. "I will come, because you are my daughter and I love you. And I hope I'm wrong. I hope the marriage works out well for you."

Dr. McKnight wasn't wrong. From Jefferson Barracks, Missouri, to Fort Ripley, Minnesota, to Fort Riley, Kansas, to Fort Halleck, Nevada, it was always the same. Her husband was a martinet, hated by his men and distrusted by his superiors. It was only because he was an academy graduate that he was tolerated at all, and he was tolerated best by being passed from one command to the other.

"It's your fault," he yelled at her on the night he learned that there would be still another transfer ahead, but with no promotion.

"How is it my fault?"

"I know that Colonel McDermott likes you. He finds you attractive. You could have been a little nicer to him."

"I told you what he wanted," Julia said.

"If you knew what he wanted, why didn't you give it to him? You are married to an army officer; it is your duty to do everything you can to advance my career."

"Even if it means sleeping with a fat, ugly colonel?"

"Oh, don't be so sanctimonious. You could hardly wait to lift your skirts when we first met, and you know it."

"I'll not sleep with anyone for you. If you are going to get promoted, you are going to have to earn it. Why don't you sleep with the colonel's wife?"

"I'll not have you talk to me like that. You will obey, do you understand?"

She didn't answer.

"I said do you understand?" He slapped her hard.

As Julia told about being slapped in the face by her husband, she put her hand to her cheek and grew silent for a long moment. Cal, who was still holding her other hand, lifted it to his lips and kissed it. He said nothing, understanding that when she was ready to talk again, she would.

"I should have listened to Papa," Julia continued. "He turned out to be a brutal officer, brutal to his men, and brutal to me.

"He was also a thief, and when he got caught stealing from the army, he was broken down to private, then drummed out of the service. I was going to leave with him, after all he was my husband and I had taken an oath to stay with him in good times and bad. But I couldn't, I just couldn't do it. I had had enough, so after he left the army, he went one way and I went the other. I had no idea what I was going to do. I no longer had a sponsor, and that meant that I had lost my quarters on the post. I knew I couldn't go back to New York and face my father. After all, he had advised me against marrying him in the first place. I don't know how it was that he was able to see something in Enid that I didn't see. But, oh, I wish I had listened to him."

"Enid?" Cal asked.

"Yes, Enid Prescott. That is my husband's name. He comes from a fine old Virginia family, and I have no idea how he turned out the way he did. He wasn't like this when he was a cadet, but then of course, I was only able to see him at very formal events.

"While I'm getting everything off my chest, Cal, I may as well tell you the whole story. I took a stagecoach from Fort Laramie, and on the coach I met a woman who was very intuitive. Well, now that I think back on it, she didn't have to be all that intuitive. I was crying, after all, and she saw that I was recovering from a black eye.

"She was very nice to me, and I found myself telling her my story. It turns out that she was a madam, and when she offered me a job, I took it. I figured why not? I had already debased myself.

"I stayed with her for just under a year; then she closed up her house, took her money, and went back to Chicago. That's when I started working for Bagby, and that's where I was when Mr. Jensen brought you into the saloon.

"I'm so ashamed of myself. I have made such a mess of my life."

"You can't say that," Cal said. "You say you have made a mess of your life, as if your life is almost over. You are just starting, and you were in the right place at the right time for me. Smoke and Dr. Urban have both told me I wouldn't even be alive if not for you."

Cal chuckled. "Unless you think saving my life wasn't all that important."

This time it was Julia who lifted Cal's hand to her lips. She kissed it.

"Cal, saving your life is the most important thing I have ever done."

"Then look at it this way," Cal said. "Everything you have ever done in your life . . . marrying that son of a bitch, meeting that madam on the stage . . . and especially working as a bar girl in that saloon, was done just so you would be there in the right place and at the right time, exactly when I needed you."

"Why, Cal, you are a fatalist."

"When you live the life I've lived, for me to be here now, working for the greatest people in the world and sitting here in the swing with the greatest woman in the world, yeah, how could I be anything but a fatalist?"

Cal pulled Julia to him and kissed her deeply. She offered no resistance.

CHAPTER THIRTY

Brimstone

"We'll give it one more week," Smoke said to Hardegree. "If Hannibal doesn't try it within a week, I don't think he's going to."

"You may be right, but I think we'll keep someone posted in the church belfry for at least another month," Hardegree said.

"Yes, I think that would be a good idea," Smoke said.

"But, you have to wonder how many men Hannibal has left. Four have been killed here . . . eight, if those last four were Ghost Riders . . . and how many at Brown Spur?"

"Five," Smoke said.

"Plus the two you and Cal killed out at the Condon ranch, remember," Pearlie added.

"And one in Denver," Smoke said.

Hardegree laughed. "Damn, Smoke, maybe they don't have enough people left to come after our bank."

Ten Strike

"The British General Wellington was a brilliant tactician," Hannibal told his assembled men. "He achieved victory by not letting his enemy know how many men he had or from which direction they would come. It was often his plan to allow the enemy to think they are winning against an inferior force, then to suddenly strike them with a much stronger force. This would leave the enemy disoriented and totally unable to mount any sort of counterattack.

"That is exactly the tactic we will use against Brimstone."

Hannibal had drawn a map of the objective. "I have studied the area very closely. Here, to the south of the town, there is a reverse slope. Because of that reverse slope I gauge that we can advance to this point without being seen, provided we walk our horses for the last two or three hundred yards.

"At five minutes before nine, Rexwell, you will make a feint with four men from the north, riding in and shooting at targets of opportunity, just as we did in Laurette.

"But proceed no farther into the town than the end of the private quarters, then turn and retreat. When you retreat, have every gun fire three shots, with one second between the shots. That way we will be able to differentiate those shots from the general shooting that will, no doubt, be taking place.

"At that time, the rest of us will come in from the South, engaging anyone and everyone we see. By then any defense the town will have mounted will have been committed to holding off the attack from the north. We shall have free run to the bank, and once there, we will proceed exactly as we did in Laurette."

"But, they'll have a lookout in the bell tower, which is the highest place in town," Rexwell said. "Even if you walk your horses up that hill, there's a chance they will see you. And they will for certain see us as we approach."

"There won't be anyone in the bell tower," Hannibal said.

"Yes, there will be. I heard them talking about it."

Hannibal smiled. "Trust me, Mr. Rexwell. There won't be anyone in the bell tower."

It was still a predawn darkness when Taylor climbed into the bell tower of the church the next morning. Hannibal had told him that there probably wouldn't be anyone there at this hour.

"What if there is someone there?" Taylor had asked Hannibal, when Hannibal gave him the assignment.

"If there is someone there, he will, no doubt, think that you are coming, either to his relief or to check on him. That will give you the advantage of surprise, and you can kill him. But do it quietly. We don't want any gunfire until it is time."

Taylor reached the belfry after a short climb and found it to be empty. Hannibal was right; they weren't expecting anyone to come in the middle of the night.

He stuffed a wad of twist tobacco into his mouth

and began chewing, and as he leaned over the half walls of the belfry, he was cooled by a gentle breeze.

From one of the houses out on the edge of town he heard a baby crying.

A dog barked.

He saw a few lights appear in the houses of the early risers, and the smell of bacon frying drifted toward him, reminding him that he was a little hungry.

Finally the sun rose, and he prepared to meet whoever would be coming up for the first watch. He heard the door open downstairs, and he took out his knife, then slipped back into the corner. As his visitor climbed up the ladder, his back would be to Taylor. It would be really easy to kill him as soon as half his body was up through the trapdoor, but if he did so, his victim would likely fall back down. Taylor couldn't allow that to happen, because that way his body could be seen by others.

Taylor needed to kill him and hide him.

The man stepped off the ladder and onto the floor, then stretched, holding both his arms up in the air. He didn't bother to look around because he had no idea that anyone else would be here.

Taylor stepped up behind him, then, turning the blade sideways, plunged it in between the fifth and sixth ribs, penetrating the heart. The man who was scheduled to be on the first watch died without making a sound.

Taylor propped him up so that his head and shoulders were above the level of the half wall. That way if anyone looked up from the street, they would think he was on watch.

The first rays of sunlight spilled in through the window of Smoke's hotel room . . . the glass having been replaced. Smoke awoke and studied the shadow patterns on the wall for a few minutes. Last night he decided that he had been wrong about Hannibal. It could be that Hannibal was feeling his losses to the degree that he no longer felt confident in mounting a Laurette-type raid.

He would discuss it with Pearlie over breakfast this morning; then they would go see Marshal Hardegree and tell him they would be moving on today.

The question, of course, would be moving on to where? He felt that the information Thigpen had given him about Brimstone had been accurate, otherwise there would not have been so many encounters with Hannibal's men. But, where was Hannibal's hideout? He had a lot of men, and like the elephants of the ancient Hannibal, that many men weren't easy to hide.

He decided that when they left here he would go back to see Thigpen. If Hannibal had decided against Brimstone, then he was going to have to find another target. Thigpen had been a valuable source of information for Hannibal in the past, and Smoke was sure he wouldn't want to let that asset go just because he had lost his liaison. Hannibal would find some way to get in touch with him, and if he did, Smoke wanted to know about it.

By now enough people in town were cooking breakfast that the aromas of bacon, biscuits, and coffee were coming to Taylor from all sides, and he was beginning to wish that he had brought something to eat with him. The problem is, it had practically been the middle of the night when he left Ten Strike and food was the last thing on his mind.

Taylor knew that Hannibal had no intention of coming into town until after the bank opened, and that wouldn't be until nine o'clock. That meant that at least one more watchman would probably show up, and at a few minutes after eight o'clock, someone else did come into the church.

"Ben? Look, I'm sorry I'm a few minutes late," someone called up into the belfry. "The wife was late gettin' breakfast on the table this mornin'." He laughed as he started climbing up the ladder. "I made her fix a biscuit with bacon for you, just to make up for me being late."

When he got to the top of the ladder, the replacement watch saw Ben on his knees, leaning against the half wall.

"Damn, are you so mad at me that you ain't even goin' to talk?" he asked.

As he had done before, Taylor waited until the relief watch was off the ladder before he moved toward him. But as he started toward him, he kicked the bell rope.

"What the hell?" the relief watch said, turning

toward the sound. He saw Taylor, and he opened his mouth to yell, but Taylor made a quick, slicing motion across his throat, severing his carotid artery and his windpipe. Blood squirted from the neck wound, the man raised his hands to his neck, and Taylor watched the life leave his terror-stricken eyes.

Then he picked up the bacon and biscuit. He was hungry, and it tasted pretty good to him.

Ten Strike

The sun was low in the east as Hannibal called his company to horse. And as if they were cavalrymen— a few of them had been—every man stood by his horse, grasping the reins very close to the bridle. The men were in company front formation, which meant that they were in one, long line.

Hannibal made an inspection troop of the line, stopping in front of Mason.

"Raise your armband two inches, so that it is in accordance with the others," he ordered Snake Eye Mason.

Mason did so.

"Peters, button that top button."

As Mason had before him, Peters complied.

He made at least half a dozen more observations of some miniscule infraction, requiring that all be corrected to his satisfaction.

When he had completed the inspection, he stepped out front to face his men.

"Men, I know that you wonder why I pay so much attention to little details. Well, there is a very good reason for it. As a matter of fact there is a very good reason for everything we do.

"It all comes down to discipline and order. A military unit that has discipline and order is a unit that can react quickly to any situation. We've been successful in everything we have undertaken because you have been exceptionally well led, and we, as a unit, adhere to those two principles of discipline and order. I told each of you as you joined the Ghost Riders that I would make you the finest military unit in the West, and I have done that. I would be proud to lead you men in battle against any foe."

Hannibal turned to Rexwell.

"Rexwell, call out the first four men," he said.

"You four," Rexwell said, pointing to four men on the end of the formation. "With horse, take ten steps forward."

The men did so.

"All Ghost Riders, including the detached detail, mount!" Hannibal called, and in a perfectly coordinated movement, everyone mounted.

"Mr. Rexwell, proceed with your detail," Hannibal ordered.

Rexwell left the encampment.

Hannibal stood in his stirrups and looked out over the remaining men.

"Left by column of twos, ho!" he ordered, and in as precise a formation as any cavalry unit in the entire army, the men rode out.

Hannibal looked back at his men, everyone trained and led by him. How foolish the army had been not to recognize his leadership skills.

He wondered if he could raise a large enough

army to carve New Mexico and Arizona away from the rest of the country. He believed that he could, and if he formed an alliance with Mexico, he was sure he could do it.

"Prestonia," he said aloud, the spoken word covered by the sounds of horses' hooves.

Yes, the nation of Prestonia, with him as its supreme leader.

That was an idea that greatly appealed to him.

He imagined how history books of the future would read.

General Enid Prescott founded the nation of Prestonia by fighting a revolution against the United States of America. Though at all times outnumbered in the field, General, later to become President, Prescott prevailed due to the brilliance of his military leadership.

He hoped that if it ever came to an actual revolution, he would be able to lead his men in battle against Colonel David Twiggs. He could imagine nothing on the face of this planet that would be sweeter than accepting Colonel Twiggs's sword in defeat.

CHAPTER THIRTY-ONE

Brimstone

Smoke and Pearlie were having breakfast at the Chatterbox Café.

"I don't know, Smoke, I don't think they are goin' to come," Pearlie said.

"This is going to surprise you, Pearlie, but I've been thinking about it, and I agree with you. I had thought that if Hannibal didn't come, it would mean a total repudiation of everything he believes about himself. I'm sure he wanted to come here—not in spite of the fact that he knows we are ready for him, but because he knows. I thought he would do it just to show everyone that he can," Smoke said. "But it may be that he is wise enough not to let common sense be held hostage to his vanity."

"Yeah, I mean he's got to be smart enough to figure it out," Pearlie said. "It doesn't make any difference how many of them there are, if we've got twenty or thirty men well positioned, we'll cut him to ribbons."

"You would think so, wouldn't you?" Smoke asked. "But—"

"But what?"

"I had come to that conclusion this morning. But now I think I was right in the first place. I believe that he will come."

"Didn't you say you had been thinking about it and decided he wouldn't come?"

"Yes, I had been thinking about it. But I don't believe Hannibal has been thinking about it. I don't think he can overcome his vanity."

"How much longer do you think we'll have to wait around here?"

"Getting a little impatient, are you, Pearlie?"

"Yeah, a little," Pearlie admitted.

"I am too, but I expect the men riding with Hannibal are getting even more impatient. He's not going to be able to keep them in check for too long. But I'll give you this. If he doesn't come within the week, we'll go looking for him," Smoke said.

One hour after Smoke and Pearlie's breakfast conversation, the two elements of the Ghost Riders were in position. Rexwell was just north of Brimstone, and Hannibal, with the main striking element, was to the south.

Before leaving their encampment, Hannibal and Rexwell had synchronized their pocket watches. Now, as the four mounted men with him waited patiently, Rexwell was looking at his watch. When the minute hand reached eleven, he brought his hand down.

"Now!" he shouted.

Rexwell and his small group approached the town at a gallop. As they reached the first house, a young woman and her little boy were in the front yard. They were the first to be shot.

The riders continued on into town, shooting at everyone they saw. The men of the town, who had thought a ringing bell would alert them, were caught by surprise. Many of them were unarmed, and those few who were armed were caught by such surprise that their resistance was weak and fragmented.

At the first sound of shooting, Smoke and Pearlie were with Marshal Hardegree in his office. The three rushed out into the street with pistols drawn, but the riders didn't get this far. Instead they stopped at the far end of the street, pointed pistols into the air, fired three, synchronized shots, then turned and rode away.

"Why are they leaving?" Hardegree asked.

"Maybe it was a feint to see how far they could get before the watchman started ringing the bell. But there's something wrong, because the bell didn't ring at all," Smoke said.

"Why didn't the bell ring?" Pearlie asked.

"I don't know, but that's a good question. I'm going to the bell tower," Smoke said. "Who's got the watch now?"

"Jack Mitchell," Hardegree said. "He should have rung the bell, he's a good man."

Smoke ran across the street to the church. He started to yell up to Jack, but thought better of it when he saw drops of blood on the floor in front of the ladder.

"They're leaving!" he heard someone call from the street.

"We must'a run 'em off."

Smoke heard someone coming down the ladder then, and he stepped into the corner to see who it was.

It was Toon Taylor, one of the two men he and Cal had captured at the Wiregrass Ranch and had taken in to Brown Spur to be hanged.

"Hello, Taylor," Smoke said.

"What the hell?" Taylor shouted as he went for his pistol.

Smoke, who already had his pistol in hand, just smiled. He waited until Taylor had drawn and brought his gun to bear, before he shot.

Taylor went down, and Smoke climbed the ladder to the top. He wasn't surprised when he saw Mitchell lying in a pool of his own blood, but he was surprised to see that Ben Pittman was also there and also dead. Taylor must have climbed up into the belfry and been waiting for them even before dawn.

There had only been a few men in the initial foray into the town, and Smoke knew that it had to be a prelude of some sort. The real thrust had not yet occurred, and he looked around from the tower. That was when he saw a large body of men approaching from the south, the opposite side of town.

"Hannibal, you think you are so smart? I read you like a book," Smoke said aloud.

Smoke began ringing the bell, which was the agreed upon signal.

Pearlie, who was standing in the middle of the street, looked up at him, questioningly.

"Men coming from the south!" Smoke shouted as he continued to jerk on the rope to ring the bell.

At first a few of the townspeople thought that the bell referred to the men who had just left, but the ringing continued, and when Pearlie and Hardegree augmented the warning bell with their own shouts, they understood and everyone got off the street.

Smoke wrapped his arms around either side of the ladder, then slid down to the bottom. He knew that they would be hitting the bank, and he yelled at Pearlie and Hardegree when he ran outside.

"In the bank!"

The two men nodded, then followed him into the bank where the teller and a customer were cowering.

"Both of you, lie down behind the counter!" Smoke shouted. Then, remembering that before they had entered the bank at Laurette the outlaws had shot it up, he signaled to Pearlie and Hardegree, and they, too, lay down behind the counter.

By now the riders were in town, and as was their custom, they were shooting at anything and everything. Smoke could only hope that the ringing bell and the shouted warnings had gotten everyone off the street.

Suddenly a fusillade of bullets came crashing through the windows of the bank, as well as the frosted-glass panel that topped the counter. After a rather prolonged fusillade, the shooting stopped.

"Is anyone hit?" Smoke asked, speaking just loudly enough for the others to hear him.

No one was.

Smoke pulled the hammer back on his pistol and waited.

"Get ready," he said.

Pearlie and Hardegree followed suit, pulling the hammers back on their own pistols.

The front door opened, and three men came running in.

Smoke, Pearlie, and Hardegree stood up, shocking the three would-be robbers by their sudden appearance. They began firing, dropping all three of the Ghost Riders. Then Smoke, Pearlie, and Hardegree targeted the mounted Ghost Riders in front of the bank, shooting through the opening left by the broken front windows.

"Let's get out of here!" one of the mounted outlaws shouted, and the attackers left at a gallop.

Smoke ran to the front door, but by now the gallopers were out of pistol range.

He looked at the three men he had killed and recognized Carl Moss, the other man who was to have been hanged in Brown Spur.

There were three others lying dead in front of the bank.

With the outlaws gone and the town now silent,

men and women began cautiously re-emerging. Hardegree made a quick check of his town, then came back to Smoke and Pearlie who were leaning against the hitchrail in front of the marshal's office.

"We turned 'em back 'n they didn't get one penny from the bank. Not only that, they lost eight men," Hardegree said.

"Eight?" Smoke asked.

"You killed the one in the bell tower, we killed the three who came into the bank, and then those three who were waiting in front of the bank. That's seven, and Doug Miller killed one as they were ridin' out of town."

"How many of our people did we lose?" Smoke asked.

"Four of our people were killed," Hardegree replied. "Ben Pittman and Jack Mitchell, who were the two watchmen, and Edith Warren and her son Kenny. They were shot when the first group rode in from the north."

"I'm sorry," Smoke said.

"Yeah, well, it could have been a lot worse," Hardegree said.

Ten Strike

"What happened? What went wrong?" Rexwell asked. "I heard the bell ringing. Wasn't Taylor supposed to keep that from happening?"

"I imagine Taylor is dead," Hannibal said.

"Yeah, so are Moss, Sutton, Pearson, and Snake Eye Mason, Anderson, Cooper, and Evans," Rexwell said. "Damn, in the last six weeks we've lost a total

of twenty-three men, and even with the new recruits
I brought, we're still down to sixteen!"

"You are right. We need reinforcements," Hannibal said.

"Three of the new replacements I just brought
has been kilt already; so was the two you brought,"
Rexwell said.

"We will get more. There are many would will-
ingly ride for me," Hannibal said.

"Yeah, well, not me. At least, I ain't ridin' with
you no more," Peters said. "Since I joined this
group, you've gotten twenty-three men kilt, just like
Rexwell is sayin'. I don't intend to be number
twenty-four."

When Peters turned to walk away, Hannibal shot
him in the back.

"Unfortunately, Mr. Peters just became number
twenty-four," Hannibal said to the others. "Clearly,
he didn't understand the concept. When you join
the Ghost Riders, you will stay until we break up. So
until that time it will be . . . what? What is our
motto?"

"One for all, and all for one!" the remaining
men shouted.

"Get this man buried," Hannibal said, with a
dismissive wave of his hand.

As the men carried Peters's body away, Rexwell
came over to talk, quietly, with Hannibal.

"We're goin' to have to do somethin' pretty
quick, I think," Rexwell said. "If not, we're likely to
have a few more men walk away, 'n they won't an-
nounce it like Peters done. They'll just leave."

"I've been thinking about another job we can

pull," Hannibal said. "It is a job that promises more profit and less danger than anything else we've done before."

"That sounds good," Rexwell said. "What do you have in mind?"

"I'll tell you when I've got it figured out."

CHAPTER THIRTY-TWO

Brimstone

Smoke and Pearlie were having a beer with Marshal Hardegree and Mark Worley in Devil's Den Saloon.

"This operation was a total failure for Hannibal. And he has lost too many men," Smoke said.

"Do you think the Ghost Riders have been done in?" Worley asked.

"I'm not ready to say that the outfit has been destroyed, but we have done a lot of damage to them, and I expect they are going to have to lick their wounds for a while before they venture out again," Smoke said. "They're not likely to hit Brimstone again."

"Thanks to you two," Hardegree said.

"Not just us, I'd say thanks to the entire town. The way you were organized gave them more than they could handle. Anyway, you don't need us anymore."

"Where will you be going now?" Worley asked.

"I haven't given up on finding Hannibal, but while they are licking their wounds, I think Pearlie and I will go back to my ranch and see how our friend Cal is getting along."

"Smoke, I want to thank you for all you've done for Brimstone. If you two hadn't stopped by when you did, we would have been another Laurette. We lost four of our citizens, but it could have been a lot worse."

Smoke drained the rest of his beer, then nodded at the two men who were sitting at the table with them. "Pearlie and I thank you for the beers," he said.

Sugarloaf Ranch

Cal was sitting out on the front porch when he saw Smoke and Pearlie approaching.

"Miz Sally!" he shouted.

Sally came to the door. "What is it?"

A big smile was spread across Cal's face. "Look." He pointed toward the two riders who were coming up the road from the front gate.

"Oh, it's Smoke!" Sally said happily. She came out onto the front porch and stood at the steps, holding on to one of the supporting posts for the porch.

The two riders rode on up to the house; then Smoke dismounted and handed the reins of Seven to Pearlie. Sally hurried down the steps and they kissed and embraced.

"Hello, Cal," Pearlie said. "Did you miss me?" he asked, teasingly.

"Yeah, like you miss a toothache," Cal replied, laughing.

Pearlie rode toward the barn to take care of the two mounts.

"Well, Cal, how are you getting along?" Smoke asked. "You look a lot better than you did when I left."

"What with all the huggin' 'n kissin' goin' on, I wasn't sure you'd even notice me out here," Cal replied. "But as you can see, I'm comin' along fine."

The front door opened, and Julia stepped out onto the porch.

"Hello, Mr. Jensen."

"It looks like you've been taking pretty good care of your patient," Smoke said.

"She's been taking real good care of me," Cal said, looking up at Julia. Julia walked over and lay her hand on Cal's shoulder. When she did, Cal reached up to take it.

Smoke and Sally exchanged a knowing glance.

"It would seem to me that things have been happening in my absence," Smoke said.

"Things? What things?" Cal asked.

"Oh, just things," Smoke said.

"Maybe," Cal said with a broad smile. "Say, Miz Sally, you know what I'm thinking might be something good to do?"

"I'm not that good at reading most peoples' minds," Sally said. "But I would be willing to guess that what you are thinking about has something to do with food."

"Well, yeah it does. I mean, seein' as Smoke 'n Pearlie are back, don't you think maybe you ought to cook up somethin' special for them? Maybe somethin' like steak and potatoes. And, you know how much Smoke likes apple pie. Why, heck, I'c even peel the apples for you."

"Would you now?"

"Yes, ma'am, and seein' as how I'm almost fully recovered now, I believe I could probably eat steak and baked potatoes and it wouldn't hurt me at all."

"I imagine you could at that. It's the apple pie you might have trouble with."

"What? Why, Miz Sally, you know I could eat apple pie with no problem at all."

Sally laughed. "Now that I think about it, I believe that you might be able to at that."

"Well, all right then," Cal said. "I'll go invite Pearlie."

"Should you be up and around?" Smoke asked.

"Oh, heck yeah, I've been up and around all over the place, haven't I?" Cal asked Sally and Julia.

"We haven't been able to keep him down," Sally said.

Cal found Pearlie giving Seven a rubdown when he reached the barn.

"Miz Sally is cookin' up a big supper for Smoke 'n you, to welcome you back home," Cal said.

"Thanks."

"Don't thank me, I'm not cookin' it. Miz Sally is."

"Yeah, but if I know you, you pro'bly talked her into it."

"Well, yeah, I did do that."

"And it is as much for you as it is for me."

Cal chuckled. "So what if it is? You'll get to enjoy it too."

"That's true."

"What was it like, Pearlie? Did you get them all?"

Pearlie grinned at Cal across Seven's back.

"I won't say that we got 'em all. But I will say that we got our fair share of them," he said.

"I wish I could have been with you."

"Really? You mean you'd rather have been riding all over the country with Smoke and me, than staying here with that pretty girl to look after you?"

"She is pretty, isn't she?"

"You've noticed, have you? Well it's good to see that you're thinking straight again. When we left, I seem to recall that half the time you weren't making any sense at all."

"Yeah, well, I guess I was a little dizzy for a while there. But my mind has all come back to me now."

"How are we supposed to know that? You've never had more than half a mind to begin with," Pearlie teased.

"You better get cleaned up before you come in. Lord, I've never known anyone to set such a store by bein' clean as Julia and Sally when they're together, like they are."

"Oh, Miz Sally, you don't know how much I've missed this," Pearlie said an hour later as he joined the other four around the dining room table. "There isn't anyone in the world who can cook better than you."

"All it is, is steak and potatoes," Sally said. "That's not very hard to prepare."

"And the apple pie. Don't forget the apple pie," Cal said. "It's been a month of Sundays since I had a good apple pie."

"Yeah, the apple pie," Pearlie said. "But I don't know what you are carryin' on about, Cal. While Smoke 'n I were eating camp food and out of restaurants and saloons, you were back here all this time eating Miz Sally's cooking."

"I'll have you know I haven't been eatin' her cooking. Fact is, she's been starvin' me to death, and that's the truth. Tell 'im, Miz Sally. Tell 'im how you were mostly starvin' me to death, givin' me only that hot water you called bouillon, 'til you finally took some pity on me and started feedin' me a little."

"I haven't been starving him to death, but I have been watching what he eats," Sally said.

"Which has been practically nothin' at all," Cal insisted.

"Must we talk about what a Simon Legree I've been?" Sally asked.

"You're right, 'n I'm sorry," Cal said. "I know that you 'n Julia have been taking real good care of me. I just wish I hadn't been shot, so I could have gone with Smoke and Pearlie."

"We've practically cleaned the Ghost Riders out," Pearlie said. "I think it'll be a while before Hannibal decides to hit another town."

"Who?" Julia asked.

"The guy who is leading the Ghost Riders," Pearlie said. "No, he *commands* the Ghost Riders. At least, that's how he has signed all the letters he has written to the editors of the newspapers. 'I am Hannibal, Commandant of the Ghost Riders,' he says."

"Hannibal," Julia said in a weak voice. She got a faraway look in her eyes.

"Well, you do have to give him credit," Smoke said. "He does operate the Ghost Riders as if they are a military unit."

"What does that mean?" Sally asked.

"I'll tell you what Louis Longmont thinks. He thinks our man, Hannibal, might be someone who wanted to be an army officer but never got the chance. He thinks he's frustrated, and he calls himself Hannibal as a way of building himself up."

"Who is Hannibal?" Cal asked. "Does anyone know?"

"That would be Hannibal Barca," Julia said. "Hannibal was a Punic Carthaginian military commander and the greatest military commander in history."

"Yes, that's exactly what Louis said," Smoke said. "I'm impressed, Julia. Of course, nobody knows what this man, Hannibal's real name is."

"I know," Julia said, quietly. "I didn't know before, but I know now."

"You know his name?" Pearlie asked.

"Yes, I'm sorry to say. I know his name."

"Who is it?" Smoke asked.

"His real name is Enid Prescott."

"Enid Prescott?" Cal said. "Julia, isn't he—"

"He is my husband, yes."

LETTER TO THE EDITOR

Dear Editor:

I suffered my first military defeat last week, but what great commander hasn't suffered at least one defeat? What is important, is the ability to learn from that defeat and put those lessons learned into another operation. The great warrior Sun Tzu has penned many precepts, which the wise commander will follow. One such quote reads: "Engage people with what they expect; it is what they are able to discern and confirms their projections. It settles them into predictable patterns of response, occupying their minds while you wait for the extraordinary moment—that which they cannot anticipate."

This will be the guideline for my next military operation.

I am Hannibal,
Commandant of the Ghost Riders.

"What I don't understand," Louis Longmont said, "is why the editors are even bothering to put that son of a bitch's self-aggrandizing letters in their newspapers in the first place. They are just playing up to his sense of self-importance."

"Evidently people are reading his letters," Monte said. "I've even heard that there are some people around the state who regard him as some sort of hero."

"Surely not," Gillespie said. "Who would regard a killer as a hero?"

"Jesse James, Billy the Kid, Clay Allison," Monte said.

"It has been my observation that one can never go wrong in believing in the worst in people," Louis said.

"Smoke, you've been closer to this than any of us," Monte said. "But you've not commented."

The four men were sitting around a table in Longmont's.

"I came home too soon," Smoke said. "I should have stayed out until the job was done."

"Is it true that you have killed twenty-three of Hannibal's men?" Gillespie asked.

"He has lost twenty-three men. I've killed some of them," Smoke said. Smoke had actually killed six-teen of the twenty-three who had been killed, but he didn't give any specific numbers.

"But he has lost twenty-three?"

"Yes."

"Good Lord, how many men does he have, anyway?"

"I don't know," Smoke said. "The last I saw of him, there were close to twenty."

"Do you have any idea where he will strike next?" Monte asked.

"No, I wish I did. I had advance information about Brimstone, so we were able to meet him there and whittle him down some. But as to where he will go next, your opinion would be as good as mine."

"Will you take Pearlie with you?" Monte asked.

"Yes. He has the same commission from the governor that I have. Beside, Pearlie is a good man to have in a pinch."

"What about Cal?"

"Don't think for one minute that Cal wouldn't give his eyeteeth to go. But I don't think he's quite up to it yet."

"How is he coming along?" Monte asked. "I haven't seen him since the day you brought him back into town, all shot up."

"He's doing very well; he's on his feet and moving around. The truth is, if I gave it another couple of weeks, Cal would probably be ready to come with Pearlie and me. But I don't think we have another couple of weeks. I think we need to go back right away, before Prescott is able to recruit any more men."

"Who? Who is Prescott?"

"That's Hannibal's real name," Smoke said. "He is Enid Prescott, and he comes by all his military talk honestly. He is a West Point graduate, and he was a captain when he got cashiered from the army."

Smoke told them everything that Julia had told him, but without giving away where and how he had come by the information.

"Ha!" Louis Longmont said. "I was right then, wasn't I? When I read his very first letter to the editor, I told you that he was a frustrated, would-be army officer. Only thing is, I was thinking he had probably applied for West Point or for a direct commission, but had been denied."

"You were right, Louis," Smoke said.

Louis picked up his wine glass and smiled at the others. "Never underestimate the intelligence of a Frenchman," he said.

"You aren't a Frenchman, Louis, you're a Cajun," Gillespie said with a jibe.

Louis put his hand across his heart. "*Dans mon cœur, je suis Français, donc, mon ami, je suis Français,*" he said.

"Now, how in the hell are we supposed to know what you just said?" Gillespie asked.

"In my heart, I am French. So my friend, I am French," Louis translated.

Ten Strike

Hannibal was reading an article in the *Sorento Sun Times* that had caught his interest. The article told of a shipment of one hundred thousand dollars, by train from Kansas City to a bank in Denver. It would be, the article said, the largest amount of money to be shipped by railroad in over a year.

"Yes!" Hannibal said aloud. He circled the article, then tore the page out of the paper and put it in his pocket.

If he would reduce the number of men sharing in the take to ten and he took three shares, he would come away with thirty thousand dollars. And with thirty thousand dollars he could return to Virginia as a wealthy man. It was very unlikely that anyone there would be aware of the shame of his dishonorable discharge, and nobody back there would have any idea of his time as an outlaw.

He would have enough money to buy a tobacco farm and maybe marry a society woman, just to spite the woman he was married to now.

CHAPTER THIRTY-THREE

Ten Strike

Hannibal had spread a map out on the table and called Rexwell over to show him what he had planned for the next mission.

"Here, between Byers and Bennett," he said, pointing to the map. "The train must cross Kiowa Creek, and this is where we will hit it."

"We've never robbed a train before," Rexwell said.

"We've never had a take of one hundred thousand dollars before, either," Hannibal replied.

"Did you say one hundred thousand dollars?" Rexwell asked with a gasp. "That is a hell of a lot of money!"

"Yes. It is enough that when we divide the money up after this take, I intend to disband the gang. All ten of us can go our own way with enough money to last for nearly a lifetime."

"Ten? There are sixteen of our men left."

"I plan to use only eight men. That will be ten,

counting you and me. Ten men will be more than enough to do the job."

"What about the others?"

"We will select the eight that we want to use," Hannibal said. "But we will tell them they must not share that information with anyone else. Then, I will say that I'm breaking up the gang and everyone must go out now to be on their own. One week later, we will meet in Bennett. I will give further instructions then."

After Hannibal and Rexwell discussed the merits and shortcomings of every remaining man in the Ghost Riders, they chose the eight men they would use: Bart Jennings, Emerson Case, Cole Simpson, Fred Martin, Marv Michaels, Josh Adderley, Walt Breslin, and Gus Kimball. They were called in one at a time, Jennings being the first.

"Jennings," Hannibal said. "I am putting together an elite cadre, and I am limiting it to only eight men. The eight men I am choosing have been selected for their courage, loyalty, and skills. You are one of the men I have chosen . . . that is, if you agree to become a member of the cadre."

"Well, yeah," Jennings said.

"Do not tell anyone else about this conversation."

"All right."

"I am going to team you up with Mo Edwards."

"Uh, Hannibal, I know you are the commander and all, but could you team me up with someone else? Edwards is one of the most worthless sons of bitches I've ever run across."

Hannibal smiled. "That is exactly why I'm teaming you up with him. I will be teaming each of the elite eight men up with one who wasn't selected. After I dismiss everyone, you and Edwards, and the other men and their counterparts, will ride away in teams of two. Once you are alone, you will kill Edwards, then come back here for further instructions."

"All right," Jennings said.

"When I dismiss you, I will be giving each of you one hundred dollars apiece," Hannibal said. "After you kill Edwards, the one hundred dollars I gave him will be yours."

"You won't have any trouble killing Edwards, will you?" Rexwell asked.

"Hell no," Jennings replied with a little laugh. "And the one hundred dollars is just a bonus. I never have liked the son of a bitch anyway."

After Jennings left, Hannibal and Rexwell met with the other seven they had selected and gave them the same instructions. Then Hannibal called everyone together.

"Men, I want to thank each and every one of you for all that you have done. But our losses have been too heavy in the last few weeks, and we failed in our last mission. I fear that we no longer have enough men remaining to carry out the type of operations that we have been conducting.

"One of the best things about operating as we have, is that none of you are known by the law. The only reward posters out are for the Ghost Riders, as a body, and for me, as an individual. And I am known only as Hannibal, which I am sure most of you have gathered by now is not my real name.

"As soon as I dismiss you, I will give each of you

one hundred dollars, at which time you are free to go. You need have no fear about going into any town in the entire state. One of the things I am most proud of is how I have managed to protect your identity. As you leave here, I want you to leave in pairs, at least until you are certain that nobody is following you.

"Goodbye, men, and good luck."

For a moment the men stood in place, as if not quite understanding that they had just been dismissed. Then, the eight men that Hannibal and Rexwell had selected, paired up . . . each of them picking the man who had been assigned to them.

"Come on, Edwards. Let's go somewhere and get us a bottle and a woman," Jennings said.

"What are you teamin' up with me for?" Edwards asked. "I always had the idea you didn't like me."

"Hell, with a bottle and a woman, what's there not to like?" Jennings replied?

Hannibal and Rexwell watched as the men rode off; then they went back into Hannibal's quarters. There, Hannibal took out a bottle of whiskey and poured two glasses.

"A frequently used army toast is 'to absent comrades.' In this case, *to absent comrades* takes on a whole new meaning," he said with a smile, as he held the glass out toward Rexwell.

"To absent comrades," Rexwell replied.

One week later, Hannibal, Rexwell, and the eight men he had kept with him were waiting at a railroad trestle on Kiowa Creek.

"The dynamite is planted," Jennings and Case said.

"We have to time it just perfectly," Hannibal said. "If we blow it too soon, the engineer might see it in time to stop. It is imperative that the engine be derailed."

It was nearly midnight, and there was only a sliver of a moon. From where they were all waiting, they could barely see the trestle.

In the distance, they heard a train whistle.

"Get ready," Hannibal said. "Once it is derailed, shoot anyone who comes out of the train."

By now they could hear the loud puffs of steam, and as the train came around a curve, about half a mile away, they could see the beam of light cast forward from the mirrored reflector of the gas head lamp.

"Wait," Hannibal said as the train drew closer.

Rexwell was holding a match at the ready.

"Now!" Hannibal said.

Rexwell lit the fuse, and it gave off a line of sparks as it quickly worked its way to the trestle.

There was an earth-shaking boom and a brilliant flash of light as the dynamite exploded. The engine plunged over the gap left by the dynamited trestle, then went nose down into the creek, which was about fifteen feet below.

The steam boiler burst with another loud explosion, and a huge cloud of white steam gushed up from the engine.

The coal tender and the express car also plunged

down the embankment, and the express car turned over onto its side, with the door down.

"Damn!" Rexwell said. "How the hell are we going to get into the express car now?"

"What do we do, Hannibal?" Jennings asked.

"The only thing we can do now," Hannibal said. "We'll rob the passengers. I want two men in each of the cars; one will go in the front, the other in the back. Let's move quickly while they are still disoriented from the crash."

The ten men moved onto the cars, some of which were derailed, but all of which were upright. Because it was the middle of the night, the first three of the five cars were made into sleeper berths, and the sleeping occupants had been thrown from their berths. There were several injuries as a result.

Hannibal and Case boarded the first car, Hannibal from the front and Case from the back. As soon as they stepped into the car, they could hear the moaning of the injured. Hannibal fired into the roof.

"I'm going to be coming through the car asking for all your money," he said. "And I will kill anyone who doesn't comply."

It was dark in the car, the gimbal lanterns having been extinguished in the wreck. The darkness worked to Hannibal's advantage because no one could see him until he was right on them. All of the passengers were too disoriented to resist, and he and Case, who was on the car with him, collected from everyone.

The two train robbers in the last car were less

fortunate. That was a day car, it had not left the track, and the lanterns had not been extinguished.

"Ghost Riders!" someone shouted, seeing the red armbands.

"This is a holdup!" Marv Michaels shouted. "Have your money out as we come—"

That was as far as he got before being shot by three of the passengers, who had figured out what was going on and armed themselves. They also shot Josh Adderly, the robber who had come in through the rear door of the car.

Ten minutes later, Hannibal, now outside and mounted, fired three shots into the air, the agreed upon signal to recover. Only six more men returned.

"Where are Michaels and Adderly?" Rexwell asked.

"I think they was both shot," Kimball said.

"Move out!" Hannibal ordered.

From the *Big Rock Journal:*

GHOST RIDERS ROB TRAIN
IN ARAPAHOE COUNTY

Lacking fifteen minutes of midnight on Tuesday last, a band of outlaws, believed to be the Ghost Riders, dynamited a trestle across Kiowa Creek. The resultant explosion wrecked the train, killing the engineer, fireman, and express messenger. The express car turned over, door-side down, so that the robbers were unable to access the safe, which contained a shipment of one hundred thousand dollars going from Kansas City to a bank in Denver.

The only option left for making their perfidious deed profitable was to move through the cars, robbing the passengers. This they did, shooting six of the passengers in the process, five of whom died. It is believed that their take was quite small. They also lost two of their number, the outlaws killed by armed passengers.

Sugarloaf

"Why can't I go with you?" Cal asked.

"Cal, you're a good man, and if you were fully re-covered, I wouldn't think of going without you," Smoke replied. "But to be honest, if you went with us now, you would be more of a hindrance than a help. There would come a time when either Pearlie or I would have to cover for you. And that could put all of us in danger."

Cal was quiet for moment before he responded. "You're right."

"Smoke do you have any idea where this Hannibal is?" Sally asked.

"No," Smoke said.

"Julia has something she would like to propose to you."

"I know Enid," Julia said. "I imagine I know him better than anyone. He is a very self-centered person, as I am sure you have gathered from the letters he has written to the newspapers. He likes to be in control, and when something happens that he can't control, he gets very upset."

"So, what do you have in mind?" Smoke asked.

"I want to write a letter to the newspapers. I think if I expose him, it will make him angry enough to do something very dumb, perhaps even dumb enough to get him caught."

Smoke smiled.

"Yeah," he said. "Yeah, do that."

LETTER TO THE EDITOR

Dear Editor:

My name is Julia Prescott. I am married to the man who calls himself Hannibal and who is the head of the band of murderers known as the Ghost Riders.

Hannibal's real name is Enid Prescott, formerly Captain Prescott of the U.S. Army, Second Dragoons, Fort Laramie. It is to my shame that my husband was reduced to the rank of private, then dishonorably discharged from the army for stealing army rifles and selling them on the civilian market.

Ironically, Enid is a West Point graduate, a fine school with the motto of "Duty, Honor, Country." Enid Prescott failed to do his duty; he was, and continues to be, a dishonorable man, and he is at war with his country.

I know that this disreputable man reads the newspapers and especially the letters to the editors, as he has penned so many of them himself. Therefore I am using this letter as a means of communicating directly with him.

Enid, if there is one iota remaining of the West Point cadet who was so full of promise and idealism, the cadet with whom I fell in love, please stop the killing. It is not too late for you to recover some of the honor you once had.

With hope that you will do the right thing,
I remain,
Your wife, Julia Prescott.

CHAPTER THIRTY-FOUR

"Seven hundred and two dollars? That's it? That's all we got? What happened to the one hundred thousand we were supposed to get?" Kimball asked.

"You saw what happened," Rexwell said. "How were we supposed to get into the car?"

"I won't take my full share," Hannibal said. "We will divide this money equally, and with Michaels and Adderly both dead, that gives us almost eighty-eight dollars apiece. But don't worry, I will come up with another plan for us. One that will be most profitable."

Hannibal relaxed his rules slightly and allowed the remaining six men, of the eight he had chosen, to go into town. That left only him and Rexwell at the mine.

"Do you have any ideas?" Rexwell asked.

"Nothing at the moment. But I will come up with something."

"Uh, Captain Prescott?" Rexwell said.

Hannibal looked up quickly. "What did you just call me?"

"I called you Captain Prescott," Rexwell said. "Is that your name, sir?"

Prescott closed his eyes and pinched the bridge of his nose. "I thank you for not sharing that information with any of the others. How long have you known?"

"I didn't find out until this morning," Rexwell said.

"This morning? How did you find out this morning?"

"It's in the paper," Rexwell said. He walked over to the table and picked up the *Sorento Sun Times*. It had been there for some time, but Prescott had not yet gotten around to reading it.

Prescott read the letter to the editor, then slapped the paper down hard. He knew for a fact that news of the Ghost Riders had appeared in newspapers all over the country. Like Jesse James, Billy the Kid, and other famous outlaws, Hannibal had become a national celebrity. He didn't mind the celebrity as long as nobody knew his real identity, but because of his notoriety, this letter would appear in newspapers all over America, including Virginia.

That meant that any plans he might have ever had about retiring in anonymity in Virginia were no longer possible.

"That bitch!" he said. "I should have killed her when I had the chance. I have no idea where she is now, or I would still do it."

"I know where she is," Rexwell said. "She is in Big Rock."

"What? How do you know that?"

Rexwell pointed to a line above the letter.

From the Big Rock Journal.

"I'll be damned," Prescott said. Looking up, he smiled. "We're going to Big Rock."

Site of the train wreck

Smoke and Pearlie were there as a steam-powered crane worked to clear away the engine, tender, and express car. A large hole had already been cut in the upward-facing side of the overturned express car, and it was then that the rescuers learned that the express messenger had been killed in the crash. The money was still there though, and it was removed and taken to Denver, its original destination.

"Here's where the horses were," Pearlie said, seeing a few piles of horse droppings. "They left going in that direction, but there's no way we'll be able to track them too far."

"Pearlie, look at this," Smoke said, picking up a tear sheet from a newspaper. He looked at it for a moment, then smiled. "The article about the one-hundred-thousand-dollar shipment is circled."

"Yeah," Pearlie said.

"We're going to Sorento."

"Why Sorento?"

"Look at the folio on that page."

"The what?"

"The folio. That's the very first line at the top of the page, with the page number, the date, and the name of the newspaper. As you can see, this page came from the *Sorento Sun Times*."

Pearlie laughed. "Where did you learn about folio? Never mind, it had to be from Miz Sally."

"Why, Pearlie, do you think I can't find out things like that on my own?"

"You did?"

"Yeah," Smoke said. "I asked Sally." He laughed. "Come on, we've got a fairly long ride ahead of us."

Sorento

"Ghost Riders?" Sheriff Norton said in reply to Smoke's question. Smoke had identified himself as a Colorado Ranger when he asked the question.

"Sure, I've heard of them. Who hasn't? But we've been very fortunate, they haven't bothered us any."

"Is there anything here that you think would attract them?" Smoke asked.

"I wouldn't think so. We're a small town with very little to offer any marauding outlaws, I'm afraid. Oh, we do have the Ten Strike Mine, but it hasn't paid off yet."

"Ten Strike?"

"It's a mine about four miles south of town. It was actually abandoned about five years ago, but recently some investors have been trying to make it pay again. Supposedly, there is an untapped silver vein, but I don't think they've found it yet. They are paying their workers well though."

"How well?"

"I don't know, exactly. But it must be fairly well. When the miners come to town they always seem to have a lot of money, at least they spend a lot in the saloons, the restaurants, and in the grocery stores."

"What kind of men are they?" Smoke asked.

"Oh, they are quite well behaved. They have never given anyone the slightest bit of trouble. The truth is, Ranger, they have been a boon for the community, and we've been just real glad to have them here."

"Have you ever been out to the mine to have a look around?"

"Oh, no," Sheriff Norton said. "They won't allow it."

"They won't allow it? Why not?"

"From what I understand, all their money is coming from investors back East. It must be, because as I said, the mine hasn't produced anything yet."

"All right, Sheriff, thanks for the information, you've been a big help."

"Ranger Jensen, do you think the Ghost Riders might be coming here? Do you think I should get people ready for them, the way they did in Brimstone?" Sheriff Norton asked. "I read about what happened to them over there."

"I'm not sure but what they have already been here, Sheriff," Smoke said. He showed Sheriff Norton the newspaper page he had found at the site of the train wreck.

"I'll be damned," Sheriff Norton said, genuinely surprised. "That's our local paper."

"Yes, it is."

"But, Ranger, I know nearly everyone in the whole county. I don't see how such a group could be here without me knowing about it."

"Tell me about your miners. Anything stand out about any of them?"

"No, sir. It's like I said, they have never given us one bit of trouble."

"I'm going to take a chance and describe one of them to you," Smoke said. "I'm choosing him because he's pretty distinctive looking, and if you have seen him, you would remember it."

Smoke described Rexwell to him, but even before he finished the description, Sheriff Norton was nodding his head.

"Yes, yes," he said. "One of the men looks just like that."

"I thought so," Smoke said.

"You're going out to the mine, aren't you?"

"Yes."

"Do you want me to go with you?"

"No, I won't be alone."

After getting directions to the mine, Smoke and Pearlie rode out, approaching it not from the town but from the front range of the Vazquez Mountains. They looked down on the mine from the top of Byers Peak.

"I don't a see sign of life," Pearlie said, "not a person, not even a horse."

"It does look deserted," Smoke said. "Let's go down there and have a closer look, but be on the lookout."

The two men rode down a trail until they reached the buildings—one long bunkhouse and a smaller building that was separated from the others. The door was standing open on the smaller building.

"Smoke, there's nobody here," Pearlie said.

Dismounting, they approached the smaller building, doing so cautiously, guns drawn and alert for anything. They got all the way to the building, then stepped inside.

There were a few empty cans scattered around and some papers on the small table. Smoke went over to examine them.

"There's certainly no question as to who wrecked the train," Smoke said. "Here's a map of the railroad from Arapaho all the way to Denver. And he has the trestle at Kiowa Creek marked."

"Smoke, look at this," Pearlie said. Pearlie was over by the bunk, and he was holding a newspaper.

"What is it?"

"It's the letter that Julia wrote."

"Then he did see it."

"Yeah, but look at what it says right here."

Smoke walked over to the bunk, and Pearlie pointed to the first line.

From the Big Rock Journal.

"Damn, Pearlie! That's where they've gone!"

Big Rock

Prescott had his remaining men camp out while he and Rexwell went into town on what Prescott called a "reconnoitering mission." Their first stop was at the Brown Dirt Saloon.

Buying a couple of beers, Prescott and Rexwell took an empty table near the piano, which was silent at the moment. Two of the bar girls approached them with practiced smiles.

"Oh, I don't think I've ever seen either one of you in here before," one of the girls said.

"That's because we've never been in here before," Prescott replied. He smiled. "But I appreciate the greeting. What would it take for you young ladies to have a few drinks and visit with us?"

"Honey, we'll visit with you as long as you buy the drinks," one of the girls said. "My name is Lucille, and this is Marylou. What's your name?"

"I'm Bob, this is my friend, Pat," Prescott said. "Get yourself a couple of drinks and come on back."

The girls came back to the table, and Prescott began talking to them, entertaining them with stories and even telling a few jokes. Not until he had them in a real conversational mood, did he start asking specific questions.

"By the way, I'm looking for my sister. She wrote me a letter and told me she was here in Big Rock, but she didn't give me her address. And I have no idea where she might be."

"Honey, to be honest with you, we don't meet many of the ladies of the town. They . . . uh . . . don't socialize with women like us, if you know what I mean."

"Oh, Julia isn't that kind. I don't think she's ever met anyone she didn't like."

"Julia?" Marylou said. "Lucille, isn't that the name of the girl Doctor Urban was talking about?"

"Yes, Doc Urban did say her name was Julia. Julia McGill . . . McMillian . . . something like that."

"McKnight?" Prescott asked.

"Yes, that's it! Doc Urban said she was a very fine

nurse and, after she got finished out at Sugarloaf, he might try and hire her."

"What do you mean, finished out at Sugarloaf?" Prescott asked.

"She's looking after Cal Wood. He was shot over in Brown Spur," Marylou said.

"By the Ghost Riders," Lucille added.

"The Ghost Riders? Who are the Ghost Riders?" Prescott asked.

"Oh, honey, you mean you've never heard of the Ghost Riders? They're led by a man named Hannibal," Lucille said.

"No, they aren't," Marylou said. "Didn't you read that letter that Hannibal's wife wrote to the newspaper? She said his name was Enos something."

"Yeah, that's right. Turns out he was kicked out of the army for something. Anyway, you say you've never heard of the Ghost Riders? Why, I thought ever'one in Colorado had heard of them."

"Well, that's why we've never heard of them, I expect," Prescott said. "We're up from Texas, just passing through on our way to Wyoming. But I thought I would stop and visit with my sister for a bit."

"Oh, I'm sure she would love that. And I'm sure Mrs. Jensen would make you feel right at home. You know when I said that none of the ladies of town would have anything to do with girls like us? Well, Mrs. Jensen isn't like that. She's sweet to everybody," Lucille said.

"Jensen," Prescott said.

"Yes, she's married to Smoke Jensen. I'm sure

you've heard of him. He's a famous man," Marylou said. "Sugarloaf? That's Smoke Jensen's ranch."

"And it's a big ranch too," Lucille said. "Why, I bet it's the biggest ranch in all of Colorado."

Prescott nodded at Rexwell, who hadn't said a word during Prescott's inquisition.

"Ladies, you have been very good company, but we must be going now. I do want to stop in and see my sister. How do we get to this ranch, Sugarloaf?"

"You just go west for about seven miles, and you can't miss it," Lucille said. "There is a huge arched gateway with the name stretched out all across the road."

"Thanks."

CHAPTER THIRTY-FIVE

Sugarloaf Ranch

"Miz Sally, I was just out to the bunkhouse, and here's nobody there," Cal said. "Where is everybody?"

"Smoke sold a hundred head to Elmer Altman. They were taking them over to him. They'll be back tomorrow."

"Heck, I could have gone with them."

"You probably could have, but there was no need for you to. Don't you trust Billy Stone?"

"Well, yeah, he's a good man. But—"

Sally laughed. "Don't worry, Cal. Your position is safe."

"I know that, it's just that—"

"It's just what?"

"Miz Sally, for the last several weeks, I haven't done anything to earn my keep here. You and Julia have been doin' everything. Smoke and Pearlie are out chasing down the Ghost Riders. You 'n

Julia are cookin', cleanin', 'n tendin' to me, and haven't done a lick of work around the ranch."

"I'm sure that when Smoke gets back, he'll have plenty for you to do," Sally said.

"I hope so, Miz Sally. I mean I—" Whatever Cal was about to say was interrupted by the crash of a bullet through the kitchen window. It plunged into the wall on the opposite side of the room.

"Oh! What was that?" Julia cried.

Several bullets crashed through the windows then, and they heard the sound of gunfire from outside.

Cal ran to Julia and pulled her down. He didn't have to do that for Sally, her instincts, honed by her years with Smoke, kicked in, and she was on the floor after the first shot.

"Cal, into the library!" Sally called.

"Yes, ma'am," Cal replied. He knew exactly what Sally was referring to. There was a gun case in the library with two Winchester rifles. "Julia, stay down low, like this," Cal said.

Cal led the way, slithering along the floor on his stomach, and Julia, following his lead, was right behind him. Sally brought up the rear.

When they reached the library, Cal took the rifle down while Sally opened a drawer and took out two boxes of shells.

"If we can get upstairs, we'll be able to shoot down on them," Sally said.

"Who is it?" Julia asked. "Who is shooting at us?"

"Honey, Smoke has made almost as many enemies as he has friends," Sally said. "It could be anybody."

The three hurried up the back set of stairs to the

op floor; all the while bullets continued to fly in
hrough the downstairs windows.

"I'll take our bedroom, you take Julia's bed-
oom," Sally said.

"Julia, come with me," Cal said.

When they reached Julia's bedroom, Cal pointed
o the side of the bed that was away from the win-
ows.

"Stay down behind the bed, and don't lift your
ead up for anything," he said. "You'll be safe there."

Julia nodded, then got into position. Cal moved
o the window and saw someone running toward
1e barn. He raised his rifle, but before he could
1ke a shot, he heard the bark of Sally's rifle, and
1e man went down.

Cal saw someone stick his head above a water-
1g trough, and he took a shot. Now there were two
own. There was still shooting coming from outside
1e house, and because it was coming from sev-
1ral different positions, he knew there were several
1ore.

"Smoke Jensen!" someone called from outside
1e house. The voice came from the corner of the
nokehouse.

"Go away!" Sally shouted down. "Smoke isn't
ere!"

"I don't believe you!"

"God in heaven, no!" Julia said.

"Julia, what is it? Have you been hit?" Cal called,
1xiously.

"That's Enid Prescott!" Julia said. "That's my
usband."

Cal fired in the direction of the smokehouse,

and he saw a chip of wood from the bullet strike, but he knew he hadn't hit Prescott.

Several more shots were exchanged.

"Mrs. Jensen, I have a proposal to make!" The call came from the smokehouse, but Prescott didn't present himself.

"I'm not interested in any proposals!" Sally called back.

"I know that my wife is in there," Prescott said. "If you send her out, I will go away."

"If you think I'm going to send this girl out to you, you are crazy!" Sally shouted down.

"She is my wife!" Prescott said. "You have no right to keep her away from me!"

Cal and Sally answered Prescott's demand with more shooting.

"Mrs. Jensen, if you don't send my wife out to me, I am going to have my men burn the house down. You can't cover all sides of it, you know."

Cal saw one more of the men raise his head from behind the well, and taking a shot, he had the satisfaction of seeing a spray of blood fly into the air.

"I have lost three of my men to you!" Prescott shouted. "I have no intention of losing another man. If you don't send my wife out to me within the next one minute, I *will* set fire to your house! That is a promise, Mrs. Jensen, it isn't a threat."

"No! Don't burn the house down! It's me you want, not them!"

The words came from outside, and raising up

Cal saw that Julia had left the bedroom and was now walking across the yard toward Prescott.

"Julia! No! Come back!" Cal called down to her.

Cal dropped the rifle, and with pistol in hand, ran down the stairs taking them two at a time.

"Tell me, Julia. Did you really think that I would let you get away with writing that letter?" Prescott asked.

There was a shot fired from the corner of the smokehouse, and Julia went down.

"No!" Cal shouted, in an anguished cry. "Prescott, I'm coming after you, you son of a bitch!"

"Cal, no!" Sally called.

Smoke and Pearlie had heard the shooting a quarter of a mile before they reached the arched gateway.

"Come on!" Smoke shouted, and with guns drawn the two men galloped under the arch and the last one hundred yards up to the buildings. They saw three men with their backs to them, and they felt no compunctions about firing. All three men went down. A fourth turned toward them, and Smoke recognized Rexwell. He fired and Rexwell went down.

By now Cal was outside and running toward Prescott who, seeing that all his men had been killed, stepped out from the corner of the smokehouse and started toward Cal with his hands up in the air.

"I surrender! I surrender!" he shouted.

"The hell you do, you son of a bitch!" Cal replied in a low, menacing voice.

Cal fired once, and a spray of blood came from Prescott's left arm.

"Don't shoot! Don't shoot! I give up!" Prescott said. Only one arm was raised now; his left arm, the one Cal had shot, was dangling by his side.

Cal's second shot hit Prescott in his right arm, and now both arms were down.

"No, please! Don't shoot me again!" Prescott begged.

Cal shot again, hitting him in his left knee, and Prescott screamed in pain.

Cal's next shot hit Prescott in his right knee, and he staggered, but didn't fall.

"I want you to know, you son of a bitch, that I'm not really that bad of a shot. I hit you exactly where I intended to hit you."

Cal fired one more time, and a black hole appeared in Prescott's forehead as he fell back.

Throwing his gun aside, Cal hurried over to Julia, but Sally was already there, and she was holding Julia's head in her lap.

"Julia! Julia!" Cal called, dropping to his knees beside her.

Julia tried to lift her hand, and Cal grabbed it and lifted it to his lips.

"Cal, I love you," she said.

"And I love you! Don't die, Julia, please, don't die!"

"It won't be so bad, Cal," Julia said with a smile. "Now I really will be your angel."

Julia took a final breath; then her head slumped to one side.

"Julia!" the anguished cry came from Cal's very soul.

"I'm sorry, Cal," Sally said. "She's gone."

Cal hung his head and wept.

TURN THE PAGE
FOR AN EXCITING PREVIEW!

A boy with a borrowed badge. An Indian lawman with a new kind of firearm. And an outlaw gang that wants these pilgrims dead. WILLIAM W. JOHNSTONE *and* J. A. JOHNSTONE *tell the story of the frontier in a brilliant new series based on the guns of the West— and those who used them to survive.*

It's a repeater. It's a shotgun.
In the wrong hands, it's one deadly weapon.

Young James Mann came from Texas to find his missing uncle in the lawless Indian Territory. Then the boy's father came after him. Now they've earned the wrath of the vicious McCoy-Maxwell gang, who are about to pull off their most savage attack. But the Manns of Texas have a secret weapon: a deputy marshal named Jackson Sixpersons. While repeating rifles are spreading across the frontier, Sixpersons carries an oddity: a 12-gauge, lever-action Winchester shotgun. Soon Sixpersons will use his smoothbore to blow a hole in the outlaw gang. And when the gun smoke and blood clear, a boy must pick up the gun and use it like a man . . . to kill.

WINCHESTER 1887

by *USA TODAY* AND *NEW YORK TIMES*
BEST-SELLING AUTHORS
WILLIAM W. JOHNSTONE
with J. A. Johnstone

On sale now, wherever Pinnacle Books are sold.

PROLOGUE

Tascosa, Texas, late spring 1895

He swore softly and chuckled again. "That was . . . some . . . journey."

And Jimmy Mann closed his eyes one last time.

CHAPTER ONE

Randall County, Texas

Usually, Millard Mann found the sight of his home comforting—not that it was much of a place. A converted boxcar, the wheelbase and carriage long carried off, the rooms separated by rugs or blankets. The only heat came from a Windsor range, and when it turned cold—winters could be brutal—there wasn't much heat.

But the lodging came free, compliments of the Fort Worth–Denver City Railroad, although Millard figured he and his family would be moving on before too long. He wasn't even sure if he would get paid again since the railroad had entered receivership—whatever that was—during the Panic a couple years back, and although it was being reorganized . . . well . . . Millard sighed.

The landscape didn't look any better than that makeshift home. Bleak and barren was the Texas Panhandle. Rugged, brutal. Sometimes he wished the white men hadn't driven the Comanches and Kiowas out of it.

His horse snorted. He closed his eyes, trying to summon up the courage he would need to face his family. His wife stood down there, trying to hang clothes on the line that stretched from the boxcar's grab irons to the corral fence. She fought against that fierce wind, which always blew, hot during the summer, cold during the winter. Out there, the calendar revealed only two seasons, summer and winter, the weather always extreme.

Libbie, his wife, must have sensed him. She turned, lowering a union suit into the basket of clothes and dodging a blue and white striped shirt that slapped at her face with one of its sleeves. Looking up, she shielded her eyes from the sun.

Again, his horse snorted. Millard lowered his hand, which brushed against the stock of the Winchester Model 1886 lever-action rifle in the scabbard. A lump formed in his throat. He grimaced, and once again had to stop the tears that wanted to flood down his beard-stubbled face.

He would not cry. He could not cry. He was too old to cry.

Facing Libbie was one thing. He could do that, could tell her about Jimmy, his kid brother. He could even handle his two youngest children, Kris and Jacob. But facing James? Sighing, Millard muttered a short prayer, and kicked the horse down what passed in those parts for a mesa, leaning back in the saddle and giving the horse plenty of rein to pick its own path down the incline.

He figured Libbie would be smiling, stepping

away from the laundry, calling toward the boxcar. Yet Millard couldn't hear her voice, the wind carrying her words south across the Llano Estacado, Texas's Staked Plains in the Panhandle. Kris, the girl, and Jacob, the youngest, appeared in the boxcar's "front" door and then leaped onto the ground.

The horse's hoofs clopped along. Millard's face tightened.

Next, James Mann, strapping and good-looking at seventeen years old, stepped into the doorway, left open to allow a breeze through the stifling boxcar.

The sight of his oldest son caused Millard to suck in a deep breath. His heart felt as if a Comanche lance had pierced it. James looked just like his uncle, Millard's brother, Jimmy. Millard and Libbie had named their firstborn after Millard's youngest brother. Millard himself was the middle-born. The only son of Wilbur and Lucretia Mann left alive.

His wife's face lost its joy, its brightness, when Millard rode close enough for her to read his face, and she quickly moved over to stand between Kris and Jacob, putting hands on the children's shoulders. James had started for him, but also stopped, probably detecting something different, something foreboding, in his father.

"Whoa, boy." Millard reined in the horse and made himself take a deep breath.

"Hi, Pa!" Kris sang out.

Even that did not boost Millard's spirits.

"What is it?" his wife asked. "What's the matter?"

He shot a glance at the sheathed rifle and then

lifted his gaze, first at Libbie, but finally finding his oldest son.

Their eyes locked.

Millard dismounted. "It's Jimmy."

Jimmy Mann, the youngest of the Mann brothers, had been a deputy U.S. marshal in the Western District of Arkansas including the Indian Nations, the jurisdiction of Judge Isaac Parker, the famous "Hanging Judge" based in Fort Smith, Arkansas. Jimmy had been around thirty-five years old when he had ridden up to the boxcar Millard and his family called home sometime late summer. When was that? Millard could scarcely believe it. Not even a full year ago.

Sitting at the table, he glanced around what they used as the kitchen. It was hard to remember all the particulars, but James had been playing that little kids game with his younger siblings, using the Montgomery Ward & Co. catalog to pick out gifts they would love for Christmas—James doing it to pacify Jacob and Kris. Millard had been on some stretch of the railroad, and Libbie had been in McAdam, a block of buildings and vacant lots that passed for a town and served as a stop on the railroad.

Jimmy, taking a leave from his marshaling job, had found Millard, and they had ridden home together, to surprise the children. James had been interested in a rifle sold by the catalog, a Winchester Model 1886 repeating rifle in .45-70 caliber.

Millard frowned. What was it Jimmy had said in jest? Oh, yeah. "In case y'all get attacked by a herd of dragons . . ." Millard smiled at the memory.

Most rifles out there were .44 caliber or thereabouts. A .45-70 was used in the Army or in old buffalo rifles, and those were single shots. The Winchester '86 was the first successful repeating rifle strong enough to handle that big a load.

Millard's weary smile faded. A rifle like that would cost a good sum even considering the discounted prices at Montgomery Ward, but Jimmy had given James a lesson shooting Jimmy's Winchester '73 .44-40-caliber carbine. Millard couldn't understand it, but there had always been a strong bond between James and his uncle. Jimmy had always seen something in Millard's son that, try as he might, Millard just could not find.

His right hand left his coffee cup and fell against the mule-ear pocket of his trousers and Jimmy's badge that was inside. His eyes closed as he remembered Jimmy's dying words back on that hilltop cemetery in Tascosa.

"You'll give . . . this to . . . James . . . you hear?"

Millard looked again at the beaten-up Winchester '86. Jimmy's head was cradled by that sharpshooting cardsharper Shirley Something-or-other. He couldn't recall her last name, and never quite grasped the relationship between her and his brother. But he knew that rifle. Jimmy had tracked the notorious outlaw Danny Waco across half the West trying to get that rifle. Danny Waco's lifeless, bloody body lay in a crimson lake just a few feet from Jimmy.

Millard said softly, "I hear you."

Other men from Tascosa climbed up the hill. Waco and some of his boys had tried robbing the bank, only to get shot to pieces. Jimmy would have—could have—killed Waco in town, but some kid got in the way. Jimmy took a bullet that would have killed the boy, and then went after Waco.

Jimmy killed Waco, but Waco's bullet killed Jimmy Mann.

Death rattled in Jimmy's throat. Townspeople and lawmen stopped gawking and gathered around . . . like vultures . . . to watch Jimmy breathe his last.

"Might give . . . him my . . . badge, too." The end for Jimmy Mann was coming quickly.

Millard didn't see how his kid brother had even managed to get that far.

"Maybe . . . Millard, you . . ." Jimmy coughed, but once that spell passed, his eyes opened and he said, "Gonna be . . . one . . . cold . . . winter." He shivered. "Already . . . freezing."

On that day, the temperature in Tascosa topped ninety degrees. Winter would come, but not for several months.

"You rest, Jimmy," Millard said. The next words were the hardest he ever spoke. "You deserve a long rest, Brother. You've traveled far."

Millard had learned just how far. From the Cherokee Nation in Indian Territory to Kansas, north to Nebraska, into the Dakotas, to Wyoming, New Mexico, and finally in the Texas Panhandle. Chasing Danny Waco and the Winchester '86 that the outlaw had stolen during a train holdup in Indian Territory.

If only he had ordered that foolish long gun from the catalog, but Jimmy knew how tight money came with Millard. Through his connections in Arkansas and the Indian Nations, Jimmy had promised that he could find a rifle cheaper than even Montgomery Ward offered.

That had brought the oldest Mann brother, Borden, into the mix.

He'd worked for the Adams Express Company, usually traveling on Missouri-Kansas-Texas Railroad—commonly known as the Katy—trains. In Parsons, Kansas, he had found the rifle, not a .45-70—which Millard thought too much rifle for his son—but a .50-100-450, one of the first Winchester had produced in that massive caliber.

Jimmy and Borden had decided it would be a fine joke, sending that cannon of a rifle to their nephew. So Borden agreed to take it by rail and have it shipped up to McAdam for James.

It never made it. Danny Waco had robbed the train and killed Borden. Murdered him. With the big rifle.

It was why Jimmy had trailed Danny Waco for so many months, miles, and lives.

Again, Millard thought back to that awful day on that bloody hill in Tascosa.

* * *

"He'll be a better man than me, Millard," Jimmy said. "Me and . . . you . . . both. Badge and . . . this rifle. You hear?"

"I hear."

Heard, yes. Millard could hear his brother. But understand him? No, not really.

"That was . . . some . . . journey," Jimmy said, and then he was gone.

Millard could hear the younger ones, Jacob and Kris, sobbing through the old blankets that separated the kitchen from the children's bedroom, Libbie trying to comfort them. James sat across the table from Millard, tears streaming down his cheeks. Sad, but his eyes were cold, piercing, frightening. Like Jimmy's could be when he got riled.

"Where is he?" James said at last.

Millard frowned. "We buried him. In Tascosa."

"You left him there?" James sprang out of the chair, knocking it over, bracing himself against the table with his hands.

The crying in the children's room stopped.

"Yes," was all Millard said.

James swore.

Millard let it pass, no matter how much that language would offend Libbie.

"You told me yourself that Tascosa's dying, won't be anything but memories and dust in a year or two. Why did you bury Uncle Jimmy there? Why didn't you bring him home?"

Because, Millard thought, *in a year or two, all that will be left here are memories and dust.* "It's not where a man's buried. Or how. It's how he died that matters. More important, it's how he lived. You've got your memories. So have I."

Reluctantly, he pushed the rifle toward his son. "He wanted you to have this."

"I don't want it." Tears fell harder, and James had to look away, wipe his face, and blow his nose.

"I don't have any shells for it," Millard said.

"I don't want it." The anger returned. His son whirled. "I want Uncle Jimmy. I want him alive. You don't know how it feels. I lost—"

"I feel a lot more pain than you, boy." Millard came to his feet, only the rickety table separating the two hotheads. Out of the corner of his eye, he saw the curtain move, saw Libbie's face, the worry in her eyes. He ignored his wife.

"You lost your uncle. I lost Jimmy, my kid brother. I also lost Borden, my big brother. Two brothers. Dead. Murdered. Because of this gun! Because—" He stopped himself, choked back the words that would have cursed him for the rest of his life.

Because you wanted this gun.

He started to sink back into the chair then remembered something else. His hand slid into the pocket and withdrew the badge, a tarnished six-point star. He dropped it on the table, read the black letters stamped into the piece of tin.

DEPUTY
U.S.
MARSHAL

"Jimmy wanted you to have this, too," Millard said. He had to sit. His legs couldn't support his weight anymore.

James Mann sat, too, after he righted the chair he had knocked over.

Letting out a sigh of relief, Libbie returned to comforting Kris and Jacob.

"The man who killed Uncle Borden—" James began, but stopped.

"Danny Waco," Millard said numbly. "Rough as a cob, a cold-blooded killer. Posters on him from Texas to Montana, and as far west, probably, as Arizona Territory. He killed Jimmy, too, but Jimmy got him." *Revenge,* Millard thought. *Was it worth it?*

"He took a bullet, Jimmy did, that would've killed a kid. Stopped a bank robbery. Stopped Waco. The law's been trying that for a number of years. Folks in Tascosa, even Amarillo, said Jimmy was a hero. Died a hero."

The curtain drew open, and Libbie came into the kitchen, her arms around Jacob, a sobbing Kris close behind.

"Maybe," Kris said, "maybe we can buy a monument—one of those big marble stones—and put it on Uncle Jimmy's grave."

"Maybe," Millard said. Jimmy's grave had been marked with only a busted-up Winchester, another '86, that he had used, somehow, to end Danny Waco's life. Not even a crude wooden cross or his name carved into a piece of siding.

"Put a gun on it," Jacob said, still sniffling.

"Maybe." Millard managed a smile.

"A gun on a tombstone?" Kris barked at her brother.

"Uncle Jimmy liked guns!" Jacob snapped back.

"That's ridiculous," Kris chided.

"Hush," Libbie said.

The children obeyed. Millard stared at his oldest son, who sat fingering the badge, his shoulders slumped, at long last accepting the fact that Jimmy Mann was indeed dead, wouldn't be coming back ever again.

Jacob became interested in the badge and left Libbie's side. He moved toward his big brother and looked at the piece of tin. "Why'd Uncle Jimmy want you to have this?"

James didn't answer, probably had not even heard, and Jacob looked at his father for an answer.

"I'm not sure," Millard said.

"Uncle Jimmy didn't make James a lawman, did he?" Jacob asked.

Millard tried to smile, but his lips wouldn't cooperate. His head shook. "No, he couldn't deputize anyone. At least, not officially."

"Was Uncle Jimmy a good lawman?" Kris asked.

Millard shrugged. "I reckon. He did it for some time."

"Can we go see his grave?" Jacob asked.

"Sure. Sometime." Millard, however, had little interest in seeing the dead. Maybe that was why he left Jimmy in Tascosa. He had not gone to Borden's funeral, mainly because of the expense and time such a journey to the Midwest would have taken. He had never been to the graves of his parents.

Never had he cottoned to the idea of talking over a grave. The dead, he figured, had better things to listen to than the ramblings of some old relation.

James left the boxcar without speaking.

"Where's Jimmy going?" Jacob asked.

"James," his sister corrected. "You know he don't like being called Jimmy. That was Uncle—" She stopped and brushed back a tear.

"But where . . . ?"

"Just for a walk," Libbie answered with a sigh, stepping toward the open doorway.

Alone with his grief.

Millard felt some relief. His son had walked out with the badge, turned toward the corral. Walking away his troubles, his thoughts. But at least—and this really made Millard feel better—James had left the .50-caliber Winchester '86 on the table.

CHAPTER TWO

Mountain Fork River, Choctaw Nation

An ounce of lead ripped into the hardwood, sending splinters of bark into Jackson Sixpersons' black slouch hat. The old Cherokee dived to his right just as another slug tore through the air and thudded into a tree. He rolled over and brought up the big shotgun, not lifting his head, not firing, just listening.

Many years earlier—too many to count—he had learned that in gunfights, it wasn't always the quickest or the surest who survived, but the most patient.

Another bullet sang through the trees.

Sixpersons freed his left hand from the shotgun's walnut forearm and found his spectacles. He had to adjust them so he could see clearer, but all he saw above him was a blur. "Sweating like a pig," is how that worthless deputy marshal he partnered with, Malcolm Mallory, would have described it. Idiot white man. Pigs don't sweat.

He found one end to his silk wild rag and wiped

the glasses free of perspiration. His right hand never left the Winchester, and his finger remained on the trigger.

A Model 1887 lever-action shotgun in twelve-gauge, it weighed between six and eight pounds and held five shells that were two and five-eighths inches long (ten-gauge shells were even slightly bigger). The barrel was twenty-two inches. When Sixpersons got it, back in the fall of '88, the barrel had been ten inches longer, but he had sawed off the unnecessary metal over the gunsmith's protests that the barrel was Damascus steel. Thirty-two inches was too much barrel for an officer of the U.S. Indian Police and the U.S. Marshals.

"Did you get him, Ned?" a voice called out from the woods.

"I think so. He ain't movin' no-how," came Ned's foolish reply.

"He was a lawdog, Ned," the first voice, nasally and high-pitched, cried out. "I see'd the sun reflect off'n his badge, Ned."

"He's a dead lawdog now, Bob."

"Mebbe-so, but you know 'em federal deputies— they don't travel alone."

That reminded Sixpersons of his partner. Where in the Sam Hill was Malcolm Mallory?

Footsteps crushed the twigs and pinecones as someone moved away from Sixpersons.

The Cherokee lawman rolled to his knees and pushed himself up. He was tall and lean, had seen more than sixty-one winters, and his hair, now completely gray, fell past his shoulders. His face carried the scars of too many chases, too many fights. He kept telling his wife he would quit one of these days, and she kept telling him as soon as he did, he would die of boredom.

In the Indian Nations, deputy marshals did no die of boredom.

Sixpersons rose and moved through the woods— like a deer, not an old-timer.

Tucked in the southeastern edge of Choctaw land just above the Red River and Texas, that part of the country could be pitilessly hard. The hills were rugged, the ground hard and rocky, and trees, towering pines and thick hardwoods, trapped in the summer heat. The calendar said spring. The weather felt like Hades. He didn't care for it, bu passed that off as his prejudice against Choctaws, Cherokees, being the better people, of course, cared little for loud-mouthed, blowhard Choctaws.

He could hear Ned and Bob lumbering through the thick forest, thorns from all the brambles prob ably ripping their clothes and their flesh.

Sixpersons figured where they were going, moved over several rods, and ran down the leaves-covered hillside, sliding to a stop and disappearing into an other patch of woods. Ten minutes later, he pushed through some saplings and stepped onto the wet rocks that made the banks of the river.

The country was green. Always seemed to be green. The water rippled, reminding him of his thirst, but Jackson Sixpersons would drink later. I he were still alive.

He stepped into the river, the cold water easing his aching feet and calves, soaking his moccasins and blue woolen trousers as he waded across the

Mountain Fork. A fish jumped somewhere upstream where the river widened. He had picked the shallowest and shortest part of the river to cross and entered the northeastern side of the woods. He moved through it, heading back downstream, hearing the water begin to flow faster as he moved downhill.

How much time passed, he wasn't sure, but the water flowed over rocks—running high from recent spring rains—when he dropped to a knee and swung the shotgun's big barrel toward the other side of the Mountain Fork.

Bob and Ned burst through the forest, fell to their knees, and dropped to their bellies, slurping up the water, splashing their faces, and trying to catch their breath.

Through the leaves and branches, Sixpersons could see the two fugitives clearly. Luck had been with him. Well, those two boys weren't bright or speedy. He wet his lips, feeling the sweat forming again and rolling down his cheeks.

"C'mon, Bob," Ned said as he pushed himself to his feet. "This way."

Sixpersons waited until they were near the big rock in midstream, not quite waist-deep in the cool water. Only then did he step out of the forest and bring the Model 1887's stock to his right shoulder.

He did not speak. He didn't have to.

The two men stopped. Their hands fell near their belted six-shooters, but both men froze.

Slim men with long hair in store-bought duds, they had lost their hats in the woods. Their shirts were torn. One of them wore a crucifix, another a beaded necklace. Not white men, but Creek Indians—Cherokees didn't care much for Creeks, either. Jackson Sixpersons didn't consider these two men Indians. Not anymore.

They were whiskey runners, selling contraband liquor, some of it practically poison, to Indians, half-breeds, squaw—men, women, even kids. Jackson despised whiskey runners. He had seen what John Barleycorn could do to Cherokees . . . and Creeks . . . and Choctaws . . . and Chickasaws . . . and all Indians in the territories. He recalled all too well that wretched state liquor had often left him in.

He had, of course, been introduced to bourbon. Grew to like it, depend on it, even became a raging drunk for twenty-two years. Until his wife told him that if he didn't quit drinking, she would pick up that Winchester of his when he passed out next time and blow his head off.

No liquor, not even a nightcap of bourbon, even when he had an aching tooth, had passed his lips since '89.

Ned and Bob could see the six-pointed deputy U.S. marshal's badge pinned on Sixpersons' Cherokee ribbon shirt. Sixpersons figured he didn't have to tell those two boys anything.

"He can't kill us both, Bob." Ned, the taller of the two Creeks, even grinned. "He's an old man anyhow. Slower than molasses."

Jackson Sixpersons could have told Ned and Bob that they would likely get two or three years for running whiskey, maybe another for assaulting a federal lawman, but Judge Parker, being a good sort, did show mercy, and probably would have those sentences run concurrently. It wasn't like those two faced the gallows.

Instead, he said nothing. He never had been much for talk.

"Reckon he's blind, too." Bob grinned a wild-eyed grin.

Silently, Sixpersons cursed Malcolm Mallory for not being there, but waited with silence and patience.

"Die game!" Bob yelled. He clawed for his pistol first.

The shotgun slammed against the Cherokee marshal's shoulder. His ears rang from the blast of that cannon, but he heard Bob's scream and ducked, moving to his left, bringing the lever down and up, replacing the fired shell with a fresh load.

Most lawmen in Indian Territory favored double-barrel shotguns, and Jackson Sixpersons couldn't blame them. There was something terrifying about looking down those big bores of a Greener, Parker, Savage or some other brand. With cut-down barrels, scatterguns sprayed a wide pattern.

Yet that master gun maker, old John Moses Browning—old; he had turned thirty-two in '87—knew what he was doing when he designed the Model 1887 lever-action shotgun for Winchester Repeating Arms. That humped-back action was original, even compact considering the '87s came in those big twelve- and ten-gauge models. When the lever was worked, the breechblock rotated at lightning speed down from the chamber. Closing the lever sent the breechblock up and forward, with a lifter feeding the new shell from the tubular magazine and into the chamber. This action also moved the recessed hammer to full cock.

A double-barrel shotgun could fire only twice. The '87 had four shells in the magazine and one in the chamber. It fired about as fast as a Winchester repeating rifle.

Jackson Sixpersons didn't need five shots. Ned's shot hit nothing but white smoke, and the big twelve-gauge roared again.

When the next wave of smoke cleared, Ned lay on the rock, faceup, his chest a bloody mess. The current had swept Bob's carcass downstream a few rods before he got hung up, facedown, on some driftwood on the far bank.

Birds had stopped chirping. Sixpersons set the shotgun's half-cock safety notch, rose, the joints in his old knees popping, and stepped into the stream

He reached the rock, closed Ned's eyes, and looked for the pistol the Creek had carried, but the weapon must have fallen into the river. It was likely nearby, but Sixpersons wasn't bending over to hunt for some old pistol. Likely, he would get wet enough just dragging the dead punk across the cold, fast flowing river.

Cursing in Cherokee, then English, he moved toward Bob's body. At least this one had the decency to die near the bank. Sixpersons laid his shotgun on dry ground and pulled the dead whiskey runner onto the bank. The blast had caught Bob in the stomach and groin, and he had bled out considerable. Still heavy, for a corpse. Probably from all the buckshot in his belly.

Sopping wet by the time he got Ned onto the bank, out of breath, and sweating, the deputy cursed the two Creeks. "Die game." He shook his head. "Die foolish."

After wiping sweat from his forehead, he looked at the woods he would have to travel across. Getting those two boys to Fort Smith would prove a big challenge, and that caused him to laugh. He had taken Deputy U.S. Marshal Jimmy Mann deer hunting up in the Winding Stair Mountains where Jimmy had bagged a twelve-pointer with a clean shot from his Winchester. But it was Sixpersons who had butchered the deer and hauled it those grueling four miles back to camp.

Shaking off the memory, he reloaded the Winchester before he drank water from the stream or wrote in his notebook—still dry—what would pass for a report on the attempted arrests and subsequent deaths of Bob Gooty and Ned Yargee, whiskey runners, Creek Nation.

He found a couple corndodgers, stale but salty, and a tough piece of jerky in his pocket. That was all he had to eat. The rest of his food lay in his saddlebags on the horse he had tethered to a pine back near where the whiskey runners had camped. Their horses had run off when they started the ball after Sixpersons had demanded their surrender.

Three miles. Not as many as he had had to cart that deer Jimmy Mann had killed. But there were two carcasses this time.

It would have been easier in the old days. All he

would have had to do was cut off their heads, stick
those in a gunnysack, and carry them to the Indian
court. But Judge Parker and the Senate-confirmed
U.S. marshal, Mr. Crump, frowned on such things
in the civilized world.

And the ground was too hard to bury the Creeks
and come back later with horse and pack mules.

Sixpersons was ready to call it quits, just leave
them there for coyotes and ravens, and forget any
reward that might have been posted, when he heard
a horse's whinny.

He came up with the Winchester, aiming at an
opening in the woods a quarter-mile downstream.
A dun pony stepped out and into the water, and the
shotgun was lowered.

The rider eased the horse out of the river and up
onto the bank, grinning at Jackson Sixpersons.

"Howdy," Deputy Marshal Malcolm Mallory said.

Sixpersons didn't answer with word or nod. The
fool hadn't even ridden out of the woods with pistol
or rifle ready.

"Dead, eh?"

The Cherokee's head bobbed, though it was one
stupid question.

"You kill 'em?"

He answered. "No, Wild Bill Hickok shot them."

Mallory laughed like a hyena and dismounted,
which was one good thing.

"I'll hold your horse," Sixpersons told him. "You
put the bodies over your saddle."

"But—"

"How else are we getting them back to Virgil
Flatt's tumbleweed wagon?"

* * *

Deputy U.S. marshals did not work alone. At least, they weren't supposed to. It was too dangerous. But sometimes Jackson Sixpersons wondered exactly what U.S. Marshal George J. Crump, appointed and confirmed by the Senate back in April of '93, was thinking.

Working with Malcolm Mallory and Virgil Flatt, Sixpersons might as well be working alone.

It was Flatt's job to drive the tumbleweed wagon, which was basically a temporary jail on a wagon bed. Iron bars were affixed to the reinforced wooden floor, with a padlocked door swinging out from the rear of the wagon. The roof leaked, and if the prisoners got too rough, they could be chained to the floor. Painted on the side of the wagon was U.S. COURT.

Under Judge Parker's orders, the driver of the wagon was not allowed to carry a gun. So in essence, the party of deputies was limited to two—Jackson Sixpersons and Malcolm Mallory. The way the Cherokee did his math, basically one.

The sun was setting, but the day had yet to cool by the time Sixpersons and Mallory reached Flatt's camp. The two deputies had found the dead whiskey runners' horses and transferred the bodies to those mounts. Ned and Bob were pretty much bloated by the time they reached camp, causing Flatt to curse and moan.

"We'll pack them down in charcoal when we reach Oaksville," Mallory said, the one sensible thing he had spoken all day, maybe all week.

"Who kilt 'em?" Flatt asked.

Mallory tilted his hat toward Sixpersons, who wa rubbing down his horse.

"Got coffee boilin'." Flatt did something un usual. He filled a tin cup and took it to Sixperson

The Cherokee knew something was wrong. Be sides receiving the coffee, he could read it in th tumbleweed wagon driver's eyes. He accepted th cup, stepped around his horse, and waited.

"Trader come along, headin' for Texas," Fla said.

Sixpersons waited.

"I give 'im some coffee and a bit of flour." Flatt' Adam's apple bobbed. "He give me a paper. New paper, I mean." He reached into the rear pocket his duck trousers, pulled out and unfolded a new paper. "*Democrat*, only two weeks old."

Sixpersons took the newspaper.

"Second page. Well . . . it's . . ." Flatt stepped awa

Sixpersons opened the newspaper, saw the stor just above an advertisement at the bottom of th page for Straubmuller's Elixir Tree of Life.

"What is it?" Mallory asked.

Sixpersons read.

Flatt answered. "Ex-marshal, Jimmy Mann. Seen he kilt Danny Waco, the old border ruffian, over i Texas, but he got hisself kilt doin' it."